Song of the
Silence

A novel
by
Barry Brailsford

Song of the Silence

Being the fourth Book of the Chronicles of the Stone

BARRY BRAILSFORD

A Stoneprint book of
Journeys into Ancient Wisdom

SONG OF THE SILENCE

© 1998 Barry Brailsford

ISBN 0-9583502-6-4

PUBLISHED BY STONEPRINT PRESS

PO Box 12-360, Hamilton, New Zealand

Phone 07-854-1502, Fax 07-854-1503

DESIGNED AND PRODUCED BY

Wenetia Publications, Hamilton, New Zealand

PRINTED BY

Kyodo Printing Co(S'pore)Pte Ltd, Singapore

TUATARA ILLUSTRATION

Tony Schaufelberger

ILLUSTRATIONS

David Walmsley

OTHER BOOKS BY BARRY BRAILSFORD

Available from Stoneprint Press

The Tattooed Land

Greenstone Trails

Song of the Stone

THE CHRONICLES OF THE STONE

being

Song of the Circle

Song of the Whale

Song of the Eagle

Song of the Silence

Song of the Sacred Wind

Also author of

Song of Waitaha

published by Ngatapuwae Trust

DEDICATION

To the ancestors who kept the dream of peace alive and carried it forward in trust.

To the peace makers who honour the ways of the Ancients and carry the gentle way into tomorrow for our children and our children's children.

ACKNOWLEDGMENTS

In honouring the mountains, rivers and lands where many of these words were written, I acknowledge Dame Te Atairangikaahu and the people of Tainui.

My thanks to Cushla, Karen & David, Gary & Raywyn, Raffi, Lisa & Sadhana, Tony & Tamzin, Amy, Rob and Tia, and Cheryll, for the many kindnesses that made this book possible, and to Andy Pona who so joyously shares the old lore.

The last words within these pages were created within the lands known as the Birth Place of the Gods. To all who gifted their love and labour to build the home that shelters this work we send our heartfelt thanks. We think of you with great fondness and wish you well as you journey with the stone.

Lastly, I bring to these pages my family, for they are never far from my thoughts.

Contents

Gather close if you seek
the door to other realms.
Open wide the corridors of the mind
to walk the trails of light
through the dark valleys of the night.
Listen to the words that dance
to songs long forgotten.

Stone is the ancestor of all.
It is of the beginning
and the timeless spirit
that joins star to star
and age to age.

Out of stone comes life.
We are of the stone
and the stone is of us.

Hold it close and feel its power,
hear its song and prepare
to enter realms known
but long forgotten.

Journey well friend,
and may the good go with you.

The
Cry of the East Wind

Follow the way that takes you ever beyond the way.

The old one sat very still. He seemed ageless, beyond time, bound to this world, but touching many others. His mind traversed the wondrous mountains of his home in Tibet. Although an ocean away, the image of towering, snow-covered peaks was ever with him.

Resting beneath the Rampart of the Eagles, Ii-chantu reached out to those who gathered to hear his stories. His gentleness invited all into magical realms. Thus it was that his first words slipped quietly into an expectant silence...

'A much venerated monk, a master, who was making a long and sacred journey with a student at his side, came to a flooded river. A woman, with a small child in her arms, stood before it weeping. Because his vow was one of separation from women, the master sent the young monk to ask her why she was crying. No woman had even touched the cloth of his robe in all the years he could remember.

'She must cross the river, master. Her other child is ill, and needs the medicine she hurried to obtain before the rains fell to close the way. The river is not deep, but runs too swiftly for her to make safe passage.'

The master went to them, picked up the child and gave it into the hands of the startled young monk. Then he asked the woman to climb upon his back, and without another word stepped strongly into the rushing waters. It was a long slow crossing, but a safe one.

The woman smiled her gratitude and with a prayerful bow hurried home to tend her sick child. Meanwhile the young monk looked on the actions of the master in amazement. Knowing vows held fast had been broken, he was deeply upset, but said nothing. All that day, and the next, his anguish grew until it was too much to bear. Eventually, he staggered under the strain of what had happened, and stopped. He felt compelled to speak, but it was the master who broke the silence.

'You wish to ask a question of me. You wonder how I could break my vows and allow a woman to ride upon my back. The answer is simple. That was her need. My heart answered her cry for help.'

The young monk thought deeply about this. It was the beginning of his journey into the deeper realms of the spirit. And there was more, for the master spoke again.

'I accepted the burden of the woman when I stepped into the river, and left it beside those waters when I set her down on the other side. My step was light in the days that followed, but yours was heavy. You took up a burden not your own, carried it from the river and over the mountains, and found it grew heavier day by day.

'You did not venture to ask the question that would set you free. I saw your heart was captured by your mind. Young one, you teach me much upon this trail,' said the master with a gentle smile.

His story over, Ii-chantu sat silently in thought. How far he had journeyed from his home. How welcome he felt amidst the Hai-da people, and all who gathered to honour the good.

Then a searing hurt, long thought healed, called up a shadow from the depths. Once again the old one found himself within the vastness of the Red Desert. Once more he was taken back in time, propelled into that place of grieving where he lost so much within the harsh lands where the Dragon breathed its fire. Without thinking he spoke.

'My heart answered her cry for help, but my hand was too slow to meet her need. Age sat too heavily upon me.' Anguished words whispered so low no one caught their meaning.

Silence now. Only the sigh of the East Wind answered his desolation. Yet, when he heard its gentle song, he smiled, for it carried the promise of life renewed. Life born of the rising Sun and the new dawning. Hope soared again.

The Fire of the Dragon

Seas of sand, tides of ancient memory. Empty of life yet never still. Empty of sound but never silent. Empty of imprint yet forever remembering.

Dust! Red dust, fine red dust that smeared the skin and clung to everything, drifted on a restless breeze. It hovered over them like smoke then curled down to embrace their shaded shelter. Some named this the Silk Road, but others told the truth and named it for the fire it was, the Dragon Road. It was the place of the damned if travelled without camels or horses, and a caravan master who knew the lore of the desert. Few ventured into this harsh world of shifting sands on foot and survived to speak of its terrors.

Six filled the airless space beneath the cover erected to shield them from the fire of the Sun. Six who found this world of shifting sand and swirling dust alien in every way. They were born of the high mountains, the realm best known as the Roof of the World, a land of deep winter snow and swift waters, of high summer pastures, of scant forests and few villages. A magical place bounded by stone, a wilderness of soaring pinnacles of rock crafted by the hands of the gods to reach for the stars. An implacable, unforgiving altar to the majesty of the universe, all lifted high to hold the most ancient of spiritual creeds within its palm. Home of the peace-makers, abode of the gentle ones who sought to follow the path of compassion.

Death was no stranger there, it visited without favour, sat within the snow-tossed storm winds to catch the unwary and steal their warmth away, moved with the avalanche to cover all below, stalked the rock shelters and stout stone dwellings in equal measure when the summer crops failed and winter shrouded all. Death was not feared, it just was, a companion on the road, the reaper of the spirit.

Red dust stirred. A child cried out in its sleep. Thirsting for cooling water, dreaming of lifting a handful of snow to its parched lips, yet slipping ever deeper into the furnace from which there was no return. Its mother spoke words of comfort. Soothing words that reached through exhaustion and suffering to gift reassurance.

Time shimmered and shaped, today slipped into yesterday and tomorrow stood clear of the shards of the past. Sharp memories had broken through to awaken old pain held deep within Llana. She was that mother. It was her youngest child who whimpered in her sleep beneath the shade cloth. Yet, five years had passed since their journey into the desert. Five dangerous years that had brought them into lands of the Hai-da to stand beneath the Rampart of the Eagles. The red dust was of another time and place, yet it still swirled through her mind to intrude upon this day.

Only four had survived that harsh desert trail that brought her to this moment. Two had given their lives for the dream that led the old one on, and without regret, for they had trusted the purpose. Their quest had called them from their mountain fastness to the ocean, and the frail vessel they had launched upon the tides to sail beyond the horizon. Thus had an aged grandfather, a lone woman and two children committed their lives to the widest of oceans. All done at the urging of the old one, who had known with utter certainty they would meet five swift ships on those waters. Five that had sailed to honour many nations and the future of all peoples.

Each step across the desert had been made in the hope of one day meeting those strange craft. Only now, did Llana know they had not even been constructed when her grandfather had led them from their home to journey to the sea. Her Hai-da friends assured her the idea of such a waka, and such a voyage, had not even been in their minds until her family was two years into their walk to the waters. All this was of the mystery where time folded over time, and the old one sat within the silence to hear its song.

Ii-chantu came strongly into her mind, the father of her father. *Choose your grandfather well*, was her favourite saying. Sometimes it was said with a laugh to honour the wisdom he brought to their lives. At other times it was said with sadness when she weighed that against the cost.

Llana sobbed, giving way to grief long thought assuaged. Then Ii-chantu arrived from nowhere to hold her close. With a knowing, learned of ancient lore, he saw deep into those he met. And no one was more precious to him than this beautiful young woman who was blood of his blood and more, for they shared a vision that asked much of them. Too much, it seemed, when old hurts surfaced again and again.

'Why now, my precious one?' he asked. 'Why do the memories flood back at this time?'

'The red dust gathers because you plan to walk that trail again,' she replied. 'It is the only way to reach the mountains of the moontides and the sacred rock that joins us to the stars. You will lead peoples from many nations into the dangers we fled. And each and every one is a dear friend. Grief and the fear of another loss brings forth my tears.'

'There is truth in all you say. The mountains call, and the trail of sorrow stands between, yet there will be healing in the journey. You will walk beside me, and the children, for it will be our homecoming. And the friends you speak of will open the way and travel with us to the Roof of the World.'

'Do you not shrink from the danger, grandfather? Isn't it too much to face again? How can you commit the children to the ordeal?'

'Before I answer, dear one, let me tell you a story. It is of our people and true in every way...

> *In a land of high mountains covered in snow, an old man gifted a small stone to a little girl. It was a rare stone found only in a distant river visited by very few. Although only three years old, the young one accepted it with respect and clasped it tightly in her hand. Some days later she returned to the old one and gave to him a stone she had found in a little stream near her home. It was like many other stones, but precious beyond words for the gifting.*
>
> *He accepted it with ceremony and gave it a place of honour within his dwelling. Thus began a regular gifting of stones, one to the other, over the next year, for there was joy in this and much laughter.*
>
> *One day the old one rose early to walk a high trail to rocks carved with power and mystery by rain and wind. There he greeted the rising Sun in prayer and gifted to the land one of*

the rare and beautiful stones gathered from the distant river visited by few. To place it safely beyond the hands of others, he ventured into the depths of the shaped rocks, into the wildest realms where others did not go. There he found, high upon a pinnacle of rock, a cleft within the stone that was filled with water. To that hiding place he gifted the treasure in the knowledge it would remain secure for all time.

The old one told no one of his journey into the rocks of power and mystery, and kept the secret of the stone on the pinnacle from all his friends. Soon after his return the snows fell to close the high trail and give birth to winter.

When spring came again to the mountains the little girl, who was now four years old, was taken by her mother for a long walk into the valleys. They enjoyed such journeys and made them often. This day they came to a place where the rocks were carved by the wind and rain into shapes of amazing beauty.

Along the way the little one told her mother she was going to find the most precious of stones this day.

'That is not possible, my little one,' was her mother's gentle reply. 'That stone is only found in the valley of the distant river visited by very few.'

When the young girl saw the carved rocks that reached proudly to the sky, she ran amongst them with joy. Alone and unafraid she went deeper and deeper into the halls of stone that surrounded her. And, when she came to a pinnacle of rock like no other, she climbed to its summit and found within a little pool of water the rare stone that was only found in the distant river.

Her mother was surprised and excited by the little one's discovery, and as soon as they returned, took her daughter to see the old man. When they arrived the girl stood before him and said with pleasure...

'Here is your stone.'

The old one smiled, for it was indeed the one he had so carefully hidden within the depths of the carved rocks. Accepting it from her he gifted it back, saying, 'It is yours to have and hold.' But once again, the girl presented it and quietly left.'

'Three things within this story will stay with me for the rest of my days. The first is that the little girl heard the song of the stone. Long before she reached the rocks that held the rare one, she heard its cry. And trusting in that voice, despite the words of her mother, she found it hidden where no one else could have uncovered its presence. The second is that having found a treasure of such beauty, she was able to let it go. A deeper knowing and a generous spirit moved within her when she left it with him. And in the letting go, she set herself free to grow into a remarkable woman filled with love and wisdom.'

'Why do you share this old story with me, grandfather? Is it merely to divert me from the harsh questions I have placed before you?'

'No, dearest granddaughter, I share it for the third reason, the one that matters most.'

Without further words, the old one placed a small silk pouch on the ground before them.

'Open it,' he said with a smile.

Llana carefully drew apart the cords and tumbled two stones of rare beauty into her hands. Her mind struggled to catch threads of memory grown cold, found faint echoes of days long gone, and discovered something truly wonderful. She gasped with surprise.

'It was me! I was the little girl who found the stone. It all comes back to me now.'

'Yes, my dear one, that stone was my gift to you, and this one was your gift to me. Both come from the river that is distant and visited by few. Both hold the song of the stone, and both speak with a clear and compelling voice. Our destiny is of the stone and the stars. We walk this trail of danger because the stone calls us to that path. We may turn aside from it, but in making that choice we turn away from the truth of who we are.'

'How did I forget the magic of these stones, grandfather?' cried Llana. 'They open the gates of memory to warm my heart. There was so much wonder in my childhood, so much that I have put aside and will one day take up again. Grandfather, you never lost your way. You have remained forever the child.'

They smiled, bound close by so much shared over so many years. Each contemplating the magic of days spent in the home at the Roof of the World, and journeys made.

'Thank you for your story and the stone. The little girl in me remembers and feels stronger,' said Llana.

They sat in silence for a long time. Comfortable in a place beyond words, supported as they sought balance within the pain and the joy. The Sun went to its rest, and stars gathered within the growing darkness. And still they sat and waited upon the spirit that was their life. Each held a stone of rare beauty, and with it the remembrance of days of wonder. And each sought within the brightness of the stars one that called them home. Finding it, they shifted within, journeyed deep into themselves to reach out to the universe and hold a star and a stone in one hand. Such was the trail to wisdom.

Gentleness and strength born of other realms were the mark of the old one. He also remembered the hardship of the journey and the sorrow that sat within it. Red had been the dust of that desert, and dark the day that had brought them to the parting. Six had walked through the night to cheat the Sun of its burning bounty. Night after night they had staggered on with goatskin water bags to sustain them. Few of the wells had been spaced for foot travellers. Each time they found water they had to carry as much as possible. Yet, none had complained, for they trusted the words of the old one and his purpose. That was the greatest part of his burden now. That, and the loss of family.

Words came again. 'Grandfather, you have woven back into my life coloured threads that were hidden beneath the cloth of time. Will you now lift more of that covering aside and share your story? I know little of your childhood, and have a growing need to learn more of the path that led us to the ocean trail, and brought us to the Hai-da Nation and all who gather here. Forgive me if this is not the time and I presume too much.'

'My story is like no other I have ever heard. It is as much the story of my grandfather's journey as my own. He never left our village and never met with others from distant lands, yet he knew more of the wider world, and worlds beyond that world, than anyone I know. Some who came to honour him for his wisdom in the gentle realms of the Buddha, fell into confusion when they discovered his mind and heart embraced the teachings of the Master and more besides.

'Everyone who tried to claim him for themselves, who wished to place him within one creed or kinship of the mind, found he eluded their grasp. Some named him Seer of the Stars, others Seer of the Heart, for he walked with a compassion which found room for all creeds that were of the Source. Those who saw the truth within him, and tried to gather to his side, attempted to elevate him to the place of a Master, were sent away to be their own teachers. Those who knew him best, and became true friends, saw him simply as an old one of mystery who went often to drink from the wells of silence.'

'So the old one was almost beyond description, an elusive star, a being who was too bright to capture. I like what I hear, and see he gifted you more than you may ever know.'

'That is also the truth of it, dear one. My parents gave me totally into his hands. I don't know if that was their idea or at his command. On reflection I think it was the latter, for there was a presence and power about him that few could resist. Yet, all was bound within gentleness.'

'Tell me of your life with him?'

'It was extraordinary in every way. With a deliberation I find remarkable now, but accepted as normal when a youngster, grandfather disciplined my mind, and helped me harness its power while setting it free. He broke all the rules. Not just a few, all of them.

'From the beginning he stretched my senses. With deliberation he jolted me out of time. My day might begin at sunset or dawn or any time between. We would spend night after night sitting under the stars, then day after day watching the shadow of the Sun pass over the land. Sleep was sometimes short and sometimes long. There was no pattern and no expectation.

'Food was also an irregular matter. It was sometimes plentiful and sometimes meagre, and always presented at different times of the day and night. Fasting was followed by the slow build-up to a feast. On one amazing journey we travelled through the mountains for twenty-one days without food or water. When I asked him why we did not hunger or thirst he said... *We are living on prana, the light of the stars.*

'As a seven-year-old I accepted that. Hunger had no place in my life when the universe provided for all my needs.

'Sometimes we talked for days and then we walked the mountains in silence. I found comfort in all the facets of disorganisation he structured about our lives. Then, when he was sure of that, it all changed. Time and food and discussion fell into place within the normal bounds again. Yet we knew with certainty those boundaries were of our making and not others. They could be, and were, put aside with ease if circumstances asked that of us.

'Having stretched the wider physical realms to sit easily around me, he then proceeded to open my mind to other senses and other realms. My eyes were trained to focus into the smallest of worlds, and to open to the distant horizons. Then he taught me to see with my eyes shut, to let images travel unheeded into the darkness and play across my mind. The power I honed there only became real to me when he revealed that what I saw of my mother was happening that very moment. To assure me of this we recorded her journey through a morning, then visited in the afternoon to hear if my understanding, and her activities, matched. No further test was needed, for all rang true.

'It was much later that he opened the hearts of people to me. That journey is usually only made on the tides of pain. The early death of my mother was perhaps the key that opened the doors into the turmoil of another's trail. It is a difficult power to hold, for it means I can never close my eyes to the troubles of others. Yet, on that pathway of compassion I have learned I cannot walk the truth for another. We make the journey of the spirit alone. No one else can make it for us. My role is that of the gatekeeper who points the way. Others must choose for themselves if they wish to walk it.

'He attuned my ears to the world of subtlety. He took me into the place of the sacred sounds that are of creation. I will speak no more of that at this time, for it is a road we will explore together later. Power beyond all imagining sits within that realm. It opens the way to healing and to hope eternal, to a wondrous world that reaches out to infinity. Within the realm of the song of the spirit, he taught me how to find the mystery within the voice of the stone, the music of the waters, the cry of the trees, the melody of the birds and the sound of the rainbow. Beyond that again we came to the awesome song of the Silence.

'Do I tire you with these words? Should we leave the rest for another day?'

'No! I hunger for your words, for in them I see how you have been shaped, and how all you are touches into my life. Your story opens into mine. In it I find solace and understanding, strength, insight and direction. If you have the will to go on, please continue, grandfather.'

The old one did, and talked long into the night to describe a lifetime of learning. When he was done, they knew the most difficult words still remained unsaid for they were choked by pain. Despite all they shared, they had not left the red dust behind.

Aria found them sitting in the dawn light, having talked through the night. They waited to greet the new day, thinking no one would find them on this gentle slope beside the soaring Rampart of the Eagles. Yet, neither was surprised when Aria came to them. Her mind and heart was drawn to a source of pain with a certainty that was very rare. They smiled with understanding. It was time to wash the red dust from their lives forever. The Sun brought the promise of healing and new beginnings.

'Aria, you come in answer to our cry for help. We have carried a heavy burden for too long and seek to be free of it. Will you sit with us and hear of the journey that set our little craft athwart the course of your vessels?'

'If that is your need, it is mine also.'

Thus did Ii-chantu begin the story of why he committed his family to make the long journey. He spoke quietly of the gathering of the Darkness in other lands, of the rise of the Altec Nation and the use of human sacrifice by its crazed leader to extend his power. All this he saw by flying his mind to the source of the hurt that fed the Darkness. Without restraint he described the desecration of the sacred Long Stone of the Altec Nation within the Temple of the Heart.

'When they held the naked body of Keeper of the Long Stone across its cool surface, and cut out her heart, they defiled the Mother. The most sacred of covenants was broken as the blood of the innocent splashed across that Tu Ahu, the ninth anchor stone of the Web of Life. From that moment of distortion, the balance of the Darkness and the Light was threatened. All Creation stood on the edge of Chaos.

'This you know well, Aria, for you also felt the cruel hand of the Black Robe forces of the Altec Nation. Your people were dragged from their lands to have their blood gifted to the knife and the stone. You responded with courage and wisdom, and in the company of Eroa, Utini and Hera began the resurgence we know will one day turn the tide and restore the balance that holds the Web. Gentleness and trust were the weapons chosen by those who gathered about you to meet violence, for they knew to confront anger with anger and hate with hate was not the way. That path only led to pain that would visit many generations to come.

'I saw your plight and followed your journeys from afar. My heart went out to you when you rode the Dark River, and when you fled to the Island of the Tall Standing Ones to place the Ninth Tu Ahu anew. I mourned the loss of the vessel named *Kekeno* when it was seized by the Octopus. That was when I knew I could no longer merely observe from afar. I went into the Place of Silence and folded time over time to see the weave within its distant design. There, I saw the gathering of the waka and the course they would take to reach the Hai-da.

'My plea to my family was to let me go, to set me free of the mountains that I might meet the waka on the ocean. I planned to travel alone, but found they also felt the call of that trail, and without further discussion began to prepare for the journey.

'We made good progress out of the mountains, for we walked within our own world. Our journey filled our days with wonder and contentment. Even the two children were aware of the events that called us ever onward, because we shared everything. Our prayers were with you when you bravely sailed to the Islands of the Double Sea to go to the healing waters and gather the stone of love, the one named pounamu.

Day by day I visited your waka to honour the trail of the whales and add my strength to yours. Ra found the deepest songs of the whales with my assistance. That door was mine to command, for our ancestors also sailed the long trails in days long gone, even to the waters of pounamu. It was my hand that moved within the sacred lake to bring the stone of stones into alignment. It was with joy that I saw you raise the Tenth Tu Ahu on that remote island in the waters of the Ice Mountains.

'There has been strength in our journey. It has taught us much. Yet, one hurt remains unhealed in both of us. I have denied that until this moment, but see my need is as great as my granddaughter's. We ask you to help us walk once more into the death of our life companions.'

They sat quietly wondering how this healing might begin. Aria had seen this need within Llana for a long time, but was surprised to hear the depth of the old one's pain.

'I would like to place those last days of sorrow before this new day, and this rampart of stone,' said Llana. 'If my grandfather agrees I will begin, but I ask him to take up the words if mine fail.'

'We had almost conquered the desert. The red dust and the heat were still with us, but in the distance the hills that marked the end of the desert loomed higher. Then the skies darkened and the wind gathered in strength to grow suddenly colder. Thunder rolled along the horizon, and lightning forked through dark clouds that shrouded the late Sun. Then the rain came, heavy rain that hit the dry land with the sound of stones dropping on timber. Within moments we were drenched and bedraggled, laughing at our plight, and glorying in the water denied us for so many days. We fell down and sat in the dust now turned to liquid mud. Then, we felt the cold of the rain and the chill that gathered to the howling wind.

'There was no shelter in that open place, so we left the higher ground and entered a long gully that gave some protection from the sweeping wind. We followed it down, hoping to find a cave, and after a time were jubilant to come to an overhang of rock that provided the shelter we sought. Habeli, my life companion, a man of strength, who was the anchor of our journey, left us to see if he might gather small pieces of wood for a fire. Only wind-blown debris was present in this wild place, but along the way we had always gathered enough to feed our cooking fire. So I was surprised when he returned after a short time with an arm full of good pieces, and within moments had started a bright fire.

'We changed into dry clothes, and settled down to enjoy the night despite the raging storm without. Sleep came quickly as the fire died, for we were all exhausted. I woke feeling apprehensive and uneasy, but lacked direction for my fear. Then I heard it. A roar that was not of the thunder that still beat upon the night. This was of the land and it was terrifying.

'I shook Habeli awake, and as I turned to arouse the children I heard his exclamation of horror... *the firewood... the wood was too easy... too high up the slopes... a huge tide comes... flee now!*

'Even as we scrambled out of the shelter into the dark of the night, the floor of the gully turned into a small stream. Within moments it was up to our knees. Grandfather and I, each carrying a child, began to climb the steep bank to escape the rising waters. The flow that caught at us now was of little account. What was gathering was the dread that drove us on. We knew the wild roar that brought me out of my sleep was closing upon us swiftly. A flood-tide was swiftly running the gullies and would soon find ours. Higher ground was our only hope.

'I gained height, then slipped and fell and slithered back into the waters. Manoa cried with fright, and this time I took his hand for the ascent. We were last now, and in the greatest danger. I cried out to Habeli to help us, but he was desperately attempting to haul grandmother Palin to safety onto the plain above. She seemed too shaken to help him.

'The roar of the approaching waters filled me with terror now. I clawed my way up the slippery slope, dragging my little boy behind me. He understood our need and worked frantically to lift himself higher. We helped each other rise ever closer to the level of the plain. And we did not make it.

'The flood-tide crashed into this narrowed way and surged over us. We clung to a protruding rock just below the summit. It saved us, providing anchors for our hands and feet when the angry waters tried to pluck us from the land.

'I heard a cry in the darkness, looked into the torrent as lightning flashed, and saw nothing but a swirling red tide that swept inexorably by.

'Grandfather's voice reached me. Hope flared. He was calm and reassuring and urged us to reach for the long sash he lowered to help us climb to him. As the water receded, I tied it under the little one's arms and helped him climb over our guardian rock to safety. In the same way I also won freedom from the waters.

'Only four of us stood on that place of safety. I was stunned into a silence so deep it was as if the storm that surrounded us was stilled. *Habeli! Palin!* was my first cry.'

'Gone,' said grandfather. 'One cry in the darkness, then silence. Taken by the waters. I reached out to take Palin's hand. Our fingers touched, but could not hold. I was too slow, too old.'

'We survived the night to greet a dawn clear of all cloud. The Sun rose on a land swept clean, a land waiting to be sucked dry once more. I find it hard to speak of the desperation I felt as I stared across that ravaged land.'

Tears flowed now. Tears so deeply wrought that Llana's whole body heaved as she grieved. Aria held her close, rocked her like a child and sang to her in a whisper. The words that flowed were of the ancient days, of courage and nurture and the need for comfort and a comforter.

'I will bring this sad story to its end,' said the old one. 'We lost all except the clothes we wore, and the Sun was already standing high. Our only path was to follow the gully that was now empty, and drying fast, in the hope our loved ones were somehow carried to safety. We walked wearily on, talking of the possibility of them surviving, and slowly built a tower of hope with words. That carried us through the shallow depressions where the flood-tides had flowed, and out to a flat plain where they had dispersed and emptied into the sands.

'It was there, on the edge of the desert, that we saw the first signs of life, and they heralded only death. Birds of prey circled in the distance. The first we had seen in all our days in the desert.'

He paused as Llana was shaken by a terrible sobbing. Every step taken now was etched in her mind as if graved deep in stone. The sand, the fading light, the circling birds and then, as they grew closer, their sounds. Hope, despair, expectation and uncertainty, all swirling through her like an ever-changing tide.

'We hurried on as the Sun swung low, and came upon a feeding circle of buzzards. As we closed upon them, they reluctantly moved away to stand and watch. Hand in hand, we approached their table to find one body resting there. My beloved Palin.'

Sharp, painful memories overwhelmed him. Llana stepped into the silence to take up their story, for she knew they had to complete this circle to reclaim their lives.

'Our farewell was brief. Grandfather placed her name there, then each of us left loving words to journey with her spirit. Even the children gifted something special for the trail, a fond remembrance of love shared, a happy event, whatever came from hearts torn by the sadness of this parting. It was done with a chorus of waiting birds circling our little party.

'We left without looking back. We did not cover her body as some do, for that is not our way. The birds that came to clean her bones were a blessing, for they truly set her spirit free.'

Llana paused as if waiting for a question. Knowing it sat at the edge of Aria's mind, she put it there herself.

'And what of Habeli? There were no other buzzards circling for as far as the eye could see. Nothing moved to reveal his fate. We can only wonder. Was his body buried beneath sands shifted by the waters, or was he cast up on another place alive? We stayed and searched for one more day, and then left the red sands behind. Left them holding fast to their secrets.'

An eagle cried on high, then swept past the tree that held its nest. It brought them back from the grief of the Dragon Road to the world of that moment. Leaving the slopes beside the Rampart, they walked to the shore, where Aria led them into the waves until all were immersed in the cleansing waters. They accepted the sharpness of its touch, welcomed the healing shared, and emerged to leave fresh footprints in clean white sands. Lighter now, freed of burdens they had carried out of the clinging dust of the desert, they stepped strongly into the Sun. Freedom and compassion had walked hand in hand to honour the night and the birthing of a new day.

Llana smiled upon the world. She had found the courage to live with the mystery. The last image that filled her mind, as she drifted into sleep, was the face of her beloved Habeli.

The old one stood straighter now. He knew the dream they walked was bigger than all of them. Each had a role, and each came to it freely, honouring their path, their truth and the journey. Once again, hope whispered on the East Wind.

***

'Silence is of the sacred and has its own song,' said the Story Teller to himself. He felt joy in returning to the Chronicles and the company of those who gathered to share the stories. Old faces and new faces sat within the circle. They filled him with hope. He smiled as he sensed the first question and looked up.

'The Christ found his vision in the emptiness of the desert. Others have also followed that path. Why the desert?'

'You speak truly, my friend. The vision quest often means going into the wilderness, a place of aloneness. For some it is the journey into the trackless desert that sets them free to find the deepest truths. For others the dreamtime, that awakens the spirit and provides direction, is of the mountains or a long ocean voyage.'

'The aloneness is met in many places and in many different ways. It is not just the abode of the desert, the mountains or the sea. Some say the long night of the soul, that wondrous journey into ourselves, is called depression in this age. Whatever, the name gifted to it, fear is the one faced on that trail, and fear is the one overcome. Beyond fear stands freedom and the truth that is the vision.'

The Stones of Lore

Carve me truly in stone. Cut through the realms of time to shape the sacred and hold it close. Sing to me and set me free.

Hltanuu and Pana sat beside the Stones of Lore, the four slabs of wondrous power that stretched across the approach to the Hai-da village. They were sisters of the mind, born of different parents, yet bound as one within the trails of the spirit.

Images set free within the dancing flames of the fire, first brought their minds together across the vastness of the ocean. Joy flowed in that linking of one to the other, and confusion and fear as the dream woven there unfolded. These beautiful young women had journeyed far from the flame that opened the way, and been sorely tested by the sacred fire that burns to reveal the inner truth.

'We have journeyed well, my sister,' said Hltanuu. 'You held all in place from this little island. Your vigil beside these stones anchored our long trail into the frozen lands of the long night without end. The power you harnessed through the Stones of Lore, and focused to join with ours, brought the Eleventh Tu Ahu into being. Together we added another coloured strand to strengthen the Web of Life. Together we honoured the call and stepped out to join with those who work to hold the balance.

'I am with child now,' confided Hltanuu. 'Kaho will be a wonderful father.'

This news saw them join in a gleeful embrace that took them off balance and tumbled them down the grassy slope. Their laughter rippled along the shore to bring a smile to Ii-chantu, who sat quietly nearby within the shade of a young tree. He knew its cause, and was overjoyed to think a little one would, in the fillness of its time, be with them. Hltanuu and Kaho gave so much for the journey. The universe replaced tenfold all that was gifted in love.

'If these two are my daughters in spirit if not in name, then surely the little one will be my grandchild,' was the thought that surfaced to bring contentment to this day.

'Pana, I share my joy and my fear with you. My child enters a world that challenges us all. It comes with its own trail of truth to follow, another sent to dance this journey into the future. That is my joy. Now I place before you my fear.'

Pana knew well the demands the spirit made on the mother. Although younger than Hltanuu, her child was born beneath the Rampart long before the journey to the icelands. She also had to walk through the fear and hold to the trail.

'A dream shifts and shapes within the night to call me from my home,' said Hltanuu. 'It opens the way to a distant land uplifted high, a world of mountains forever cloaked in snow. Ii-chantu's hand moves within this vision that emerges from a flame that lights the darkness. My fear is for my child, for the dangers that will beset us all if that call is answered.'

Pana not only shared the fear, she also shared the dream. It came to her as well when she looked into the flames of the circle fire in the Lodge of the Elders. Before Pana could respond, Ii-chantu appeared and sat beside them.

'The fire reveals the truth,' were his opening words. 'A trail opens to us, and you are called to answer its challenge. Yet, in all this there will be protection. Your children are of the dream and revel in its shape and sound. Hear my words and know all is as foretold.'

The young women sat in silence now. Lifting their minds to a higher realm, they found the stillness that gave them courage. As ever, Ii-chantu had arrived with perfect timing to bring them into the wider wisdom of the dream they shared. There was no need to give way to fear. Calling it out of the shadows, they faced it squarely in the light, and walked beyond its false facade of power to the freedom that gave them strength. Turning to each other they smiled with relief.

'Ii-chantu, thank you for your gentleness and the nurture you bring to us,' responded Pana. She paused, thought for a moment, came to a decision, and said, 'Tali-a-tali and I want to ask a boon of you. Will you be a grandfather to our children?

The smile that spread across the old one's face was broad and bountiful, and filled with thanks. He accepted their invitation of kinship by joining his hands in a prayerful way and slowly bowing his head.

'Thank you, Ii-chantu,' said Pana, who had wanted to ask this of the old one for some time. Far from kin, called to strange lands and challenged by mystery, she yearned for the counsel of this elder.

'There is one further need that I wish to lay before you,' continued Pana. 'I sense some of the Stones of Lore remain hidden. This idea has grown stronger day by day. I believe all were not revealed by the wave that gifted the others to the light. Do I see this truly?'

'It is so. Others lie hidden beneath the four we see. They now cry out to be revealed, for the stars call them forth. It is time to hear their song,' concluded the old one.

'Mystery is folded within mystery,' said Hltanuu. 'I also felt the presence of a power hidden from my eyes, and spoke with Matuku and Huru of that feeling. They merely smiled in a knowing way, so I let it rest. Ii-chantu, speak more of this if you will.'

'You have already opened this new trail with your own minds. I merely come to assure you there are markers and a clear direction. It is time to gather the elders into the circle, to share the dream revealed, and to uncover the last stones gifted by the Ancients.'

Pana and Hltanuu sat with Tali and Kaho in the circle that surrounded the fire. Many had gathered in answer to Kun-Kwii-aan's call to meet in the Lodge. Few knew of the mystery that drew them hence, but all had been told they would hear of exciting matters bound within the Stones of Lore.

Kun-Kwii-aan took up the sage stick and offered its fragrant smoke to the four directions, while chanting soft words that opened the doors to the spirit lands and the red trail of courage. Finally, with a smooth sweep of his hands, he made the sign that announced they were now poised over the sacred crossroads, the place where all realms meet. It was done with the dignity and grace of one who had seen much of this world, and waited patiently to enter the next. When he finished, and turned to address those assembled, his words were simple and direct. .

'The rainbow shines on the edge of the storm clouds, and the darker the clouds the brighter its light. That has been our journey together. We stood tall to meet the storms and were honoured by the many blessings of the rainbow. Trust, and wisdom gifted by our ancestors, gathered us into this hoop that is built on the strength of many nations. With purpose bound in courage, we destroyed the battlefleet of the Black Robes without recourse to weapons that cast life aside. With the help of the Dakula and the Inuit, we crossed the frozen lands of the Tundra to secure the Eleventh strand of the Web.

'Since our return we have rested, waited, listened and grown restless, for we all know the work is incomplete. The balance still tilts in response to hands bloodied by savage acts of ill intent. I sense the Stones of Lore are about to ask us to prepare our waka to go to the tides once more. I now ask those who urged me to bring us together, to share their words. So be it.'

Upon closing he sighed and sat quietly as if in meditation. Then as the silence gathered strength he signed with his hand for Hltanuu to speak next. When she stood, her first words took Kun-Kwii-aan by surprise.

'I stand to speak for Pana and Ii-chantu, but first I ask for permission to speak for myself and for Kaho, my life companion.'

Hltanuu turned to Kun-Kwii-aan, her grandfather, to seek his sign of assent as tension built within the circle. It was freely given.

'Grandfather, the seasons to come will gift to you another great grandchild,' announced Hltanuu with a smile. Laughter and joy greeted her words. The elder smiled with contentment. The unease that had gathered was quickly gone. Now it was time to speak of the deeper matters that waited in the shadows to be set before the flame.

'The Stones of Lore have not given up all their secrets. Other carved blocks remain hidden. We ask for the right to bring them into the light. We suspect they hold the key to the trail ahead.'

This exciting news was met by a thoughtful silence. All knew Pana, Tali and Ii-chantu had retrieved from the stones ancient wisdom that would serve the nations well in the days to come. Now they were hearing of more stones buried deep. Excitement and expectation built. It was time to take those hidden treasures from the darkness. None raised their hand to deny the way.

It was High Sun when the first Stone was revealed, and late in the day before the others were cleared of all covering. It was no easy task, as the four hidden ones lay beneath the four revealed. Strong arms and thick ropes were needed to shift the masking stones aside.

As was the way in the beginning, Matuku and Huru, the Little People of the Stone Nation, were the first to step forward to greet the sacred stones hidden for so long. They chanted in a tongue rarely heard to call forth ancient memories. Everyone knew they were embracing lore long thought lost and marvelled at the power that moved with their words. Then the Hai-da stirred and came to pay homage, and the other nations, for all wished to honour the wonder of the past.

Through all this, Pana and Hltanuu stood to the side with Ii-chantu. Their work began when all left. Only then did they enter the Silence to hear the song of the stone.

'One stone remains on this wondrous Island of the Rampart where the eagles soar with power. The other seven are destined to leave this land. Their journey is to other lands. All this I see,' said Ii-chantu, 'but not their destination or their purpose.'

Encouraged by the vision of the old one, the two women went deeper into the space between, into the Silence. No one broke their journey, all was stilled, all sound closed from them as they moved with courage into the realms that held the sacred forever sacred. When Hltanuu knew they were free of that place she shared the words gifted in that wondrous sphere.

'Each stone knows its destination and its purpose. This one speaks of its journey to the Menehune of Kauai,' said Hltanuu.

'And this one of the Island of the Tall Standing Ones, the land that is now home for me,' added Pana.

'Hinau will be pleased,' continued Hltanuu. 'The third cries out for the shores of Aotearoa, the land of her people. It is destined for the Islands of the Double Sea.'

'This one sings of a vast southern land that is of the dreamtime, and the keepers of its story,' cried Pana 'It seems reluctant to speak, for it carries a voice that is very old indeed. I know not its destination, but see it reaching those shores after voyaging to the Island of the Tall Standing Ones. So much mystery here, and so much resting upon wise decisions!' exclaimed Pana.

They stood before the last three stones. No one spoke as they listened intently for word of their journey. All was quiet, no sound at all, just silence.

'Something blocks the way into these stones,' said the old one. 'Five are open to us and three closed. Perhaps Matuku and Huru can help us.'

Hltanuu went to find them, leaving the others to sit with the mystery. She returned quickly with the Little People striding purposefully before her. Few could match the speed of their short legs when they were in a hurry.

'The silence is not a block, the stones do not deny you knowledge,' said Matuku. 'The first five hold in place work already done. They anchor that part of the weave that is complete, rest in places that have already been joined into the wider dream by you or others. They are locking stones. They mark important parts of the long journey that brought us to this moment. The other three stones are, as yet, without alignment or direction. That does not mean they are not instilled with memory, or lack the knowledge of their destination. You hold the keys to their homes, you are the creators of the dream.'

They sat before the Stones of Lore and thought of what the Little Ones had shared. They had expected words from on high, and now had to look for words from within. The circle was theirs to walk, the responsibility theirs to shoulder, and the wisdom theirs to honour.

'Ii-chantu, you see one trail leading to your homeland on the Roof of the World. That vision was with you when we left the Inuit in the lands of ice. Is that the destination of one of the carved stones?' asked Hltanuu.

'No! It is of another place. While I see our trail reaching into the highest mountain lands, I do not see the Stone on it. We need to think of their purpose within the dream, then we may find answers to their destination.'

'The placing of the last Tu Ahu is the dream,' added Pana. 'When we have joined the Twelfth to the stars, the Web of Life will be restored, and the Darkness and the Light will be in balance.'

'The eight Stones of Lore somehow place a lock upon the Web,' continued Hltanuu. 'This the Little People have shared with us. We have discovered much, have learned much about the destination of five of them. All travels forward in trust. Let the remaining three sit within the mystery. Let us be content to prepare for the trail that opens today, and let the ones that await tomorrow, look after tomorrow.'

That night Pana shared their news with Tali. He was excited when he heard that one stone was to go to Kauai. His people had returned to the ocean after the passing of many centuries. They had rediscovered the magic of the long tides and the stars that guided them far beyond the horizon. Their commitment had saved *Waka Turuki* from the waters where the winds died, and thus made the creation of the Tu Ahu possible. Now they were to become the keepers one of the Stones of Lore. Once again the magic of their land would be joined with the wonder of other lands.

Then Tali's mind reached beyond his homeland to explore the new trail that opened. The Roof of the World, the land known as Tibet, an intriguing realm, beckoned. His imagination knew no bounds as it created the picture of his waka sailing through an ocean surrounded by the tallest mountains in the world. When he shared this wonderful vision, Pana gently set him on a truer course.

'We must cross a vast desert to reach Tibet,' said Pana with a laugh. 'Ii-chantu has shared that part of the trail with me. We sail only as far as the Middle Kingdom of the Khan, and then move on the Silk Road that is but a world of red dust.'

By the time the Circle of the Keepers met, all within the village had already discussed the journey to be made. Everyone was eager to hear their answers on the who, the when, and the how of it.

The moment of decision had arrived, and with it the sadness of parting. Seven carved Stones were destined to go to sit in seven different places. Only two waka would sail to the Middle Kingdom, the others would voyage to Kauai, the island of the Tall Standing Ones, the shores of Aotearoa within the Islands of the Double Sea, and a vast land beyond.

'How will this be accomplished?' thought Pana, who knew she was destined to go with Ii-chantu on the trail to Tibet. She could not imagine being apart from Aria and Eroa, could not bear being separated from Hera and Utini, or without the company of Ra and her sister Tai. Her question was soon answered. After all the waiting, their lives were committed in an instant, by others who walked closely with the wisdom.

'This is the way the design unfolds,' said Kun-Kwii-aan, who had been asked to preside to honour the Hai-da.

'*Waka Turuki* will return to its own land with three of the stones. One to sit with the Ninth Tu Ahu, the other to be carried to Hinau's homeland of Aotearoa, that holds the spirit of the Tenth, and one to be set ashore on the large continent to the west of the Islands of the Double Sea.

'*Turuki* will be accompanied by the second Menehune vessel to be escorted through the waters where the winds die. Then that craft will sail to its own waters to deliver the stone to Kauai.

'*Siigaay Kaa* , our Hai-da vessel, voyages with *Kohatunui*, the first Menehune waka, for the Middle Kingdom of the Khan. These two craft, carrying the three remaining stones, will brave the unknown lands of the west. They break new ground, while the others hold safe that which is already won. All is of the greater purpose and the peace.'

This was indeed the parting of the peoples. Friends of long standing would soon be separated by the widest of oceans. Silence greeted Kun-Kwii-aan's words. Everyone knew this was how it had to be, but found no comfort in that understanding.

Now Eroa stood to speak. He placed the Stone Bird of the Ancients before the fire, and stepped back from it to share his thoughts.

'The Tall Standing Ones call me home. Yet, that is not to be, for another voice echoes off the walls of valleys remote and beautiful. I give *Waka Turuki* into the hands of Soleti, my brother of the long tides. May he find safe passage by the light of the brightest of stars.'

'It's all happening so fast,' thought Hltanuu. 'Who will be named for the journey to the Silk Road? Where is my place in this weaving of the nations?' Her thoughts were interrupted by Matuku and Huru standing as one, and calling Hana and Kanohi to their side.

'We also sail with *Turuki*. It is time for us to return to the Halls of Stone. Those who hold the anchor call us home. Kaho goes forward in our name. He carries the power of the Circle of the Stone into the unknown. All this has been decided and stands as firm as the Rampart that overlooks this village.'

Hltanuu sighed with relief. Kaho, her life companion was set free by the elders of the Halls of Stone to make the journey. Her joy was complete when Hera and Utini stood to share their decision.

'We are bound by the prophecies of the Ancients,' confided Hera. 'Our trail is carved in the stone and the stars. We sail west with those who follow the cry of the albatross. We voyage to the Middle Kingdom of the Khan.'

Thus did the party that journeyed to honour the placing of the last Tu Ahu come into being. No one mentioned Ra or Tai, and that was not an oversight, for all knew they were committed to that trail from the moment Ii-chantu spoke of it amidst the snow of the north.

Ii-chantu smiled. He was overjoyed to see who gathered to walk the next dimension of the dream. His family had travelled far, and at immense cost, to bring them to this moment. The last Tu Ahu would be like no other ever placed.

> Later, Ii-chantu went apart from the others and sent his mind into the Altec lands where the Darkness was first unleashed to tilt the balance. There he found the man he sought, hunched over a stone table mumbling angry words of dark intent. His face and hands were scarred by the searing power of lightning. A pain he brought upon himself by sending it against others.
>
> Mata-u-enga was his name, and hate his coin. He knew this Tu Ahu was the hardest to bring into being, and saw a way to deny the twelve who would walk to honour it. The architect of the Black Robe scourge was about to invoke his next array of demons to send against those who stood bravely to hold the Light.

***

The Story Teller waited to see if the questions would come. No one stirred or was uneasy in the silence. Then the first voice opened the way.

'Grandfather, again and again the stories come back to the power of stone. We can see the Stones of Lore hold wisdom carved deep by ancient hands. I understand messages cut as symbols into stone. But I cannot understand how uncut stone can carry knowledge that can be heard.'

'It is truly so. I have met many people who tune into stone. Perhaps they go beyond it to receive knowledge within another dimension. In that way it would be a transmitter and receiver. I cannot explain that, but accept the evidence of my own eyes.'

'What about Ii-chantu looking in on Mata-u-enga from afar?'

'This is the same. I have sat with people who do this with ease. Their information has always been accurate and they are people of integrity.'

'Where does the scientific world stand on these phenomena?'

'Some dismiss such seemingly strange powers out of hand. Others keep an open mind, accept such matters as unexplainable, but valid occurrences. I detect a shift here. More and more we begin to realise that to dismiss something simply because it is not proven, is to limit greatly a deeper understanding of the world around us. It narrows what is possible.'

'Are we on the verge of a new science, one that gives another definition to proof, one that embraces wider dimensions of experience?' asked someone in a quiet voice.

'Perhaps we are. Perhaps we are beginning to recognise the God Factor in Mathematics, Physics, and Biology. Perhaps that is the measure of the evolution of the species,' replied the old one.

The Trail of the Albatross

Only the wind knows the winged one's journey. Only the wind provides the power of flight. Only the wind brings the soaring bird home through the circle of the night.

Eight wondrous carved stones stood clear of the land that had cloaked them since the Age of the Ancients. Stones of Lore destined to provide an outer circle to sustain the Web of Life. Seven of which would soon be carried on the waves by waka dedicated to their journeys.

'They are of enormous weight,' sighed Eroa, who stood with sweat glistening on his back. He had shared the labour of shifting the stones closer to the shore. The master carver was awed by the beauty crafted by his forebears, the Ancients. For these stones were shaped exquisitely on all five sides and carved with majesty. Only the use of levers, and a three-sided hoist, would confirm his suspicion the underside also carried messages bequeathed by the ancestors.

'Tell me, Matuku, and if you will, Huru, what think you of these treasures?'

The Little People were once again washing them clean with water. A task they accomplished with much fun and constant words of reassurance to the stone. The flow of words was not interrupted by the question.

'How beautiful you are,' said Matuku as he cleaned sand out of the curving cuts. 'How perfect in every way, and how important for the future. Yes, you are about to move out into the sunlight and travel on the waters. That's what stones carved for the trails do. You have slept within the darkness far too long. It is time to awaken to your work and enjoy the magic of the light.'

Eroa laughed. He understood that although Matuku spoke to the stone, he also answered him.

'Eroa, they hold more power than I have seen in any other stone,' confided Huru. 'Yet they are hardly awake. They have slept so long, their voices are so quiet few hear them speak. This will change as they take on the fullness of their power once again. It is an awesome thing to know them and to give them nurture. Understand they will grow stronger as they hear the songs of joy that are the way of peace.'

'And there is danger in awakening,' added Matuku. 'The Dark One, the hand that sent the battlefleet against us, knows they have been set free to enter the circle. The moment the covering sand was swept aside he felt the power bound within them. He fears it, and probes its weaknesses and ours. All will not be secure, until they have completed the journeys foretold in the stars so long ago. And along the way they must be protected from the imprint of Mata-u-enga, the Commander of the Black Robe forces.'

'Each stone must have a keeper, a guardian who shields it from the harsh words and the pain sent forth to frustrate the dream. Those who spill the blood of the innocents upon the stone, will endeavour to bring blood between the designs' graved here, and the power of the Ancients. If they succeed, they will turn it away from the Light, and toward the Darkness. Then the balance will be undone again. There is still much to do, and a constant need for vigilance and courage.'

Eroa quickly absorbed these words of warning, for Ii-chantu had already prepared much of the ground for this message. They sailed once more into adventure and challenge. He would have it no other way. Others gathered now in numbers. It was time to set the first stone on its way. Time to commit all to the tides again.

Turuki sat very low in the water. Three huge shaped stones rested on the joining platform that bound the two hulls together. They would need little ballast for this journey, and could not expect a swift passage through the waves. Yet, that was of no account, the needs of the stone stood paramount.

It had been a difficult task to place them high upon the platform without the aid of the magic of the Little Ones. What they might achieve in moments with a single low chant, others took a day to accomplish with the aid of many strong backs and tall timbers that provided the means for the long pull and the hoist. Yet all was done as requested. No words of ancient mystery had been set free to lighten the stones by shifting the space between. No mind trail was opened to move them effortlessly into place. There was too much danger in that, too much opportunity for Mata-u-enga to project his own designs into the stone to twist its memory and distort its purpose. They could not take that risk.

Within four days all seven stones were secure within waka. On the brightness of the next moon they would sail for distant waters to begin their work to hold the balance.

Tali-a-tali, Pana, and Hltanuu sat with Kun-Kwii-aan, the ageing chief of the Hai-da. They came together to plot a course that would bring *Siigaay Kaa*, the Ocean Walker, to the lands far to the west. Only the Hai-da retained the songs for that journey. The weave within the ancient sounds that reached out to the marker stars was worn now, and filled with occasional discords. Yet, they felt enough of the harmony remained to carry them along a true trail to safe landfall.

'Who sails with us to carry the songs that open the way?' asked Tali. He yearned to know who would command the companion vessel that would lead him along the trail of the stars and the rivers of the ocean.

'Two will stand together to guide the Hai-da waka through the tides,' announced the old one. 'I will carry the songs, and Kaho, the strong companion of my granddaughter, will command the vessel. Age gathers about me like a shroud, but that sits lightly with me as I drift in and out of time. It merely binds me ever closer to the stars that guide us over the waters. No one is better suited to guide the helm. My old hands are of little help at home, or on the tides, but that is not the need of this journey. All that is unchanging is of the mind and the courage.'

Hltanuu thrilled to hear those words. She knew her beloved Kun-Kwii-aan might not live to return to the place of his birthing. Yet, she knew the old one would be happiest giving his last days to the waves. The Hai-da spirit, the vision of the ancestors, the tall red-haired ones of pale skin who sailed so far to come to this land, was in sure hands. Then she remembered Kaho was the new commander. No one would serve them better. All was as it should be.

Dawn gave way to the sound of laughter and song. Four waka were launched upon that tide with the Stones of Lore standing proudly above the waves. No one shed a tear for the journeys made and those ahead. No one acknowledged that for many this was the final parting. All looked steadfastly to the future and held fast to the understanding they were forever one. Time and tide imposed no separation. All were sisters and brothers, a family of many colours joined within the dream of peace.

Kaho stood at the long steering oar of the Hai-da waka. Kun-Kwii-aan sat on one side of him and Hltanuu on the other. Each day she looked more like a woman who carried the seed of another. Three generations rode this trail. Symbols of birth and rebirth, the continuance of what has been and what has still to come into being.

'Hold fast to the North Star,' cried the old one when day gave way to night. 'It was our guide on the journey to raise the Eleventh Tu Ahu, and is once again our marker as we set sail to create the Twelfth. Our course is north to the Kamchatka, the strong current that flows from the frozen lands. By its hand we will be sent swiftly westward to the Okhotsk Sea and the Middle Kingdom of the Khan. It has ever been so.'

Far to the south, the other waka sailed the trail that carried them into the fiery waters where the wind died. Only the Menehune craft with its long sweeping oars could safely cross that place of fire. They would tow *Turuki* until they caught the breath of the wind again. Then they would return across the place of death again and sail home to Kauai. Although each day brought greater separation, they voyaged with a closeness that was wonderful to know. One thought bound them, one dream and one purpose.

While those in the south faced the fire of the bright Sun, those who plied the waters of the north knew other hazards.

'The cold bites deeper,' said Eroa.

'And we have warm cloaks to ward it off,' responded Aria. 'They are in that basket near your feet.'

Five days had passed and each brought more wonders to behold. Beautiful islands and forests of tall sitka spruce and red cedars abounded. However, the massive rivers of ice that gave birth to the icebergs that drifted on the ocean, left the strongest impression. When the first ice drifted past they set a westward course to work free of the shore, and Kaho asked for a triple watch to see them through the dangers of each night.

Sea birds came to greet them often, and this day it was an albatross, a bird so wide of wing it spanned the joining platform of the waka.

'See its effortless flight,' extolled Utini. 'See how it lifts into the wind and glides higher to gather speed, then dives low to gather even more to lift again. Its endless questing carries it ever westward until after several years it comes again to its place of departure. Thus does the greatest of the travellers fly a circle that takes it around our world.'

'Why does it always fly to the west?' asked Hera, as she lunged for Tia-ho, their little one who was forever exploring the length of the waka. So much energy in one so young was the thought that saw her gather her daughter safely to her.

'The wind calls it westward. In these parts, the wind gathers its strength from the west. Its long trail is ever out of the setting Sun. We know not why the winds in this part of the world always flow in this way. As the albatross finds power by flying into the wind, it is called westward. Thus is the direction decided and followed year after year.'

'Tell me of the Middle Kingdom. What is it like?'

'I know nothing of that land. Ii-chantu has revealed little, and I sometimes wonder why. At least we will not find the Black Robes there.'

'Do not be so sure,' cautioned Hera. 'Although they may not wear cloaks of that colour, others may walk there to enhance the power of the Darkness. Our knowledge of the wider world is shallow. Within its depths there may be forces that rival, in every way, the power of Mata-u-enga. We move blindly, trusting Ii-chantu in everything.'

'Whale Ho! Whale Ho! Whale Ho!' was the cry of the Keeper of the Third Wave, who stood high upon the prow.

This cry immediately brought Eroa, Utini and Kaho together. Did an Octopus wait in hiding to attack them on this trail? That was the unspoken question that had sat with them from the outset. The song that led them on, the one carried by Kun-Kwii-aan, had five vital lines missing for these waters.

'Three things decide our fate,' said Kaho.

'Aye, that is true,' responded Eroa. 'If the Alaskan current, that carries us so strongly, meets the Kamchatka current from the frozen oceans of the north in anger, the Octopus will feed here. However, if the Alaskan waters turn and join quietly with the other, we will rise to a faster tide with speed and purpose and there will be no danger. That is the first trail to unravel.'

'If the answer is the one we dread, the whales bring us to the challenge with hope,' added Utini. 'From time lost to time, our ancestors have run the waters of the Octopus with valour born of knowledge gifted by the whales.'

'That brings us to Ra. Where is he?' asked Kaho. 'We need him now, for he is the third piece of the puzzle. This is his realm. He has been gifted the songs that join us to the whales.'

Within a short time Ra appeared unbidden, to speak with Kaho. Eroa was pleased to see he honoured the place of their new commander by going to him first. A tall lad now, a man in many ways, and their lifeline on the wide ocean.

'Kaho, we are soon to enter the waters of an Octopus. The whales sing of this and the waters move to confirm their words. Yet, this one is unlike those we have bested in the past. I understand its tentacles are very short, and although vicious, are not as strong as those that have tested us on other tides. The danger is in the closeness of the tentacles, the narrow valleys that gather power into ways that toss the vessels to and fro, and keep all off balance. This motion may tear the Stones loose and set them free to smash our craft apart.'

'Let us bind them tighter,' cried Utini.

'And warn Tali in the other waka,' added Ra.

'Prepare to meet the Octopus,' was Kaho's command that sounded through the waka. 'Lower the sail, unstep the mast and secure them against the turmoil of this tide. Let the drum-beat sound. Summon all to the blades that call on the courage of the ancestors. Be of brave heart.'

The Octopus waited. Four times Eroa and those around him had met the Doom of the Waka on the high seas. Each encounter had been different. Each time they crossed the mouth of its lair, the whirlpool born of the meeting of two rivers in the ocean, they faced the unknown. Only the whales knew which tentacle would carry them beyond the maw that was the doom. Their survival rested with Ra, with those who braced themselves at the steering oar and the whales. Above all else with the whales.

'Hold true to their line,' shouted Tali, who stood high upon the Stone on the platform to guide the three who commanded the long oar of *Kohatunui*. He looked ahead to the track Kaho cut through this gathering tide.

'Close up. Close up. We must not be shut outside the gate. Close up on their wake.'

'Tali crowds in upon us,' cried Utini, who was their eyes to the rear. 'He rides closer than any waka I have seen before.'

'He holds the line,' responded Kaho, who was clearly not concerned by the course chosen by the other waka. Trust travelled on this tide. He focused on the lad beside him and welcomed Ra's words...

Prepare to ride the tentacle... make ready for the turn... hold until the lead whale gives me direction... hold! hold! hold!... turn now!!! Turn... follow his line... follow... trust...

Tali brought them through waters cut cleanly by those who acted on Ra's calm call. Two waka went to the Octopus as one. Yet within each their focus was dangerously divided - between the shifting tides that struggled to pull them into the whirlpool, and the Stones that strained to break loose. Did they have the power within the paddles and the sweeps to stay with the whales? And if they did, would the ropes that bound the carved stones hold?

The first cry of alarm sounded in the hindmost waka. Tali saw one rope break and leapt upon the stone to secure it with another. Three companions joined him in the struggle to secure the stone that gathered dangerous power from the waves. Those who rode its shifting bulk might at any moment be tossed into the ocean. Again and again they tried to snare it with ropes, and again and again it was snatched away from them by the twisting and turning of this wild tide.

'Save the waka, let the stone fall free into the waves,' was Tali's desperate thought. Their struggle to seize it with a strong rope had failed. All was lost.

'Leave the ropes. Use timbers,' was the cry that reached him. Pana's voice cut through the urgency that held him tight. Without warning, a sweeping oar was thrust along the side of the stone to ram its blade under the bindings that anchored the front of the stone. Then another snaked through on the other side to slip under the fastenings that still held. Ropes already tied to the free end of the sweeps were quickly fastened to the platform timbers. Now two long timbers were secured to the stone and the waka. In an instant it was done, the stone was tamed, captured to be harnessed with other ropes. It was safe.

'Freedom!' was the sound that reached them. Tali and Pana laughed. Ra was standing high upon the decking of the other waka pointing ahead. 'Freedom!' could mean only one thing. Those who toiled at the blades and sweeps had carried them through the maelstrom that was the Octopus. Courage had once again opened the way. Courage and the whales.

They now rode the fast river that was the Kamchatka current. It swung them on a south-westerly track toward the distant Okhotsk Sea, the doorway to the Middle Kingdom. The stars charted their progress, as the winds held fair day after day to fill the sail.

Ii-chantu felt the presence of land long before the keeper of the Third Wave shouted...

'Land Ho! Land Ho!'

He was shaken by a wave of regret for what was about to happen. Only he knew that when they entered the Grand Harbour they would all be taken prisoner. Then, at a time chosen by the Khan's advisers, they would be paraded through the streets as criminals and taken before the August One to await his pleasure. That might mean long imprisonment, or even banishment to the wastelands where only the circling buzzards prospered. Foreign vessels entering the Kingdom were not welcomed. This was known to be a forbidding place. Yet, he had no other course.

'We must prepare the first stone carving for a journey,' explained Ii-chantu. He had asked that the waka be drawn together, that he might speak to all. 'We have little time left because ships of the Imperial Fleet will soon appear to take us captive. Trust me in all that happens. There is no other way to breach the frontiers of this powerful state. It is the stone that will set us free. The stone and the power that walks with Hera.'

Hera and Utini looked puzzled. They were not afraid, for they believed in the old one. He had saved them too often to betray them now. All stood firm, no one challenged the words of Ii-chantu.

When the silhouette of tall sailing vessels loomed ominously out of the haze that shrouded the shore, they stayed calm and sought only direction.

'I need to know what you expect of me,' said Hera. 'Prepare us for what is to come.'

'We are going to carry the Stone into the Inner Courtyard of the Khans. Within the huge city, is a smaller walled city, that few ever enter and fewer still leave, for it is the sacred centre of the Middle Kingdom.

'Try to see those who come to arrest us as the harsh face of an inner realm that is beautiful, and at this time lost to the truth of its place in the world. Understand that these people have a culture that goes back thousands of years, and that they still hold within their halls wisdom and power that truly honours the Ancients.

'Yet, much of that is lost to this generation. We have come to try to restore it to them and shift their numbers into the balance. That is only possible if we can place the Stone of Lore within the Inner Courtyard of the Khan, the central pivot of the sacred centre of the Kingdom.'

'But we cannot carry the Stone,' said Utini.

'That is true,' agreed the old one, 'but Hera can.'

'Explain this to me,' said Hera, as calmly as she could, as the Imperial Fleet sailed ever closer.

'You sent the shattered stone door, that blocked the Fifth Gate within the Halls of Stone, back to the parent rock from which it was cut. You stepped into the power of the Ancients to move within the inner structure of stone, to shift its energy into an alignment that obeyed your commands. What you have done before, I simply ask you to do again.'

Before Hera had time to protest, the old one launched into the immediate aspects of his plan. With swift words he sent them to gather eight long sweeps from the waka and lash then two by two to form stout poles. These were then placed beneath the stone after it was levered up to allow them to slide crosswise beneath its bulk. He then chose three to stand at each end of a pole. Thus were twelve arrayed each side of the stone. It looked an impressive gathering of power to lift an enormous weight. Yet, all knew they could not do so. Only with Hera's intervention, could they hope to achieve all that Ii-chantu asked of them.

Before Hera could attempt to test her power to reach into the stone, the Imperial Fleet surrounded their waka. Without a single word of greeting, sailors armed with swords boarded and attached ropes to the prow of the waka. Thus began the long pull into the Inner Harbour.

All sat in silence as strange vessels, crewed by strange people, carried them into a strange world. A vast city opened to them. It stretched across the valley and into the hills for as far as the eye could see. The roofs of the buildings were curved in graceful ways, that suggested they were designed to honour the stars. Colour abounded, beautiful colours in the stone and the tiles of the roofs. Trees filled the spaces between, and beneath them moved many people, and all were clothed in loose colourful garments.

Not so the warriors. They were armoured against the power of arrows and spears. And all seemed devoid of expression. An unreachable facade masked those hidden within. It was thus with their Commander, who with cold gestures and clear directions indicated they must now disembark.

Ii-chantu bowed low before this noble man of power. He spoke quietly, and without haste, and was heard in silence by the Commander. Then came the questions and the replies, all given in a voice that was unknown to all but Ii-chantu. With a brief nod, permission was granted. The Stone was to be brought ashore.

While this came to pass, Hera retreated into the Silence. There she asked for the power to touch deeply into the stone, and align its inner structure, to defy the pull that gave weight to everything. Utini and Aria stood close by to ensure no one came between her and the power. Aria held Hera's little one in her arms. Tia-ho was no longer a babe, she was an active, restless little one who needed to be watched closely.

Eroa moved to the stone to ensure those chosen to lift it high moved as one.

'Hoist, on the count of three,' was his order.

He looked to Hera, saw that she was still deep within another realm, and waited. All was timing now, and lore of ancient knowing that set power in motion. Then came the returning. Hera was making her way back to them and the task. Her nod announced she was ready.

'On my command! One! Two! Three!'

On that count, twenty-four set themselves strongly and with huge apparent effort, that was mere illusion, lifted the poles to their chests and stood tall. Then moved forward, on Eroa's word, to carry their wondrous burden to wide stone steps that led to the landing above.

Hera smiled. All were jubilant, but hid their wonder and their joy behind masks of unconcern. Each had a role to play in this journey, and without exception they were determined to see it through. No one contemplated the consequences of failure. Too much was at stake to allow doubt to confuse the way.

Warriors marched beside them as they were paraded through the city. Huge crowds gathered to view this procession that made its way towards the impressive arch that opened into the walled city within the city. The march of the criminals, was in truth, the march of the triumphant. With heads held high, and songs of greeting, they carried the Stone into the place from which few emerged.

High within a tall tower that overlooked the Arched Gate, the Khan watched all this in secret. He felt a power moving here, something that might threaten all he held close.

'These strange people bring a presence with them that defies my understanding,' he thought to himself. 'Should I destroy them without further consideration, or probe deeper? My advisers will favour the former, but the closed mind is a danger to itself. It sows the seeds of its own destruction. Ignorance breeds only ignorance.

No! the key is in the stone they carry. If twenty-four of my strongest men can lift it high, then that is where the matter ends. If not, then I have much to learn this day.'

Hera grew tired from the march and the concentration needed to hold the stone in alignment. She hoped they would soon be able to set it upon the ground. Even a few moments rest would be wonderful. She knew Utini and Aria still walked beside her, but could not turn her head to see them. Their nurture, their strength and their calmness, reached her. They were as important, in this moment, as she was. Together they walked into the unknown to honour the journey.

They were escorted deeper and deeper into the sacred city, until at last they came to the Inner Courtyard of the Khan. Massive stone gates opened as they approached and they entered without breaking step. With indrawn breath they stared at the wonder surrounding them as they were ushered into the central space where an ornate throne of carved stone stood in all its magnificence. The Khan sat there, still and yet ever watchful of those who brought something both intriguing and dangerous into his life.

With a nod of his head, and a signal conveyed by a simple gesture, he indicated the stone should be placed before him. Hera sighed with relief as it was set on the paved way that covered all.

No one spoke and no one moved. It was thus for a long time. Then a word was spoken by the Khan, and all became purposeful activity. The twenty-four who had stood to the poles were taken aside to sit quietly. Then twenty-four warriors, chosen for their strength, marched in and took their places at the poles. With determination etched into their faces, they awaited the order to raise the stone on high. It came without a word. The Commander stood before them and set his hands as if to clap them together, then beat out the count of three silently and lifted his palms skyward. With perfect coordination the chosen ones bent to the pull, and set their legs to take the strain, and moved the stone not at all. This was repeated three times with the same result. Then the Khan signalled for those who had challenged the weight of it, to stand apart from the stone.

He thanked them for their strength and their effort, then signalled for them to leave. He had much to consider.

Again a quiet word, and Ii-chantu was brought before him. The old one bowed low three times and stayed low until invited to rise.

'Have them lift the stone again,' was the command.

Hera and Eroa understood without translation. Hera went within the Silence to prepare herself for the task. Eroa stood in wonderment. Something stirred within him, something turned within an ancient circle that waited upon this moment. He opened himself to that power, freed his mind and stepped forward to gather the nations to the Stone once more. Insight of startling clarity revealed to Eroa how to turn this challenge to advantage.

'As before, brave hearts. On the count of three hoist the stone high, and be ready to move it, and set it down again, at my direction. No matter who stands in your way, and at whatever the cost, follow every command. Courage stands tall to walk the truth of this Inner Courtyard.'

Hera stood with her little daughter holding her hand. The child was walking strongly now, nay, running everywhere and outstripping many of her pursuers. Hera went deeper to harness the power to realign the stone once more, all this with a calmness born of the journeys made. Eroa knew when she was ready.

'One, two, three! Hoist!'

To the amazement of the gathered officials, the stone was hefted high and held. The Khan smiled, for it was as he expected. Strength played no part in this, magic moved within the stone.

'On the count of three, move at my direction,' cried Eroa. And with those words little Tia-ho broke from Hera's hand and ran to hold that of Eroa, her grandfather. Those who held the stone staggered and nearly fell, for in that instant Hera briefly shifted her focus. She almost lost her claim on the stone, and then with amazing speed, recovered and held.

Eroa, with the little one firmly gripping his fingers, took station at the head of the stone carriers. Then with purposeful steps and firm command, led them towards a low stone platform of crafted beauty. Thirty paces would bring them to this place, but before they had taken ten the warrior cohort swiftly set themselves squarely in their path. Eroa slowed in the face of this implacable line of stone-faced soldiers, but Tia-ho broke free again to dance ahead alone. Her innocence, her joy and her utter confidence carried her through the line that parted at her approach, and Eroa followed. They gained the platform and swiftly set the Stone of Lore upon it with ceremony.

The Khan left his throne and stood beside the wondrous carved one. All heard his indrawn breath and his exclamation. The Stone fitted perfectly within the raised rim of that platform. The fit was so precise, on every side, that he could only stand in amazement. Chance did not move here. Chance had no place within this moment. This the Khan knew. All was planned in days long gone by his great-grandfather, who prepared this sacred site for the arrival of this very stone. Time folded over time once again. Yesterday and today sat within a seamless cloth of many colours that embraced tomorrow.

Excited and thirsting to know more, the Khan returned to his throne, and with a single word dismissed his officials. Then he ordered the Commander to withdraw the warriors to the rear. When all were arrayed to his satisfaction, he gestured for Ii-chantu to stand before him once again.

'Tell me of these people. Some are pale-skinned and have red hair and blue eyes, others are shaded as the night and have even darker eyes, some have red skin and black hair, others favour an olive complexion that matches our own. Speak of the many coloured peoples who journey to this place with this stone,' said the Khan. 'Speak of this, and all that you feel I should know, but do it quietly for your words are for me alone. Be sure to place only the truth before me.'

Thus it was that Ii-chantu stood before the August One, to speak of all that brought so much pain to the nations. The Khan sat enthralled and signalled for a seat to be brought for the exhausted old man. He knew with all his being he was listening to the voice of integrity and shared a trail of truth. He tried to remember when he last heard honest words spoken with good intent. Too many years to count, was his sad conclusion.

The Khan smiled when he heard of the Black Robe armies, for news of that power had been but a rumour. This must not be hurried, he decided. I do indeed have much to learn. These people need rest and food, and I need to sit quietly with their leaders. What the old one shares deserves better surroundings.

Again a signal and the immediate response. The warriors left, and servants came to lead the families of the nations into another courtyard surrounded by spacious guest rooms. They were ushered into a long room with low tables heaped with an abundance of food. And on their way to that place they were shown deep tubs of warm water in which to bathe. Laughter and song, rarely heard within these solemn walls, soon filled the sacred centre with the need to dance.

The circle had turned around the magic of the stone. Joy blossomed within the heart of the Middle Kingdom of the Khan. Some said that spirit never left, for it was the legacy of the stone, but others felt it was gifted by those who entered this inner realm without fear.

Perhaps it was the little one who skipped ahead of the stone carriers who really put the magic there.

> Power unleashed is power revealed. Another saw all that had come to pass. Far beyond those shores, he set his scarred face to the stone and called on ancient lore, long hidden in the shadowlands, to aid him in his quest. For many days and many nights, he had sought the presence of those who had set his power to nought, again and again.

> Mata-u-enga, the ailing leader of the Black Robe forces, knew the day would come when the protective screen around those who sought to hold the balance, would be stretched too thin. Circumstance would call forth the need to honour power, and reveal their purpose.

He smiled when he saw them place the Stone of Lore in the Inner Courtyard of the Khan. Another victory won, and wild rejoicing, but at too great a cost. A triumph that would unravel all. The last flame is the one that burns the brightest, and the darkness that follows is more complete for its dying.

***

'Grandfather, once again you pitch us into the unknown. Yet I see others have gone ahead to prepare the way. The stone fitted perfectly into a recess created many years before.'

'That is true, my son. Much is asked of us and much is given in return. We are never abandoned, we merely lose our way from time to time. There is learning in that, learning of the best kind, for then we become our own teachers.'

The Courtyards of the Khan

Few honour the Silence now. Yet each child is born with that memory, and every one grown tall retains the ear to hear its song. It is of the awakening, the journey home, the way back to the Source. It is of the Returning.

'**W**e favour the Yangtze River Road,' said the Khan. 'My most trusted advisers say it is the best link to the Silk Road. State officials will prepare the way. Your vessels will be moored and maintained within the Grand Harbour while watercraft, built specially to reach the upper reaches of the River Road, will carry you to the beginning of the trail that crosses a high pass. All who can assist you will do so. Runners will go ahead with my instructions. The Middle Kingdom will honour your journey every step of the way.

'Even beyond the Silk Road, we will answer your call if others stand against you. Yet, in all this we understand your greatest need is stealth.'

'One moment we were prisoners, and in the next, princes,' thought Ra, as he sat with those gathered to hear the words of the Khan. 'Ii-chantu took us into the jaws of the dragon, to the source of the all-consuming fire to bring us into safety. I marvel at the sweep of his mind, and I recognise it touches often into mine. And there is more, for I know it visited me long before we first met upon the ocean. How strange it was to find the old one adrift in a little boat athwart our path all those moons ago. How strange and how wonderful.'

'Your departure is delayed, and that is my joy. You cannot leave in this season of falling leaves,' said the Khan. 'Ii-chantu will tell you the passes have closed, that the snows have come early. He may be far from home, but be assured he is ever aware of its moods and seasons.'

Some were disappointed to hear this news, for they felt an urgency that called for action. Yet there were others who were delighted to know they would have time to explore the wonders of the Middle Kingdom.

'You are invited to spend the winter in our land. All you wish will be at hand within our courtyards, and horses for journeys within our borders. Rest awhile, share all we have to offer, learn from us that we might learn from you. All is in the hands of the storm winds and the snow. Let go, await the season.

'Your arrival lifts my spirits. You have brought life to a kingdom that was being crushed under the weight of too much governance. I am, in the one moment, all powerful and powerless. The Middle Kingdom is so vast it defies the hand of one person to hold it in harmony. I am forty years of age, and have been trained to sit upon the throne since birth, yet I am frustrated.

'My influence is at the mercy of those who hold petty power within each village, town and city, who serve me only to serve themselves. They are appointed to help the nation, but that is not their daily practice. Laws pronounced within these walls to bring comfort to my people, become regulations to increase their burden in the hands of distant officials.

'There is pain within this land that can only be eased by wisdom and power far exceeding my own. I rejoice in the presence of the Stone that sits within the Inner Courtyard. It is the source of change that will bring us to a new dawning. My mind stretches to embrace the many gifts you have shared, and my heart is filled with admiration for your commitment to the good.'

All were reconciled to the need to stay until the spring thaw opened the way. Many saw opportunity in the delay. Ra and Tai were two who approached it with excitement. They planned to learn the language of the Middle Kingdom, to take advantage of the Khan's offer to provide tutors for those who wished to learn to speak in the way that was a song. And they had other plans. As they left the gathering, they captured Hera, arm in arm, with smiles that spoke of wickedness. It was Tai who set their hopes before the woman who had won them this wonderful sojourn within the Inner City.

'We have planned a day beside the river. All is prepared, and you and Utini are invited. Tia-ho, the little one you chase throughout the day, is to be in the keeping of Porea, Eroa and Aria. Please come!'

'Give me the who, and the why of this,' responded Hera.

'The four of us will go to the river,' said Ra, 'to play a little and to learn a little.'

Hera laughed, and said, 'Then it will all be play, for I have nothing to teach you. Let's be gone then.'

They went in a wheeled cart pulled by a horse, to them a new and wondrous means of travel. Every time they ventured beyond the Walled City they entered a world of colour and adventure. Beautiful trees arched over the paved roads, many walked along them to visit markets and temples, or sit within places that provided food and drink. Everyone spoke quietly, and moved at a measured unhurried pace. Flowers, little planted courtyards and trees brought serenity to the flow that was a city. This was indeed a world apart, a land that was a garden.

To reach the river, they passed through farmlands where peasants tended rice in flooded fields and tilled dry plots to grow other grains. Huge water buffalo, creatures as new to them as the horses, ploughed the lands. Everywhere they looked, the cultivators touched the earth with patience and nurture.

'You came not to play,' said Hera, when the food was eaten. 'I know that look Ra. I have seen your restless mind reach this place before. So you really want to learn. I will sleep while Utini answers your questions.'

'Hera, you know we have something to ask of you, and you alone,' said Tai.

'That was my suspicion, and I think I see the trail that opens in your minds. You want to know about the power to lift stone, the realignment that shifts its weight aside. Am I right?'

Ra's grin said it all. Tai laughed aloud.

'I am not sure if you are ready for this knowledge. Or perhaps I really mean, I am not sure if you are chosen to carry it forward. That is my dilemma. I know you will only use the power for the good, but will its use be for your good? Is it of your path, is it part of the truth of who you are? All we need for the journey is gifted to us if we ask. However, those things we take without honouring our real need are but a burden. They add nothing, except extra weight and much trouble.

'Give me your reasons. When you are ready, speak to me of the truth that is of the core of you. Then let us wait upon the spirit that moves to guide us.'

Shaded by the spreading canopy of a tall tree, they lay back and watched the clouds move slowly across the blue of the sky. No one spoke. After a time Utini and Hera fell asleep, and Ra and Tai left to amble along the river path. Everything was alive, everything sparkled in the light reflected by the water, everything was in tune with the gentle music of the land.

'What is our need? Do we seek power for the sake of power? Is this but a whim, something that is really not of our journey?' asked Ra.

Tai did not reply. She remembered a story told to her by Ii-chantu when she asked him about the different gifts we carry. She decided to share it. Sitting beside the river she took up the threads of the tale and wove her way into the words.

> *Two brothers, who were born to a wealthy merchant, chose not to follow their father into that world. The older brother left to live high in the mountains with a sect that taught the deepest of magical powers. There he studied for many years to master their teachings, by fasting often and training his mind to use the skills of their world. The younger brother became a simple monk who found much enjoyment in a life devoted to the gentle way.*
>
> *The time came when each decided to make a journey, that by chance brought them together on the bank of a mighty river. They were delighted to meet each other after so many years. Each spoke of their dedication to their chosen way. The simple monk took very little time to tell his story, for he was very humble and spoke lightly of the trail he had travelled. The older brother spent much time describing his long years of training and the magic he could perform.*

When the ferryman arrived to carry them over the water, the monk paid with the smallest coin in the realm, for that was the fare. The other brother refused to pay. He declared he would walk across the water to demonstrate the power that he had gained through long days of study. He quickly completed this feat without difficulty, and sat to wait for the arrival of the ferry.

'Greetings, brother,' said the magical one, when it arrived safely. 'What do you think of my power?'

The simple monk thought for a time, then responded with a gentle smile, and a few brief words.

'I see that what you have studied a lifetime to achieve, I have accomplished with the smallest of all coins.'

'There ends Ii-chantu's story,' cried Tai with a chuckle. 'It is one of my favourites. Does it carry a message for us as we sit beside the waters of this river?'

'It says that power for power's sake is not the path of truth. That power must be exercised with wisdom and love at its side. Aria placed those lessons before us when we travelled the trail of the White Whale to the Islands of the Double Sea. Do we have the wisdom and love needed to truly honour power? When I look at myself I am not sure,' said Ra.

'That is my feeling too,' added Tai. 'Let us return and see if Hera and Utini are awake.'

'Thank you for bringing us to this river and the joy of the countryside,' said Hera. 'We slept but a little while, and found time to share our thoughts on many things. However, of the power to move stone we did not speak. Let us all hold onto that question for three days.'

The Sun was setting as the happy four arrived at the Arched Gate and entered without challenge from the warrior guards. Those impassive sentries knew them well, for some had been included in the twenty-four who tried to lift the carved stone block.

Three days later the four met again. Hera formally asked Ra and Tai if they felt the call of the stone, and truly saw a need to explore into its inner realms. All knew the decision was already made. It was indeed time for Ra and Tai to walk into a world of awesome power. Those who held the dream close knew this young couple had been chosen to go to the frozen north with the Inuit to prepare them for the trail to Tibet. Ii-chantu and Hltanuu knew the way was open to them. Eroa and Aria were of like mind.

Ra and Tai would take their first steps on the morrow, long before the light of dawn, for that was ever the way.

Darkness. Whispering voices within the darkness. A flame cuts the gloom, one tall white candle gathers strength in the centre of the room, to open the way for soft words of welcome.

'The power to move the stone is of the Silence. To come to the power you must first learn to enter the Silence and hear the pulse of the universe. Let us prepare to enter that realm. Remember you cannot make it happen, you can only let it happen. If you push towards it, you merely move it further away...

> *Let go... wait upon the Silence... go within yourself... go deeper... open all you are to all that has ever been... drift on the tides of time into the timeless place... feel nothing... see nothing... be nothing... just be...*

Hera's gentle words shaded into the nothingness. Each travelled a different path yet in the end they came together at the sacred crossroads. A wondrous spirit moved to enfold them. They were of the Silence, the place of the joining of wisdom, power and love. Some called this realm the Oneness.

> *Return... return slowly... bring yourself back to this candle... return to this light and this place...*

Ra and Tai were astounded to see the candle had burned so low and the Sun was so high. They had journeyed half the night and much of the day. Smiles and laughter followed, for they knew they had truly gone within the Silence.

'We will go further tomorrow,' said Hera. 'We will walk that realm again. Before then, bring your body, mind and spirit firmly back to Gaia, for that is the old name of the earth, a name that is of the Silence. Do this now, relax, bathe in the waters, sit on the grass and be close to the stone. Find and keep the balance.'

Once again four gathered in the darkness. One candle waited to guide them back from the depths. On Hera's words they went quickly into ancient realms of mystery.

> *Hear the pulse of the universe... listen for it within yourself... feel it coursing through your body... remember it is of the Source...*

This time Hera brought them back to greet the dawn. They were all excited by the experience shared. Ra forgot about the need to learn to move the stone. He had discovered other realms that opened doors to wondrous places. There was so much to learn.

'I felt something very strong within the Silence, a beat, a sound that eludes my understanding,' said Tai. 'My power is of the waters, the tides of time and the spaces between. This I know, but I still do not understand how to use that power with confidence. I wait, I learn, and in the learning I begin to catch brief glimpses of its wider dimensions and its purpose. Yet, I feel so vague, so undirected, so useless.

'Ra stands so strongly with the songs of the whales, he outstrips me in the realm of the waters, leaves me wallowing in his wake and feeling incomplete. My twin sister Pana comes into her mind-speaking power, and the wisdom of the Stones of Lore, and holds in her hands our dreams and our future. How can one twin be gifted so much and bring it to its fullness so quickly, while the other languishes, sits in a waka awash with water and seems to be going nowhere? The doubting part of me says I am too slow to understand, while the trusting part reminds me everything is bounded by timing, not time.'

'Take heart, dear sister,' consoled, Hera. 'The sound you heard is the pulse of the universe. Few reach that far into the Silence so quickly. Your trail will open.'

'Did you hear it, Ra?' asked Hera.

'No! I found only silence within the Silence and amazing colours that thrilled me. They moved in wondrous ways to reach into something long forgotten. Words cannot describe the feelings and thoughts that shifted in me.'

Hera was excited to hear this. One heard the pulse and the other had seen its colours. Something both balanced and beautiful moved here. They sat quietly looking deeper into all shared.

'How intriguing,' she thought. 'Ra and Tai are twin flames that complement each other, that light up different dimensions, find the essence of diverse realms and hold them side by side. Each is the keyholder for the other. Only Tai can complete Ra's awakening. Tai, the young woman named for the tides themselves, opens the way for Ra, and Ra opens the way for Tai. That mirrors how Utini and I are joined as one.'

'Tai and Ra, you are of each other in a very special way. Fire needs water, and water needs fire for the balance, and both need air for life,' said Hera. 'I am intrigued by the way your senses interweave to make a whole. And one thing is very clear. Tai you will find the keys to the power of the waters are held by Ra, and Ra, Tai holds the keys that will one day bring you to the power to move the stone.

'We leave you now. It is your journey, one you must make hand in hand. We go that you might travel the Silence together. Learn to share the pulse and the colours. Only when you have achieved that will we gather as four again.'

As they parted, Hera repeated words placed before them in the beginning...

> *Remember you cannot make it happen, you can only let it happen. If you push towards it, you move it further away.*

Tai and Ra knew much was asked of them. Their need to journey within, and a yearning to embrace wider realms with power, flowed strongly now. What began as youthful curiosity had quietly taken on a serious face. And it opened into far more than they expected. The Silence was taking them deeper into themselves and each other. Their relationship was revealed as never before. They were two sides of one stone, woman and man, each unique and strong, each independent yet entwined, each born of the Source. Yet within that magic they saw there was separation, for they still stood outside the loving touch, the circle of creation.

Hera saw this clearly and Tai sensed it. Hera because she had known the anguish of not being betrothed at her birthing. She remembered the joy of meeting Utini and discovering their colours ran true, each to the other. She recalled how long they had waited for the completion of their love, how she had needed time to heal the wounds left by the violence another had laid so heavily on her body. She remembered the terror of the violation, the subsequent loneliness that had set her aside from others, and the arrival of Utini and Aria to free her from that burden.

Tai thought, 'I am eighteen and Ra must soon be sixteen. His age is uncertain, for none know the birth stars of the foundling babe now grown tall. He is the man I love, and I know he honours me in that way. Others our age have children. Pana, my twin, is the mother of a beautiful child. Yet we have yet to lie together as life companions. I need direction. We need help.'

'Hera, you have awakened a need within me,' confided Tai, when she sat alone with her a few days later. 'Everyone knows Ra and I seek to share our lives, that we will one day seek the blessing of the elders for that journey. Yet, we have not sealed that union. I fear Ra is beyond my reach, that we are destined to remain friends and nothing more, that I will never experience the closeness you share with Utini.'

'You are older than him, Tai,' said Hera. 'Think on that, remember at the outset he was the younger, the child who looked to you and Pana for comfort and friendship. That was in the early years, then he changed. When we sailed the trail of the whale he outgrew all of us, he became a man, the one who took responsibility for guiding us through the Octopus. He slips in and out of the world of the child and the man without knowing he is doing it. That is his strength, and in this matter his vulnerability. Deep down he seeks to hold you close, to lie beside you and share the long night of loving. But I feel he fears that step, holds back from it because it carries both gain and loss.'

'I do not understand,' responded Tai in confusion. 'I see only gain. Where is the loss?'

'The gain is that Ra the man will walk tall, but the child in him feels he will be diminished. Ra, your playmate of those early years, fears to be the true mate of the woman. The man needs you as much as you need him, but the child is confused.'

'How do I undo that confusion? Is there no hope, must we be forever bound within the world of the child?'

'No! No! No!' said Hera with a smile. 'Remember his joy when Aria and Eroa opened the way for you to be companions. He truly loves you and seeks to be the man. When you are life companions, the man will find there is still a place for the child.'

Tai felt heartened. Drew hope to her and waited, for she knew Hera was not yet finished. Her mind skipped into a better place where all she desired unfolded simply and with joy. Hera's next words merely accented that beautiful moment.

'There is a magic in loving that makes us taller, stronger and more complete in every way. Such sharing is of creation, a wondrous joining that brings heart, mind, spirit and body together in an ecstasy that is beyond words. It is of the Power, and, if held within the balance, opens the way for the inner journey of the spirit. Nothing eclipses that realm of fulfilment. It is of the core of life, of the web of all being and the wellspring of renewal.'

'Yet, there are those who seek spiritual enlightenment through a life of chastity,' responded Tai.

'That is true. There are people who choose that path, and it is one to be honoured, but does it answer your need or mine? Is it a higher way or simply another way? They have chosen to walk alone, to set themselves within a place that asks much of them, a regime of discipline that challenges them to grow and learn. Thus do they make the journey of the spirit.'

There was a long studied silence. They gazed with serious intent one on the other, then suddenly broke into loud laughter, knowing they shared a common thought. When calmness returned, Hera said with a broad smile, 'I know that is not my way or yours. We seek to explore realms far beyond ourselves by touching into each other. Man and woman joined. We embrace our deepest yearnings, share them heart to heart, joyously enjoying the excitement of the journey, and growing stronger in the knowing.'

'And children are the fruit of the meeting of those tides,' added Tai. 'It is the way of creation, the lore of love and loving. My problem is I know love and yearn for the loving. Yet, I still lie alone in the shadows of the night. What can I do?'

'Nothing,' said Hera with a smile.

'Nothing!' cried Tai in despair. 'Nothing, what do you mean, dear friend?'

'The way is already prepared for you. When you went into the Silence together you opened more doors than you can ever imagine. You have felt the pulse of the universe, and Ra has seen the colours that are woven by its power. Trust the power of the Silence, force nothing, be still and patient. Let the wish become the dream and the dream become the reality. Give yourself to the river within, to the flow that is without beginning or end, to the completeness of the circle and the tides of the cosmos. Become a child of the universe. Be.'

Tai departed still feeling a little bewildered, yet in some strange way more assured. To do nothing was easy, as long as she felt it would one day bring her to the loving way she sought to share with Ra. A long winter lay ahead. There was time to explore the wondrous worlds of the Inner Courtyard and the lands beyond its high walls. There would be time to journey together into the Silence. They would find each other for it was written thus, long ago.

They awoke one still morning to find the nearby hills wearing fine white cloaks. Then dark clouds gathered, heavy and sombre and herded close by winds that sang with a cold edge. Snow now fell within the Courtyard, drifted gently down to swirl into doorways as the breeze shifted and stirred, settled on the trees and stone walls, and covered the paths to create a beautiful white carpet that awaited each new footprint.

Tai ran to find Ra. Ra brought Utini and Hera. They called to Eroa and Aria who came with their children. Hltanuu and Kanohi rushed to greet them. Pana and Tali appeared from nowhere, and within a few moments they were all dancing to celebrate the joy of this day. Into this spinning excitement appeared Ii-chantu and Llana and the children. Smiling quietly upon the abandon of their friends, they were thrilled to walk the cleansing trail of snow again.

The cold hand of winter grasped the land to freeze the lakes and force the farmers to house their animals inside. It brought everyone closer to the fires, and opened the way for those with searching minds to explore many hidden realms. The snows spun a cocoon, a splendid whiteness that, in the one moment, both captured them and set them free. Free to sit and think, to tell stories and to share. Winter was a time of retreat, a season of acceptance, an opportunity to watch and wait and learn.

'Awake unto the Khan!' cried the voice that cut through the darkness. Dawn was still unheralded in the winter night, when those words reached Tai to startle her from the deepest of sleeps. Her muffled cry of response was answered by the opening of the door, and a harsh sweep of light that filled the room. Four royal retainers stood before her. Four tall, strong men, finely clothed. She was shaken, confused and bewildered.

'Dress quickly and wear a cloak,' was the next command. While that voice was not unkind, it lacked warmth. 'You are summoned. Say nothing and dress without delay.'

No one moved. No one made to leave or gave her privacy to prepare. So without complaint, but with growing concern, Tai dressed hastily and with care. She was not distressed by their presence, for they had all learned the people of the Middle Kingdom were different in many things, and the same in others. Her worry was around their purpose. What did it mean to... *Awake unto the Khan?* She was soon to find out.

They moved within a pool of light, for beyond the lamps, darkness cloaked all. And within that pool was captured the sound of her feet upon the snow, the beat of her heart and all her thoughts. Where the light ended the world seemed to end. Nothing stirred outside it.

A doorway opened to their footsteps. Another lived within this night, one unseen who heard their approach and beckoned them into a room of light. A long corridor led to another door, which opened, as had the other. No movement now. The four retainers stood two by two beside her, and with a silent signal sent her into the dimly lit chamber beyond, alone.

'Come closer, do not be afraid,' called a voice from the shadows.

Tai gathered her cloak about her with an instinctive, protective gesture, for she felt very vulnerable. She had recognised the voice of the Khan, and knew not if there was comfort in that, or greater threat. Then a new strength flowed, a clarity that was sustaining and filled with determination. Without leave to speak she stated her concern.

'Khan, forgive me for speaking without leave, but I wish to know without delay why I have been summoned.'

'Sit and be comfortable. You speak our language well. Few master it so quickly, for it stretches both the mind and the voice to hold its many sounds. You are indeed a woman of beauty and power.'

These words brought no comfort to Tai. She sensed the gentleness of this man, found reassurance in that, but was still beset by apprehension. Then he continued.

'Were you not betrothed to my young friend Ra, you might indeed have been called to share the remains of this night with me,' he announced with a laugh. 'Nay, to be even more honest, if he does not claim you soon, I may call you hence quite soon. Should I tell him this, or leave you to warn him of my intent?' again the laughter, and with it, a wicked playful smile.

Tai relaxed a little in response to his jovial words. He had blunted the edge of her anxiety with his jesting. Some had spoken of the Khan's invitations sent forth to other women from the waka. To summon in that way was strange to them. They had always offered guests comfort in the night. It was their way. There was honour in loving freely given. As she thought on that, the Khan broke through her thoughts to speak with sorrow in his voice.

'My people see me as a god, one with the power of life and death over others, an object of veneration and fear. Yet in all things I am but a man. If the truth be spoken in this precious time, lit only by the candle's flame, I am a very lonely man. There is no woman in my life, no companion and friend. Many share my bed. All looking for advantage, all tutored in the ways of pleasure, but unable to touch the essence of who I am, unable to hold me close and love me for myself. The Khan gets in the way of the man. The office overwhelms all the wonder and beauty that might be truly shared by a man and a woman.'

Tai knew not what was expected of her. She held her silence and waited to hear more. A thought formed, and grew, and was echoed in the next words of the Khan.

'You can help me in many ways. I need the advice of a woman, one who is betrothed, safe, secure in herself and still a virgin. One who will not create whirlpools of envy and hate by her very presence. One I can trust. One who seeks no advantage from confidences shared. I see all these things in you.'

Tai was taken aback. 'Why me?' was the thought that swirled through her mind. 'Aria and Hera walk with wisdom that goes far beyond mine. I do not know how I can help this man, for it seems I cannot even help myself in these matters. Yet, I wish to try, for he has opened his heart before this flame, and honoured me in a very special way.'

'Does your silence speak of consent? Will you hear my plea, and then decide if you will share my journey to its completion?' asked the Khan.

'I respect all you have placed before me,' responded Tai. 'If I have the means to aid you, it is yours to ask of me.'

'I wish to break the mould. I want you to help me find my true companion in life. Your vessels carried much to these shores. The Stone that fitted the place carved so long ago to await its arrival, warnings of the Black Robe threat to the balance and the Web of Life, and last, but not least, new ways of seeing the world. Nay to be more exact, a different way of relating man to woman and woman to man.'

The Khan paused for a long time, as if searching for the words he needed to express thoughts that had only recently become his own. Thoughts foreign to those who sat on this throne over the centuries.

'The women of the Middle Kingdom are of a rigid world that shuts them out of my life. I wish to break the pattern of bygone ages and start anew. I seek a true companion, one who will be both lover and friend. I seek her from amongst those who journey with you.'

Tai was stunned. This was the last thing she had expected. Her mind reeled. She thought of those who sailed from the Island of the

Rampart, sifted and sorted and found no answer. Who might stand beside this remarkable man for his long journey?

'Do you already have someone in mind, Khan?' she asked quietly. Certainty sat with her now. He already knew the one he wished to bring into his life. This man saw to distant horizons, walked a wide world and sat within it with wisdom. He knew. He would not be talking thus if he did not.

The candle flickered. The flame would soon die, would drown in the hot pool of wax that gathered at its base. Would the Khan's courage fail like the candle, give way to the flame that blazed strongly to bring its own end? She gained her answer when he reached down and set another candle to the light, gathered flame from flame, and placed it beside the one that had served this night. There was no turning back. He carried the light forward.

'The woman is known to you,' he whispered, as if fearing the walls might hear the next precious words. 'The name she carries is Llana, but beneath that rests another. How do I approach her to win her? I have observed the gentle ways of Aria and Eroa, the joy of Hera and Utini, the closeness of Hltanuu and Kaho, and the magic of your sister Pana and Tali of Kauai. I have learned I have much to learn, but this I know is the key. She cannot come to me by command. The caged sings a sad song.'

'Your words are filled with wisdom,' said Tai, who began to feel relieved. This man had indeed learned much. He was open to change, yearned for it and was prepared for what might be. 'A woman of the other nations seeks a man not a master, a friend and a lover, and someone who will leave her room to be herself. My words merely echo your own conclusions.'

Tai paused. She now knew her role was that of the messenger. In this she needed guidance from others.

'Khan, let me carry this forward quietly. To this end, may I share the essence of our meeting with Aria and Hera? Be assured they will carry it no further, not even to their companions, if that is your wish.'

'Do so. I trust you in this. It is time for you to leave. Forgive me for breaking your sleep and asking so much of you. I know age brings wisdom, and that some would say I might gain better counsel from women of greater years. Yet, I also know youth carries innocence in stronger measure, and often a simplicity that brings us quickly to truth. Please accept this amulet to honour all we shared this night. And may none see it as payment for favours gifted beneath the covers of the night.'

The Khan laughed at his last words to assure her he spoke once more in jest. As he held the treasure before her, Tai saw a precious stone catch the light of the flame to send forth a brilliant blue light. It was wonderful, a cut piece of exquisite beauty set within a finely crafted cusp. All was bound with grace into an elegant chain of gold.

Thus did they part. Tai to return through the darkness with four to guide her to her cold bed, and the Khan to his thoughts of a companion who would share his life. The last words that drifted into his mind as he found sleep, were, 'Llana is my chosen one, but if she does not find favour in me, I shall ask Ra if Tai might become my companion. A woman of such joy should not be left alone night after night.'

Tai awoke with a start. Ra was calling her name and rapping on the door. She remembered the events of the night, shook her head, and for a brief moment, wondered if she had dreamt it all. Then she saw the amulet and smiled.

'Enter!' she cried as Ra burst through the door. 'Come and see what the Khan has gifted to me. Isn't it beautiful?'

Ra took it from her outstretched hand and gazed on it with awe. It was indeed both precious and beautiful. Then he looked at Tai in a strange way. Sat very quietly and looked at her again, this time appraising his friend of so many years with close interest. Seeing her in a new way, and at the same time wanting to ask more about the gift and fearing to hear the answers. Tai broke the silence.

'Ra, you have a question about the gift. I see it churning through your mind. The amulet is indeed from the Khan, and by his own hand, and it was gifted in the early morn before the rising of the Sun. But that is all. He wished to speak privately with me, and, as is his want, waited not for the dawning. He recognises and honours our betrothal. You are pronounced his friend, but by his very words, one he thinks is rather slow in one matter of note.'

Ra smiled in answer to Tai's words. He knew she would share nothing more about her private meeting. That was easy to let go, but the Khan's words about his slowness turned again and again through his mind. For one who found joy in the swiftness of his mind, and the speed of his hand, they sat heavily upon him.

'In what way am I slow?' he asked Tai. And, when she merely smiled, he took the question to Aria, who gravely shook her head and sent him to Eroa, who solemnly referred him to Utini, who passed him on to Hera with a sigh.

'Who said you are slow?' asked Hera.

'Tai brought the words to me from the Khan,' replied Ra.

'Then it is the Khan you must see,' said Hera with a smile. 'I know the answer, and so do all who you have questioned so diligently this day, but what begins with the Khan must end with the Khan. It is the custom.'

Thus it was that Ra found himself sitting in private audience with his august friend. Many times they had shared in this way. Mutual respect and honesty marked their words, and it was from that understanding that the Khan spoke frankly of Ra's slowness in the matter of his companionship with Tai. He left in confusion to seek the aid of his brother of the long trails.

'What am I to do?' asked Ra.

'Talk to her,' said Utini. 'Go to Tai and share the turmoil I see etched upon your brow. Few speak so openly to each other, or with such simple truth. The Khan reveals something you have set aside, something you have hidden from yourself. Bring it into the light. Walk around it together.'

That evening, when they went aside from others to walk the Courtyard through a fresh covering of snow, it was Tai who spoke first. She felt the whole matter of their relationship was getting out of control, and Ra was being placed under a weight that was not fair to him. She was the prime mover in that, through the words relayed from the Khan.

Tai remembered well Hera's words... *Trust the power of the Silence, listen, force nothing, above all else be still and patient.* Her reference to the Khan's jovial comment would have been better left unsaid.

'Ra, I know what troubles you, and feel I am to blame for your distress. We were betrothed after we travelled the trail of the whale. Others know that and we know that. It is enough. What follows will come to pass in its own time.'

Ra took her hand in his and they walked for a long time in silence. He seemed lost for words, moving through shifting sands and uncertain of where to stand. Tai felt for him, saw the boy within the man in all his vulnerability, and wept within for his hurt.

'Ra, do you wish our lives to be bound in companionship, or would you sooner be set free of that agreement?'

'Tai, I cannot give you an answer. It would be easy to say yes, but there would be no truth in that. I am confused. I thought I knew, and now I feel unsure. Expectations created by others sit heavily upon me. I need time and I need space. Time apart from people, time to think and to see the way ahead.'

Walking hand in hand, they returned to the warmth of their rooms. They did not speak again. Silence covered all, and fresh snow flecked their dark cloaks with the blessings of the heavens.

The next day Ra departed on horseback with twelve of the Khan's royal guards as escort. He had decided to seek guidance in a distant monastery in the mountains to the north. Two moons were his gift to that journey of the spirit. One to look into himself, and one to look out to the wider world and the tides of life.

Tai was sad to see Ra go, as were others who had treated his situation with lightness. They too found it hard to see the boy as the man, for the boy had been such a joy, one forever bound in memory. It was right for Ra to go away for a time, to be apart.

The separation, nay the chasm that now placed Ra and Tai in different parts of this huge land, brought Tai and the Khan closer together. In Ra's absence, Tai gave more and more time to her study of the language of the Middle Kingdom, and the Khan insisted on tutoring her in the more difficult aspects of its classical forms. He enjoyed her company and she his. There was understanding now, and a deepening friendship born of the growing closeness of Llana and the Khan.

Three women had put their minds to the Khan's need. It was Tai's idea to have Llana accompany her for the lessons. For one nurtured within the mountains of Tibet, the language of the Middle Kingdom was a close relation. In the beginning, Llana came reluctantly into the presence of the Most August One. Aria and Hera accompanied them on the first occasion. Llana only returned a second time on Tai's insistence. The third visit saw the turning of the tide, for it was then that the Khan's warmth won her over. By the fourth and fifth sessions, Tai began to feel she was becoming one paddle too many in this canoe. Yet, for many weeks they continued to use the lessons as the stage upon which to dance to the music of a growing love. Thus did the weave created by Aria, Hera and Tai move and shape in answer to the Khan's dream.

The balance of Tai's day was now given to journeying into the Silence. The pulse that echoed there grew stronger, until the day arrived when other sounds began to form around it. Although very subtle at first, they carried her deeper and deeper into the mystery. There she discovered a sacred sound that she imagined came out of the Nothingness, the Void beyond. She held it close and realised it was, in truth, emitted by her own heart.

Tai found nothing strange in this, for her heartbeat was the throb of life, a mere echo of the pulse of the universe. Now she heard its song, a beautiful measure, a wondrous rhythm that moved her far beyond the magic of its insistent beat.

Yet that understanding was merely a beginning, for soon after she heard the song within her throat. It was music of another kind, a sound that needed no rush of air to give it form. Like her beating heart it was just there, a voice projected without conscious effort. And the mystery deepened when she felt a pulse, and its accompanying song, gather in the centre of her forehead.

'It's voices in my head now,' began Tai, when she eventually took her news to Hera. 'I go into the Silence and my body begins to sing. What think you of that my friend?'

'Glorious and wonderful,' replied Hera with glee. 'I cannot begin to tell you what you are discovering, and the power you are gathering to yourself.'

'Try, dear sister, or I will think my mind is losing its balance.'

'I have not experienced all you feel and hear. My entry to the Silence is at another level, one exclusive to the voice of the stone. I have been tutored in the realms you walk, I understand them and their uses, but have not been granted the means to set them free. Only Ii-chantu can bring you to mastery of the pulse of the universe and the music that echoes within the Silence. Let us visit the old one, and let us do it now.'

Ii-chantu rested beside a glowing fire tended by a woman, who sat quietly beyond its brightness. The jade Buddha sat serenely on a small wooden altar. Food and drink prepared for the old one rested on a flat stone. The scholar was completely at home, a favoured one who was cared for in every way.

'She hears the music of the chakras, explores three of the first seven and does it well,' said the old one with a smile. He, too, was excited to see Tai begin to move into her power. It was time for him to join her in her quest.

'You have entered the realms of the sacred sounds,' explained Ii-chantu. 'People think language came from...*out there somewhere...* but it is actually born within. It is of our own being, founded in the voices emitted by the power of our bodies.'

'Did you see the colour of each sound?' asked Hera.

'No!'

'Perhaps it's too soon for you,' said the old one. 'Let us go into this together on the morrow. Rest now and enjoy the quietness of the day. Walk a little and sit beside the waters to find the balance.'

When Tai departed, Hera and Ii-chantu shared their thoughts. Both knew Tai had leapt into the deepest of rivers, and laughed at that, for they knew she was born to know the power of the waters. They wondered why she heard the sounds, but failed to see the colours. They agreed Ra played a part in this matter, that he was both the impediment and the solution to flow of the river.

'What news of Ra?' asked the old one.

'Nothing for one moon now,' replied Hera. 'Not a single word from him, even though the Khan sent a courier to bring back a message. He returned to say the young master had not broken the vow of silence he placed upon himself. That he eats well, smiles when attended, sleeps often, walks far beyond the walls and is in good heart.'

'The heart is the key in this,' said Ii-chantu with a wry smile. 'He has a dancing mind and a soaring spirit that but awaits the joining of the heart. May it be soon, for I know the Darkness gathers to send another challenge to our journey. The scarred one wrapped in Black Robes, the vengeful one who sent lightning to stop us setting the Eleventh Tu Ahu within the land of night without end, gathers his strength for another assault. When you placed the Stone of Lore within the Courtyard, he sourced that pulse of power and scanned this realm and all within it. I watch his progress day by day and begin to see the shape of his next thrust. Ra may be needed to stand with Tai to counter it. We are far more vulnerable than most imagine.'

'And what news of Llana?' asked Hera. 'We know the Khan invited her to visit the tomb of his father. Few have ever made that journey of remembrance with him, and they have always been family. She loves the man. Is that to your liking, old one?'

'It is as written,' replied the grandfather of the woman who filled the life of the Khan with such joy. 'The winds of change sweep into the Middle Kingdom. She is born with power that will aid his purpose, and bring comfort and nurture to his path.'

'And you my friend,' asked Hera. 'How fare you, where does your trail lead?'

'I also find comfort in this land. There is mystery here and learning that excites me. I could happily sit in this courtyard to see out the last of my days. But the distant mountains call strongly, and the highest cry out for the last Tu Ahu. The one that is like no other. I think often of that journey and the means to bring it to completion. Power alone will not serve us. Only love, wisdom and power joined can place the magic within the circle.'

They parted, but did not meet on the morrow as decided, because Tai was too exhausted to enter the Silence that day. Hera and Ii-chantu understood, for young women sometimes tired when the moontides flowed. Concern was put aside. Another day was but another day in this season of winter rest. Yet a brief moment with Tai would have sent Hera to fetch Ii-chantu, for she was sorely tried, at risk unto death if not treated with skill born of the light.

'Awake to attend the sick,' was the cry that brought Hera out of sleep. Utini answered the door, greeted the retainers, helped her gather medicines and wrap herself in a warm cloak.

'Tai is very ill. The retainers who came shared this, but nothing more. What can I do to help?'

'Go for Ii-chantu. Do not delay, for this illness has moved with a speed that defies the ordinary. The girl was well but two days ago. She glowed with inner strength and fine health. Something born of the Darkness walks here!' cried Hera, as she left hastily. 'Call Aria to us, and Pana!' were the last words to reach him as he ran across the snow to find the old one.

It was a sad dawn. One for hushed voices and sombre thoughts. Those gathered to attend Tai feared for her survival. Hera saw the danger in all its starkness, recognised the hand of ill intent, and knew they would need strength and presence to bring her safely home.

Aria, Hera, Pana and Ii-chantu sat in a quiet place to consider their next move in the struggle. This was a battle for the life of one they all held dear, a contest of wills and a clash of powers over the body of Tai. With temporary blocks in place, and lines of life joined, it was time to plan the final victory. Crisis cried out for quick action, but healing that would last was of another place. Patience and the stillness held sway over lasting wisdom.

'She went too far into the Silence alone. She made herself vulnerable, exposed her inner self without the protection of the colours. She could not see them, could not weave the rainbow to keep the Darkness at bay, and thus opened the way for the shafts sent by Mata-u-enga,' offered Aria.

'Ra is the key to the colours,' added Hera.

'A shadow found entry to her being, one sent forth by the malevolence of Mata-u-enga. It fed upon her energy, leeched away her resistance, and probed deep to separate her from her power,' continued Ii-chantu.

'There is more to this,' confided Hera. 'She felt guilty over Ra's departure, for she blamed herself for causing him pain. That hurt tilted the balance against her, and opened the door that gave entry to the shadow. We failed to see her weakness, failed to stay close, failed to understand the uniqueness of the bond between Tai and Ra.'

'There is grave danger in that separation,' said Pana. 'Ask the Khan to send for Ra immediately.'

'We know the cause, and have the means to send the shadow back to its source,' said Aria. 'Let us now call forth the shafts of hate, embrace them and send them home with love.'

They hastened to Tai's side. It was done with power and purpose before the Sun swept aside the last of the night. Love harnessed with assurance drew the dark shafts from the body of the woman who lay before them. Then with reverence for all life, and generosity of spirit, they despatched them to the realms of the highest good, or if they chose, back to the master who fashioned them thus. All saw Tai stir as the words and the power wrought the healing. It was done. Time alone would reveal the depth of the damage and the life she might hope to lead in the days to come.

As they turned from the healing, the clatter of hoof beat on stone broke the silence. Something stirred in the courtyard.

'Take my horse! Lead me to her! Hurry, please hurry!'

Heads turned. Ra ran to Tai's side. He arrived unbidden, had reached the Arched Gate before the courier sent to call him hence had cleared the stables. He knew his purpose, for his wild ride had begun two days ago. Once again, time had folded over time with a gentle shift that brought him to meet her need. Twin flames, destined to shine as one, could not be denied.

Tai recovered slowly. She slept day after day to the concern of Ra, who was ever at her side. But those who nursed her knew she was free of the shadow and gathered strength in rest. Change hovered over everything like a gentle breeze. Change that brought nurture and commitment, change that put all at risk for the needs of the other, change filled with hope and yearning.

Few words passed between Tai and Ra, yet all saw love declared in their smiles. They were ready to step into the river together and accept its direction. In the joining of the tides they would seek life, and in the seeking grow to know each other, and themselves. Their lives were woven into the Silence. When they moved as one and came into the fullness of their power, the stone would shift to the sound of their song.

Thus was it written and recorded in the season of snow and the days of learning. And all the while one of the Stones of Lore rested within the Inner Courtyard of Khan. None fully understood the power set within its being, or the realms embraced by its presence. Yet all found reassurance in its mystery.

All the world was larger for its existence, for it spoke of today and tomorrow, and reached into antiquity to honour the wonders of all that had ever been. The beginning and the end met within the images carved deep into its surface. Hope sat within the balance carved there, and love moved on distant tides of time.

***

The Story Teller forgot those gathered this night, as he let his mind travel freely. In that moment he felt overwhelmed by the forces that moved to shape life. He thought of the many tides flowing through lives both young and old. Saw the vulnerable ones within the ebb and flow, those caught between the shadow and the light, those held across the inner and outer realms, and those drowning in the pull of daily life. He felt the many stresses generated to send them into turmoil and beyond the reach of the Silence.

'Grandfather, you take us into paradox again. Earlier you told us the Khan had everything, was all powerful, and yet in many ways was utterly powerless. Is this always the way of government?' asked one who was intrigued by the world of politics.

Before he could respond, another said, 'Ra and Tai were twin souls, two sides of one coin, yet they came to a place of separation. Is conflict inevitable in everything?'

*Seizing the pause, before a further question filled the space,
the old one said, 'The lore of opposites, the lore of change, and
the lore of harmony all revolve around conflict and the
resolution of conflict. The very existence of one idea creates its
opposite. That is the wonder of the balance. And that new
counter within the balance creates tension. You might call
that conflict, but remember it is a force for change, and from
that change can come harmony. And when harmony is
achieved, it of itself creates its opposite to honour the balance,
and the new tension, and the next resolution, and the
harmony that follows. All is change.'*

*'Such a world of endless cycles of change frightens me,' cried
someone in a quiet voice.*

*'Change is life and life is change. The fear you share is in all
of us. It can be a friend or a foe. Change, conflict, call it what
you will, is forever in our face and is the key to our journey.
We can react to change in one of two ways - in a protective
stance that attempts to shut the door against its intrusion, or
in a learning stance that invites change to teach us. We may
run away from change, stand and fight it, or embrace it with
joy in the dance that is life.'*

The Lament of the Stone

Seek the inner realms of stone, find its essence and therein find yourself.

Dark clouds sat solemnly in the east to block out the Sun. They gathered to close the line of life renewed with each dawning. Massing at awesome speed, driven by unnatural winds, the Darkness cloaked within the clouds stirred the ocean into frenzy and disarray.

Those who lived beside the Supreme Harbour of the Middle Kingdom felt the presence of the storm long before the first winds sent sweeping rains to lash their homes, and savage the vessels that rode at anchor. It touched the hairline, raised a shiver in the spine, set the teeth on edge, and alerted the senses to danger in ways different and powerful. Only the foolish took no heed of messages sent ahead of time.

The city, and the villages scattered through the surrounding hills, were alight with activity. Those awakened to the sound of the storm hurried to respond to its warning. Windows were shuttered and animals hastened to shelter. Children who had risen early were ushered to the safety of the home.

Lightning flashed and crackled. Trees bent to the wind and broke with explosive sound beneath its unrelenting blows. This was like no other storm that had ever reached these shores. Hurricanes of awesome destructive power sometimes shattered the calm of the hottest season. They were born of the heat of the ocean and fed of its bounty. This storm was birthed in the depths of the coldest of days and born of mystery.

Ii-chantu knew its source. 'This storm of the Darkness. It is sent by those who strive to bring us down,' were the words he shared with all who gathered to hear of its power. 'Tai took the first blow, a savage storm of the mind, and this is the second. The target of this fury lies anchored in the Great Harbour. Those who harness this maelstrom with ill intent, seek to destroy our waka. Tali's vessel has been safely hauled ashore to scrape the hulls. *Siigaay Kaa*, the Ocean Walker, is the one in danger.'

'Surely there is more to this. Mata-u-enga would not reveal his hand so openly for such a prize,' suggested Kaho. 'We could rebuild in one season.'

'You speak truly, there is a greater design. The waka of itself is nothing, but it holds everything. Remember two Stones of Lore are lashed to its deck. They are the prize. If he sinks them in the depths of the bay, he wins a huge victory.'

'Alert the Khan. Gather the crew,' shouted Kaho. 'Bring horses for them. We must beach our craft, send it high upon the shore before the Black Robes sink it in the tides.'

'Save the Stones!' was the cry that echoed through the Courtyard.

Two hundred quickly gathered to race through the city to challenge the Darkness. Men and women both, all committed to the struggle and prepared to risk their lives to save the Stones. Some, like Ra, had learned to ride the horses, while others crammed into horse-wagons driven by the Khan's men. It was a wild ride through streets littered with limbs torn from the trunks of the tall trees. The way was deserted. Only those driven to answer a higher call ventured forth this day.

Two wagons overturned and some people were injured. Speed was all now, and courage within the darkest of dawns. The Harbour opened to them. Ra and Kaho were the first to arrive, and with them the Commander of the Imperial Fleet of the Middle Kingdom. Cool heads were needed to meet the challenge of this tide.

The ship rode her anchors like a plunging dolphin. Leaping and straining to meet the enormous waves, the vessel struggled to ride free of the climbing waters. Yet each rising wave sent its crest across the splashboards and into the twin hulls. Water gathered and swirled within, weighed the waka down and slowly stole its power to lift to meet the challenge.

They needed to board the craft. Needed to bail it free of water, steer it before the wind, and beach it on the far shore. First they had to board it in numbers, but could they breach the waters between, the gulf that separated them from the stricken vessel? Kaho, who saw all this and more, was in earnest conversation with Mokoio, the Fleet Commander of the Khan.

'A vessel comes,' cried Mokoio into the teeth of the wind. 'The Khan has offered his own craft. It is the largest and always ready to meet the next tide. It arrives soon, but will it be in time?'

'I must send swimmers now. Bailers to stem the tide. *Siigaay Kaa* sits lower and lower in the waters,' shouted Kaho.

Thus did Ra and eleven others, who hoped they had the strength to swim to the craft, dive into the churning waters. Cries of encouragement swept across the widening gap as they struggled to reach the stricken waka. A murmur of sadness rippled through those who watched when only ten emerged from the tumbling waves to climb over the heaving sides of the vessel.

'The Khan's ship comes swiftly to us,' cried Mokoio over the scream of the wind.

As foretold the mighty craft swept down from the east with the wind propelling it rapidly across the waves. It rode the tempest with power. A sure hand held the great vessel on course. Kaho wondered who possessed such skilful hands.

'The Khan honours us by taking the helm,' said Mokoio. 'Few know these waters as he does, or handle craft with such sureness.'

Kaho was surprised to know the August One was the helmsman. He had no idea the leader of the Middle Kingdom was at home on the ocean. Those thoughts were snatched away by the force of the wind as the craft turned towards *Siigaay Kaa*. The waka was still afloat but too low in the water to last much longer.

Out of nowhere a huge wave built and crested. It lifted the wallowing vessel high, then hurried on to thrust it sideways. This assault bore the bailers and the wallowing craft to the limit of endurance. The first anchor rope parted with a crack that carried over the waters, and within an instant, the second released the vessel to the roiling tides. Ra's anguished cry of despair cut across the wind as the waka moved at the mercy of the storm.

The Khan signalled for battle drumbeat. Those at the long sweeps were urged to bend their all to the pull. Time stood still as the gap closed.

'Prepare a towing line,' was the next command, but it came too late.

Siigaay Kaa was lifted towards the sky. Then, as it prepared to meet the next wave, was tilted and driven deep by the pounding waters of the next wave. It sank in the blink of an eye.

The gasp of pain that enveloped all was pierced by the Khan's cry, 'Hold the sweeps. Trail lines in the water. Prepare to recover survivors.'

A brave, skilful manoeuvre brought them alongside the debris that marked the last voyage of the waka. Twelve had gone to serve the vessel that had carried them on the longest of tides. Twelve, who were prepared to give their all, to save the Stones gifted for the journey. Only eight were gathered from the waters alive. Ra was the last lifted from those sad tides. He was reluctant to leave the pitiful remains of a once proud craft, and to give up the hunt for survivors. Much was asked of all of them on this trail.

Mata-u-enga had won the day. The Darkness had shifted the balance once more. The one who fed on hate, and sowed dissension with relish, had found a way to thwart their plans. Yet, all was not lost.

'The Stones of Lore are in dark waters. Too deep to be reached by divers,' explained the Khan, the day after the tragedy that cast a pall of gloom over the Inner Courtyard. 'If ropes could be attached, we might raise the Stones. We think they will still be secured to the timbers of the waka. The original ropes were replaced with even stronger ones before the onset of this winter. My engineers have tried to snag the wreck with huge bronze hooks. However, the currents that run strongly through these waters snatch them aside before they reach the bottom. They will persist for as long as hope allows, but I fear they will not succeed. There has to be another way.'

'They are also beyond the mind of Hera. Her power to move stone is denied by depth of the water,' confided Ii-chantu. The Khan had been told how Hera's power had allowed them to lift weight that defied his strongest guards.

Yet it was indeed Hera who brought the first rays of hope. She knew there was a solution. What was beyond her might not be beyond others. Yet, she would need to move gently to explore the idea that rippled through her mind.

Tai was still resting. She was stronger now, and changed at a level that was hard to define, but different in the eyes of those with minds that see beneath the surface. Ra sat with her. He smiled at Hera and said, 'I am explaining to Tai for the third time that I was never in danger on the waka. Everyone knows I was careful when I swam out with the others to serve as a bailer. And when *Siigaay Kaa* sank it just disappeared beneath us.'

'You leave too much unsaid despite repeated tellings,' responded Tai with a laugh. Ra had changed too. No barrier stood between them now, nothing.

'We have been considering how to recover the Stones from the bottom of the bay. It is too deep for divers and I cannot reach it through the waters. We have yet to find a solution.'

'Can we help?' asked Tai, who now wished to be involved in everything, despite her need for further rest. 'I have also sought answers. The stone cannot be lifted unless it is made lighter. You say it is shielded from your power by water, so my question is would it be beyond mine for the same reason?'

'Several things arise from your question. First, we do not know if you truly developed the power to realign the stone. Second, even if you had the power, we do not know if it is still with you. Was it mere coincidence that you were the one attacked before the storm was sent to sink the waka? A huge mind moves here with a plan that encircles Gaia, and reaches out to challenge the shape of the universe. Third, although you are of the waters, and may move through them to join your mind to the stone, you have still to see the colours. Without them the stone will not come to your call. Fourth, it is Ra who carries that dimension, he sees the rainbow within the Silence and can sing it into the stone. And last of all, are you and Ra able to work as one?'

Hera finished with five fingers held before Tai to mark each point. Tai looked at Ra, then turned to Hera and replied, 'We are willing to try. Only by stepping out will we find the answers marked by your fair hand. To do nothing is to fail those who died to save the Stones.'

'The attempt is best made in spring,' said Hera. 'Enjoy yourselves, and when you are ready, we will sit with Ii-chantu to explore the realms of the stone once more. Meanwhile, Ra will tell you his fourth version of the sinking of the waka, and by the fifth telling you will understand he really watched everything safely from the shore.' Hera left them laughing together. It was rumoured Ra now stayed through the night.

Spring came with a glorious burst of colour. It was announced by the blossoms that clothed the trees of the Courtyard in cloaks of delight. The west wind warmed the land again and the snows departed the hills.

'We will go into the Silence together,' said Ii-chantu.

Hera, Tai and Ra sat around the brightness of the candle with the old one. They had gathered thus for one moon now, in preparation for the arrival of spring. Tai was fully recovered and Ra was bursting with energy. If will alone could lift the Stones, it was done already. They knew it was not that easy. Yet there were encouraging signs. Tai now heard the voice of all seven chakras, and Ra saw their colours as she visited each in turn. Mind linked to mind within the Silence, two became one to touch the pulse of the universe and hear its music.

'Open your eyes,' commanded the old one. 'Hold to the Silence and focus on the stone at your feet. Go within it Tai, search for the space between, move there and gently realign its essence, thread the colours through and then with good intent take all weight from it.'

Hera reached down and lifted the large stone. It was so light she felt it might float to the ceiling. No one spoke, but all rejoiced within. The laughter came like a bubbling stream when they returned from the Silence to honour the light of the candle.

'We did it!' cried Tai. 'Ra, we did it and I still feel strong.'

'Tai you were clear, and strong, and burning with purpose,' said Ii-chantu with a smile. He paused and turned to Ra to continue, 'Your support was so gentle, and yet so direct, it complemented her beautifully. We have a chance. Tomorrow, if you feel ready, we will work with the stone in water.'

'Thank you, stone,' said Tai, as she touched it lightly and skipped by to dance hand in hand with Ra through the Courtyard. 'Thank you, Ra, for being Ra,' she cried to the night. 'Thank you, life, for my healing.' No one felt any of this was strange. Tai and Ra had been celebrating thus for days and none knew the reason for their joy. 'Too soon to say,' were Tai's words of caution to Ra. 'Too soon for one who has been unwell for so long.'

Once again they sat in the light of the candle, but this time it sent its light to the waters of the Imperial Bath House. The large stone of yesterday rested on the bottom of the largest wooden tub. Hera sat beside it with warm water reaching to her shoulders. Tai came quickly to the stone and touched into its depths with such ease she was astonished. When Hera lifted it high, they all beamed with delight.

'It is easier in water. I am certain of that. Water aids me, lifts my power, speeds my entry and gives me greater strength,' cried Tai with huge excitement.

'Are you ready to try to call this stone to the surface?' asked the old one. 'That may not be necessary. I know the Khan has everything ready for the lifting. Special barges have been constructed and crews trained to manoeuvre them at your command. Leave that for another day if you are tired, but try now if you are ready.'

'Now! Let's do it now,' she announced with assurance.

They gathered again, and were astounded when Tai swiftly joined her mind to the stone at the bottom of the tub and called it to the surface.

'We have a good chance, a very good chance. You see, size is of no account in this,' said Ii-chantu. 'Calling stone is calling stone. All moves apace and two questions remain. Have the Khan's engineers really located the Stones? Will your mind find them beneath the tides? To reassure me on the latter will you go once more to this stone and call it forth?'

The old one went to the candle and snuffed it out. All was darkness. Tai knew she would come to this moment and set her mind to meet it. They waited, unsure of what was happening but filled with hope. Time passed, too much time and still there was no hint of success.

'I am lost. I cannot find my way,' whispered Tai in a shaken voice. 'My power has no place without my eyes. I have lost all direction.'

'Do you see the colours?' asked Hera.

'No they have gone. That is it. The colours have gone and the stone does not respond.'

'Hold Ra's hand. Join with his mind and try again,' suggested Ii-chantu with gentleness. 'You have the power. The darkness is no barrier. When the shadow entered your being it sowed seeds of doubt, but took nothing from you. Without the light, you fear the return of the shadow. Be assured it has gone far from you. Face the fear, walk to meet the doubt, and see it for what it really is. Gather up those misshapen seeds, and send them back to the Darkness with all the love at your command. Do that now!'

Silence. Silence as they helped Tai cleanse the seeded remnant of the shadow from her mind and body. An all-embracing silence that honoured the spirit. Then a cry of triumph. It was done. Tai was free of the fear of the shadow.

Once again they came to the stone within the darkness. Once again they sat around the tub and waited to hear the stone stirring to the touch of Tai's mind.

'The stone moves. Ra we have done it. The stone moves, dearest one.'

The flickering flame of the newly lit candle revealed a scene of the purest joy. Far more than the stone had moved. The balance of their lives had shifted into a wonderfully complete and sustaining place. They departed in joy.

'Hasten to the Khan,' was the cry that brought them early from their bed. Ra and Tai wondered why they were summoned hence.

The Khan was not alone. Llana sat by his side. They were frequent day companions now, but not of the night. Every action and every gesture of the Khan spoke of his love for this woman from another land. Excitement filled the air.

'Two matters touch our lives deeply this day,' announced the Great One, after the customary words of greeting. Both involve you in some way, so I wanted to speak of them in the quietness of this time.

'At High Sun we will try to bring the lost Stones to the surface. Everything is ready for our first attempt, and I wish to say we should not place a huge expectation on it. Too many unknowns veil this endeavour. I ask you to come to the challenge free of the burden of expectation. Patience and understanding are our guides in this. We will try again and again, but if in the end we do not succeed, may we be content to let the Stones go.

'My other news is filled with certainty. At the Gathering of the Nobles this evening, we intend to announce to all within the Middle Kingdom that Llana and I are betrothed, and in the autumn will be joined with ceremony new to this land. She is to be titled Life Companion to the Khan. All this is by her request and not by my command.' His laughter reinforced the jest that made light of the changes she brought to his lonely life.

'We thank you for your part in this. Friendship is a very precious thing, and often beyond the reach of one such as I. When your quest ends, consider returning to spend your lives with us. There is much we might share and much you might do for our people.'

Although no word of caution was placed there, they knew no part of this announcement must escape before the nobles were informed. So with cheerful words of congratulation, they left to begin what was destined to be an exciting day. Even if the Stones remained beneath the waves, there would be much to celebrate.

High Sun, and not a breath of wind disturbed the mirror of the waters. Few gathered close to the vessels commanded by Mokoio, for the Imperial Fleet kept casual craft away. However, many lined the shores, as word of the lifting of the Stones had travelled far and wide. Yet, there was a quietness in the crowd, an eagerness to see the task go well.

The venture was not a spectacle, but a sacred task performed by the Khan's spiritual advisers. Stone was honoured in this land and the Stones of Lore were already a legend throughout its many regions. All knew the story of the Stone within the Inner Courtyard, the one carried ashore and slotted into a place prepared in another lifetime. Mystery so powerful was succour to all.

'The floating markers place us over the first location. My engineers feel we are anchored in the most favoured waters. However, if you have other means to find where they rest on the bottom, share it now and we will work to your plan,' said the Khan.

Painstaking, careful work, over several moons, had led them to this place. Yet the Khan was humbly setting all that aside, if they came with better information.

'We thank you for opening the way,' responded Kaho. 'Everything your people have done suggests we sit above the wreck of my vessel. We respect that conclusion and wish only to proceed on your command.'

A hush fell over everything. Even the cries of the seabirds, and the sound of the waves caressing the distant shore, seemed muted. Tai and Ra stood high on the platform that joined the two barges as one. Ii-chantu and Hera were nowhere to be seen. That sat strangely with both of them. Yet there was freedom in their absence, an acknowledgment that the power they carried was truly their own.

'Are you ready, Tai?'

'Yes, Ra. Let us join hands and begin. Delay serves no purpose.'

The Central Sun was their candle now, the universe the room they entered to find the Silence, and the love of two joined as one, their Power. Ra felt Tai open the way and followed. Heard the pulse as never before, and saw her move through the chakras to call on all she was to summon the seven colours to these waters. He aided her to find their brightness, and held the balance for her journey to the Stones. Searching now, probing the waters, reaching out to honour stone caressed and cared for in days long gone. Linking mind to mind and heart to heart, to set the spirit free to touch the essence of the stone. Yearning to feel its presence and to bring it home.

'Hold me! Ra, hold me!' cried Tai. 'Hold me as I probe the depths. Be my lifeline as the darkness beckons and the shadows shift in the tides.'

Words welled up. Words gifted at another time in another place...

Go deeper... open all you are to all that has ever been... drift on the tides of time into the timeless place... feel nothing... see nothing.... be nothing... just be...

Siigaay Kaa filled her mind. A wreck appeared amidst the changing light created by the currents that stirred the sands on the ocean floor. Although twisted by the collapse of the joining platform, it was entire in every way. The stones were there. They lay on broken timbers, still strongly secured by the ropes, but canted at an angle. 'It is but a dream,' was the thought that surfaced from the depths she explored. 'A dream filled with wonders, shimmering shafts of light and fish that swim with grace to bring colour to this underworld of the waters.'

'Tai, move on. Call the stone to us,' were the words that brought all into focus. They helped her shift from the drifting realm of dreams into the place of action. Purpose gathered to her.

Tai responded, entered the stone and swiftly moved the alignment to bring it home. Trusting now, working by instinct to weave the colours strongly, singing to the stone, and all the while holding close to Ra.

Suddenly her vision shifted, blurred, filled with clouds of swirling sand and frightened fish that darted to and fro. No grace now, just panic as the world below shifted. Change born of magic stirred in the depths. Light suffused all, grew stronger and was joined by primal sound birthed in the creation. A cry reached for the heavens. The stars sang to welcome its arrival.

'I think the stone moved,' whispered Tai.

'I feel that too,' replied Ra. 'But will the ropes part to set it free?'

Silence now. The Khan at their side. Mokoio and Kaho standing close, all looking intently into the waters. Nothing moved. Then the sound came again, stronger and pitched to reach into the heart. Closer now, something surfacing, a loose timber, one spar set free to ride the tide. Nothing more.

Turmoil growing within. Concentration binding Ra and Tai. Expectation now, despite the warnings to set that aside. Bubbles surfacing, then an eerie cry of release. Movement beneath the waters, light erupting skywards amidst cries of amazement as the stones leapt from the deeps. And they brought *Siigaay Kaa* with them.

'Secure strong lines quickly,' cried Mokoio when he recovered his voice of command.

Skilled seamen instantly met the wreck on the tides and it was done. *Siigaay Kaa* was firmly lashed between the barges, and the hulls were cleared of water to ride higher on the tide. Dishevelled, battered, joining platform askew, splashboards broken, it was to the untrained eye a shattered mess. But to Kaho and those who knew, it was still sound because the hulls had not been smashed. All else was easy to replace and refit. The waka that was lost had miraculously returned to serve again. Another legend was gifted to the Middle Kingdom in that moment. The song of the stone, and the magic of the singers, would bring joy to many around the winter fires when the snow lay heavy on the ground.

Hera and Ii-chantu appeared from nowhere to embrace Tai and Ra. They were jubilant. Overjoyed, for their wildest dreams had been surpassed. They had prayed that the Stones had remained bound to the wreck, had stayed together, because then their journey to the bottom would have been cushioned by the buoyancy of the hulls. It would have been a slower descent into the tides, and at the end a softer landing. Set free of the timbers, the stones might have hit the seabed reefs with enough force to shatter. Yet, once safely at rest on the bottom, they hoped the ropes would rot and part, to allow Tai and Ra to call the Stones to the surface without the hindrance of the sodden timbers. But the bindings had not rotted. Instead the water had swelled their fibres to make them hold even tighter. No one had foreseen the raising of the waka. That the young couple might pull the stones with such power was incredible.

Tai and Ra were at a loss, bewildered, overwhelmed and exhausted. They needed rest, then the excitement that embraced the barges and rippled out from the crowds on the shore took hold. The clamour of thousands filled with wonder lifted them, they felt stronger. Much had been achieved upon these waters, and there was more to savour as Aria and Hera gathered them close and took them below to a place of quietness.

Tai knew she had come into her power with purpose and new presence. In the end, the shadow sent to bring her down had merely made her stronger. She revelled in the joy of that, and the wonder of the world she walked with Ra. Their babe would make its journey to greet the Sun in the time of nurture when the leaves left the trees. The seed quickened. It would gift to them an autumn child.

Ra had survived the challenges put before him, and found a place to honour both the boy within and the man he was becoming. Few would see a change in him, for the Ra of the quick and playful mind, the one who sings the songs of the whales, the seeker of the question beyond the question, the adventurer of the spirit and the student of the mystery, would ever stand tall. It was not a matter of being different in any way, just a matter of him accepting all he was, honouring his frailties and his strengths, and finding contentment in both.

They came ashore to a thunderous welcome. The city gathered, the people from the hill villages and the lowland farms gathered, the fishing people gathered, all came to share the splendour of this day. *Siigaay Kaa* was safely hauled ashore by a multitude of willing helpers, under the watchful eye of Kaho and Mokoio. Then the Khan stood on the deck of his ship which was moored at the long wharf, to speak to the assembled people. Llana was in attendance at his shoulder, and in the company of Eroa, Aria, Utini, Hera and others from the many nations.

Tai and Ra were asked to stand before them to receive flowers and gifts arranged for the occasion. The beautiful treasures bestowed by their friend belied his suggestion he came to this first attempt with no expectations. Kindness sat close to this Khan.

Kaho rose to thank the Khan, and the people of the Middle Kingdom, for restoring his waka to him. Ii-chantu then rose to add his words of praise for the recovery of the Stones.

When all was done, the Khan called the Keeper of the House of the Nobles to him. They spoke briefly, and then an order was given into the hands of the couriers of the realm. The highest born in the land were summoned to gather with all haste. As most were already nearby, the royal command was quickly answered. Each came with five retainers and the furled flag of their House. Arrayed before the Great One in serried ranks according to ancient tradition, they awaited the word of their Keeper to reveal the magnificence of their colours. On his command they were unfurled to dance in the rising wind and create a beautiful ocean of pulsating colour.

'He is going to do it now,' whispered Tai.

'You mean he will not wait until this evening,' replied Ra quietly.

Tai merely nodded, for all was ready, and a hush fell over the House of Nobles and the people. The Khan rose to his feet and stood to embrace the silence that reached so far. He waited upon the words that would signal a new era for the Middle Kingdom. By this very act of announcing the new way in the presence of the nobles and the people, he set the seal on it with power. Thus would action and word be joined.

'This day is like no other in my life. I hope in the years to come each and every one of you will remember it thus. Not for me, for my few words, for my pleasure in the moment, but for the changes it brings in your lives. The winds of change have been gathering in the desert of the red dust, the one crossed by the Dragon Road. It tells us a dragon stirs within this land and the nations beyond these shores. It brings the fire of renewal into our lives, gives us once again the opportunity to learn to work together, one with another, neighbour with neighbour, house with house, district with district and nation with nation.

'We have created chains that bind us to ways that have long lost their meaning. Men and women have been locked into patterns that deny them both the freedom to grow and learn. The balance has gone from our lives. Our children are bequeathed a world that has lost its direction and wider purpose. We stagnate as a Kingdom, seal our strengths behind closed doors and live beneath a yoke of order that confines and crushes the human spirit. I am the inheritor of that system, the one dedicated to carry it forward. And I choose not to follow that way.

'Law is meant to be the guarantor of freedom, not the tormentor of the innocent. True law is the mark of the highest good, not an excuse for some to wield power unjustly over others. True law is the gift of the wise, not the instrument of the oppressor.

'Nobles of the Most Honourable Houses, I invite you to sit in session to find a new way. I invite you to pledge your lives, before all assembled here, to honour the good. I invite you to find the courage to become the leaders of a Kingdom founded on truth, justice and the nurture of all the people. I ask you to honour traditions bound with the integrity of our ancestors, and reject customs and practices that do not serve their dream.

'Those who choose not to serve me thus may leave. If you seek to serve with a divided heart it is better to walk away. Your choice will be honoured and accepted for as long as you walk in peace. Others will stand where you choose not to stand. That will be the way. If you wish to leave, lower your colours and do it now.'

No one moved. Every flag flew high and the people cheered.

'We stand together in this. The path ahead is not an easy one, but worthy of our lives. Be brave, and be true to the dream we place beside these waters and share with the land. All I am, I gift to you and those we serve. And there is more, for on this day of new beginnings, I announce a betrothal.

'Before all gathered here, and in the presence of the House of Nobles, I, the Khan of the Middle Kingdom, pledge myself in constancy and love to the one named Llana, who was born of the land at the Roof of the World. If this pledge is accepted by the one I ask, she is to carry the title of Life Companion to the Khan.'

All who knew the custom of the Middle Kingdom were stunned. Never in living memory, or in recorded history, had a Khan publicly asked a woman to be his companion. In the past, such matters were by his command alone. Their amazement was even greater, when Llana stood before the Khan, and responded to his pledge in a clear voice that carried far.

'Khan, Keeper of the House of Nobles, people of the Middle Kingdom, friends of the long journey, grandfather Ii-chantu, I stand before you all to accept the pledge placed upon these waters. May we all honour the dream of a new beginning, that is my wish and my purpose. I gift my life to the dream and the welfare of the Middle Kingdom. So be it, and may it ever be so.'

Wild and excited applause followed her acceptance. The voice of the young woman reached into the crowds, and her words were taken up and relayed on. Within days, each and every word would be echoing off the mountains in the remotest reaches of the Kingdom. The winds of change had indeed found a strong and beautiful voice.

'His timing was immaculate,' said Ra

'This was the perfect moment,' responded Tai. 'He seized the wonder of the recovered Stones and wedded that to the changes he envisages for his people. I am tempted to stay here to help them see it through.'

That was but a passing thought, for both knew the snows were retreating from the high passes that led to the Silk Road, the one some called the Dragon. That trail was their challenge, and the need of the many nations that sought to recreate, for all time, the Web of Life and restore the balance.

> Not all celebrated the recovery of the Stones. The joy of many may be the envy of others. Those who gathered their Black Robes around them in the darkest of realms were filled with anger. They had laboured long and hard to seed hurt within Tai, and gather the storm to sink the waka.

> Time ran out. Time moved with too much purpose. Time served the good. It was time to interrupt its flow, to distort and reshape it to serve the servants of the shadowlands. Time to spin threads of discord. Perhaps even time to destroy time itself.

***

'Grandfather, my question may seem a foolish one, but it cries to be heard. How did we lose the powers Tai and Ra used to touch the stone?'

'Your question is in no way foolish. I believe the answer is woven into the story. Our power is diminished by separation.

When we see ourselves as greater than others, when we place humankind above other creatures, above and beyond the realms of the birds and the fishes, outside the world of stone and the colours, we give away our power. Only when we see we are part of everything, joined to creation, bound to all the realms and integrated into the Web of Life, do we begin to call on our full potential.'

'Why did they have to enter the Silence?'

'Only there could they let go of all that created separation,' confided the old one. 'Remember they were told to... drift on the tides of time into the timeless place... to feel nothing... to see nothing... to be nothing... just to be... In the Silence they found themselves again, found the truth of who they were, and connected with all that has ever been.'

'Is the Silence there for all of us. It is still within the reach of everyone?'

'Nothing has gone beyond recall. The Silence awaits us all. It is of all our journeys and is visited more often than you realise. You have all sat within it at some time. It awaits your return.'

The Distortion of Time

The sands of time are like the candle that measures the passing of the light. They fall within a glass that holds no sense of days long gone or still to come. They mark the Eternal Now.

Dawn found the old one restless and aware of the need for action. Yesterday his granddaughter had been presented to the Middle Kingdom as Life Companion to the Khan. Yesterday the Stones had been raised from the ocean bed and with them the waka. All had celebrated long into the night, all but the one named Ii-chantu.

'Time outpaces us,' he said aloud to himself. 'Something important moves within the realms of time. Those who work to frustrate the balance have caught us unawares on two counts. Tai suffered for that, and the Stones. We have grown less vigilant, have found such comfort in this beautiful sanctuary that we may have lost our way. No, that is unfair. The snows closed the trail and bound us to winter over in warmth and nurture. Some needed that, even I have found strength in delay. But I sense the wheel turns too fast now, favours those who seek to send us into the tides of chaos and threaten to bring us down. I need to know more, I must risk another journey into the dungeon of the servants of the Darkness.

'Mata-u-enga has changed his course. He now meddles with time. I must know more. But first I need to ask Aria and her friends to watch over me when I slip beyond these realms to explore another.'

None of them complained when word came for them to sit with Ii-chantu. The grandfather of all never called them lightly. If he saw a need they were bound to respond.

'It is the only way,' said Ii-chantu with a sigh. 'Each journey into the cold halls of their shadowed place of power makes me more vulnerable. They grow aware of my presence and hope to set a trap to capture me. I need you as my anchor, I need your strong minds to call me home. Leaving is easy but the return is filled with danger. They would rejoice in holding me in the emptiness between, forever.'

'Can you tell us more? Why must you take this terrible risk? We need you here, you are dear to us, you are the elder who guides our faltering footsteps. Without you we would be lost,' cried Aria with deep concern.

'The Black Robes are trying to reshape time. They foolishly tamper with powers beyond their understanding. In their ignorance they may distort far more than they suspect. I need to move amongst them, I need to see them at work if I am to counter their designs. Too much has already been put at risk by my failure to venture into their presence during the season of the snows. Time waits for no one.'

After brief words of instruction, the old one sat within a circle formed by Aria, Hera, Hltanuu, Pana and Tai, each the finger of the hand that would reach out to guide his return. Aria held the power, she was the one asked to bind all five as one. Each sat with a candle placed before them to light the way home, and to turn aside the shadows if the old one was pursued.

A sound of sacred timbre filled the room, held, then faded as the mind of the old one departed on its long journey across the ocean. No one spoke, they gave all their being to holding Ii-chantu close. The candles burned low.

'He has been gone too long,' whispered Aria. ' Hltanuu and Pana, send your thoughts to him. Find his need.'

Once again these two sisters of the far-reaching mind were joined to serve the nations. Born of different lands, but gifted with the same voice to reach across the universe, they linked hands and went into the space between. The candles slowly burnt lower to mark the passing of time.

Deep anguish marked the faces of Pana and Hltanuu, as they penetrated the hurt that folded over the caverns of the Red Conclave. Probe met probe. More pain now as the shadow people honed their minds to capture those who intruded on their sanctum. Holding firmly to the light, they searched within that growing clamour of hate-filled minds, and heard the whispered words of Ii-chantu.

'Call me home now!'

Five sat expectantly before five candles that would soon die. Two shuddered and moaned as they struggled to put aside the fear that embroidered the dank walls of the caverns. Then they smiled as they found the strength to embrace the darkness. Joined by intent, they sent healing to all within that hollowed place, and, as in other days, healing was rejected. When this was done the old one stirred, opened his eyes and smiled.

'Pana and Hltanuu, thank you for reaching out to me. Your guiding hands set me free of the warp they were weaving with time. I was in too deep to find the return trail. You broke their hold by splitting the focus of their minds.'

'What did you learn?' asked Hera.

'They are trying to bend time, to speed it up and thus shift the span of the seasons. This will distort the memory of the trees, bring them to a cycle that is so short they will never again produce good seed. The birds will nest in spring, but the seasons will turn so fast upon each other their chicks will come to winter long before they are able to survive the cold. Likewise fish will fail to produce young. The rhythm of the ages will shift so far few creatures and plants will survive. All life is threatened.

The land will also suffer. With such rapid changes, with short hot summers and deep cold winters following so quickly upon each other, erosion will send the hillsides into the rivers, and constant floods will scour the valleys. People will starve, nations will collapse and a climate of fear will open the way for Black Robe conquest.'

'Can they succeed?' asked Aria.

'Yes! They have the means. But if we move now we still have time to save the ancient lore of time. Call our people together. Tell the Khan. Delay is the danger.'

The Khan, and all invited to the Imperial Hall, listened to Ii-chantu with growing apprehension. The thought of black magicians bending time, to destroy life as they knew it, was difficult to comprehend. Yet they had seen a young couple raise massive stones from the ocean. Nothing seemed impossible in that moment. When the old one finished, the Khan invited comment.

'We could discuss this matter through the remainder of the night and still have no answers,' said Eroa. 'I suggest we invite Ii-chantu to open the way by sharing his thoughts on how to annul this threat. Let his understanding guide us at the outset.'

Thus did the old one speak again. Until invited to suggest the remedy he had felt constrained to be silent on that matter. Now that the Khan had assented to Eroa's suggestion he was ready to share all.

'There is only one amongst us who can intercede to close the prime portal of time. Only she has the power and the means. I speak of Llana. And she can only succeed with the help of a great circle that joins many hands.'

'I know of what you speak grandfather, and understand the price. I am honoured to accept the challenge and to join within the circle,' responded Llana with a break in her voice.

'Can you explain the price?' asked the Khan with gentleness.

'Walking the inner realms of time, entering the before and the beyond, may shift Llana's age,' explained Ii-chantu. 'She may grow younger or older, or she may stay the same. All this is conjecture, for none I know have ventured into that place in my lifetime.'

'May we have time to speak of this alone?' said the Khan. 'In our absence explain to my aides what is needed for the making of the circle. Everything you desire is at your command.'

Nine hundred and ninety-nine men, women and children gathered in the Inner Courtyard of the Khan to form the circle, that was in truth three circles. The outer one was created by grandmothers and grandfathers, the next by parents and the inner one by children. The Stone of Lore was at the centre. Thus were three generations arrayed to stand tall to propel Llana through time. Without that span of youth and old age, without the commitment of all who linked hand, heart and mind, she would never breach the inner realms to close the portal. Only their commitment allowed her to shut the door of time on those who worked to break it down.

All waited on the return of the Khan and Llana. They arrived hand in hand to walk calmly to the edge of the outer circle. As it parted they both stepped through, to Ii-chantu's surprise, for this was to be Llana's journey, hers alone. They passed through the second and the third circles together and came to the Stone of Lore. With calm assurance, and a courage that touched all who knew the dangers they faced, they stood side by side to enter the unknown as companions.

'If time steals age from them, or adds it to their years, they are prepared to share that burden together. By standing as one they will age as one,' thought Ii-chantu. 'A wonderful bond of love enfolds them. They could have no greater protection.'

'Stand tall and strong for our journey,' cried Llana. 'Gift your strength to us and your caring. Do not break the tie, hold steadfast hand in hand, until I speak again to free you of the burden. Do this for the turning of the seasons and the ordered cycles of the Moon and Sun. Do this for the time-worn pattern of the tides that rise and fall on the shore. Do this for the continuance of the ancient lore of time. And do it now.'

Some said a wondrous sound filled the Courtyard, and others spoke of colours that swept swiftly around the circles. All agreed that time shifted in some strange way, for in an instant, day changed to night. Then power gathered on the outer rim and wove its way across the spaces between the circles. Its passage was marked by clear blue light. When it reached the two who embraced beside the Stone, it enveloped them, grew brighter still, and sent a vivid shaft of light into the darkened skies.

'It is done! It is done!' cried Llana. 'Time holds, the seasons are secure. I release you from the circle. Rest now, for you have given much this day.' The voice that spoke with such assurance was younger than before.

Those who moved to light the way for the Khan, and his chosen one, were amazed to see he walked with the step of a much younger man, and the woman beside him was but a woman of nineteen years.

'Have we become younger together?' whispered the Khan to his companion. 'You look extraordinarily youthful.'

'And you also,' was her happy reply.

The arrival of her grandfather, and many friends, cut short their words of amazement. All the old one wished was done. They had set to rights the realm of time and the price asked had not been too high to bear.

In another land, in caverns deep within the earth, stunned figures cloaked in black slowly struggled to revive. Some lay on the cold stone floor and others were slumped over tables. The closing of the portal they had begun to open with such disregard for life, had sent back to them all the anger and pain harnessed to that purpose. It arrived multiplied tenfold, and with a such a harsh sound it shattered the hearing of some forever. Others felt its force within, bent double, writhing and screaming until falling into unconsciousness, a blessed relief for minds twisted too far, and torn apart by a massive shift in time.

One took little of the pain. Mata-u-enga saw the return of their dark energy long before the others, and set about him a black shield to deflect it. He survived, but others did not. In the days ahead he would create anew the Red Conclave with knowledge birthed by harsh experience. He swore it would be stronger than before, and totally committed to the victory of the Darkness over the Light.

'Bring a fiery torch to me,' he shouted. 'Clean away this mess! We have designs to weave, blood to let and a sacred task to fulfil. Bring me light.' He said far more than he knew.

The Inner Courtyard of the Khan was very quiet now. Those who celebrated the power of the circle had recently gone to their rest. Only two still walked beneath stars that held true to ancient trails in the fullness of the Moon. They found comfort in that sight, for it was of their making. Order, the time-honoured order of the heavens, was secure. Time still honoured time.

'You made a hard decision, dear one,' said Llana. 'I had no choice, for to hold back was to invite the end of all. But for you there was another way, a safe way that would ensure you survived to meet the needs of your people. Yet you chose to stand beside me, never knowing the outcome, but honouring love and trust. It was your sure hand that brought me back to the circle so quickly. It was your presence that meant the shift was swift, and the distortion so small we were only changed by a mere fifteen years. The universe gifting time to us, honoured the trail we travelled together, and will continue to do so in the many years left for our journey.'

'Let us go to your children now. We promised to see them tucked safely in bed. They have a younger mother and stepfather to share their life. May we hope we did not lose our wisdom with the years we shed. We will need all of it for the work that beckons. All of it and more. Rest beckons, there has been almost too much magic in this day,' said the Khan with a chuckle.

They departed hand in hand. It was ever that way now. Both content and secure in their commitment. As they passed the Stone of Lore, Llana paused. She searched her mind and found lodged there words that tumbled through time, words gifted by the stone, the memory of all.

> *Stone children awaken... answer the call of prophecy...*
> *honour the message of the Stones of Lore... move on the wide*
> *waters... bind the stars to the land... sing of the sacred... hold*
> *and heal... heal and hold... hold and heal...'*

'Others with wiser heads than mine should sit with this riddle,' said Llana. 'It is tomorrow's business, I have other plans for this night.'

Those called to answer the demands of Mata-u-enga sat very still. Within each and every one of them, fear contended with ambition. Power was the food they sought to feed the ego. Power that grew in the soured soil of other people's pain, the fruit nurtured in envy, anger and hate. Power that threatens to corrupt the very essence of the spirit.

'Serve me well,' said the master. 'Serve me well or I will serve you ill.'

***

'Time, time, time, so much tied within time, or loosed by time,' thought the Story Teller. He waited, and was not surprised when someone asked him to say more about time.

'We move to many tides of time,' he said. 'Time measured as the candle burns low, time marked by the rise and fall of the tides, time revolving around the waxing and waning of the Moon, time scribed by the cycle of the Central Sun, and time bounded by time. Yet these are but some of the many cloaks worn by time.

'The Ancients taught us time is far more than the sum of all we see, the movement forward that gives a place to yesterday, today and tomorrow. They spoke of the eternal now, of time that embraces all seasons, past, present and future, in one moment.

'Nay even more than that, time without moment. They taught that if we could move fast enough, time might stand still, or slip sideways, or reverse. Space travel and work in astrophysics confirms their understandings. Speed alters time, thought alters time, and the moving spirit alters time.'

The Fork in the Trail

Journey to the sacred crossroads, the parting in the trail, where east and west embrace the rim of life's greatest circle. Mark it well, for there the spirit meets the greatest challenge and knows the deepest joy.

High Sun found the leaders of the nations sitting with the Khan. They were pleased with all achieved in recent days. The healing of Tai, the recovery of the Stones and the waka, and the saving of the seasons.

'We have won time,' said Eroa with a smile to those assembled. 'Yet all know the snows retreat and the high trail calls. The Khan has organised vessels to carry us on the Yangtze River Road and we thank him for that service. Much has been done to help us to journey to the Silk Road and beyond. May we now decide the day of departure and those called to this difficult trail?'

The Khan spoke to confirm all was arranged for the trail party. Then he looked to Llana and said, 'We come with a message from the distant realms of time. One received within the circle of yesterday. But I am not the carrier of the words.'

Llana took up the threads to share the message gifted during her journey to save the realm of time...

> *The Stone children awaken... answer the call of prophecy... travel the high trail... move on the wide waters... heal and hold...*

Mystery walked the land again. Excitement grew as everyone let the words travel widely in the hope they would find a home. Only certain minds could walk around them with the insight to set the meaning free. Brave Mira, who drowned when *Kekeno* went down, was one with that ability. Kanohi was able to take on the cloak of the seer to explore intent, but he was journeying home. Among those who sat within this circle only Hera and Ii-chantu might have the measure of the message.

Silence provided room for penetration. No one looked at the two who gave them hope. It was the old one who spoke first.

'We come to the moment of separation. There is a fork in the trail. This I see but little more.'

'Truth walks with the old one,' continued Hera. 'The trail forks, one way is over the mountains and the other over water. Nay, it is clearer still. The second trail is on the ocean, for we are gifted the words... *move on the wide waters.* The stones that *awaken* are the ones we recovered from the sea. The voyage is for them and their destination is unclear, but the stars will be our guide.'

'This news changes everything,' said Eroa. 'We have to decide who goes overland and who by sea. That is only the *who* of things. Then we face the *where* and the *how.* Hera and Ii-chantu, I ask you to go deeper into the mystery, to discover where the Stones are destined to go. Others may be able to help you. Spare no one, for time watches overall.'

That evening five sat around a fire. Ii-chantu had called them together. Hera and Aria sat opposite Ra and Tai, and the old one closed the circle.

'Seven more will arrive later,' said Ii-chantu. 'Meanwhile let us find out the destination of the stones.'

Silence followed. No one had advanced that part of the mystery despite long contemplation. The words gifted to Llana gave no indication for the *wide waters* were indeed very wide.

'Let us ask the Stones,' said Aria. 'They should hold the song of arrival. Let us simply ask them for direction and let us do it now.'

They called for a wagon, and within moments were hurrying to the Harbour and the Stones. Tall guards stood around them night and day, but gave way to the five who entered. The Khan had asked that Ii-chantu be given access at any time of his choosing. Aria stood before those wondrous treasures crafted by the Ancients, and with a song of antiquity, opened the way to the stone. Then she turned to Tai and Ra and said, 'They know your voice, and the colours you hold, and wait upon your inquiry,' and stepped back.

Tai lit a candle and placed it between the two Stones. She sat before them with Ra at her side and moved into the Silence. She was gone a long time. All were relieved when she returned to Ra, who had served as her anchor. Lines of tiredness scored her face, but beyond them were etched lines of hope.

'Each has a different destination. They journey together on a long haul towards the setting Sun. Then in a land named Su-meria, they await the arrival of the twelve who travel the Silk Road. United, all sail on until they come to the Red Sea and the Kingdom of Egypt. One Stone stays within that realm and the other goes on a long sea voyage to Hengeland.

'The last Stone is guided by the songs of the sacred wind. It creates the final union, the linking of stone to stone and star to star. It is the Master Stone, the source of the music that aligns the balance with the spheres. All this I recite, for little of it is of my understanding.'

Two arrived, then soon after five more to bring the numbers now assembled to twelve. Ii-chantu had sent them word of the new place of meeting. The Khan and Llana were the first, and Utini, Kaho, Hltanuu, Pana and Tali the last to sit around the Stone. Twelve, the number for the long trails gathered. Tai slowly repeated the words she heard within the Stones, and then sat quietly while others teased their way through the information.

'Send for Mokoio,' ordered the Khan. 'He has sailed the mysterious western waters.'

Mokoio came within minutes. He had been forewarned of the meeting and the possibility of consultation. Once again, Tai recited the information.

'Su-meria, and the wondrous land of Egypt, are charted in the ancient logs of the Imperial Fleet,' responded Mokoio. 'We can align all the stars that bring a vessel to both those lands. In my younger days I dreamed of reaching those shores, of sailing in the legendary waters of the River Tigris. However, Hengeland is unknown to me, but I will ask the Keeper of the Charts to search for its location.'

All were relieved. They knew the first destinations of the Stones, and although they were destined to part, all would meet again in

Su-meria. Adventure called and decision beckoned. Who was to walk the land, and who to sail the wide ocean?

'The sea trails are the domain of Kaho, Hltanuu and Kun-Kwii-aan, the elder of the Hai-da, who is too weary to be with us this night. To them we add Mokoio who has experience of the distant waters and would bring much to the voyage,' said Eroa.

'The Silk Road party needs Hera and Utini, and Eroa and Aria to place the Tu Ahu, under the direction of Ii-chantu and Llana,' said Kaho. 'If Hltanuu sails with me and Pana travels the land trail we could be ever aware of each other through their mind-link. Tali must decide if he is to send the Menehune vessel on the voyage, and if so, if he is to be in command. Ra and Tai would serve us well on both trails.'

'And what of me?' asked the Khan. 'I feel the land trail calls strongest.'

All were all taken by surprise. None thought he would leave his kingdom to make a long journey, be it by land or sea. Llana had hoped he might, but had not voiced that wish. Their discussions went backward and forward and reached no conclusion. Eventually it was decided to leave the decisions until the next moon. There was much to do to prepare for the two journeys that opened to them.

Ii-chantu took no part in any of that. He was content to sit in the warmth of the Courtyard to tell stories to the young.

'Would you like to hear the story of the students in the forest?' asked the old one.

The usual chorus of delight launched him into the tale.

> In a distant land of mystery, a revered teacher gave a stick to each of his students and took them to the edge of a great forest. He told them to walk into its vastness, and when they knew they were alone, to break the stick in two and return.

That evening all the students had appeared with their broken stick, but for one. He did not return the next day, or on the one that followed. Eventually he arrived on the fourth day, dirty, hungry and clutching his unbroken stick in his hand.

The other students thought him foolish and said that he had failed. However, the master asked that the late one be washed and fed, and then invited to sit with him.

'Tell me about your experience,' said the teacher. 'Tell me why you were away so long when the others completed the task that very day. And tell me why you returned with your stick unbroken.'

'I walked and walked until I was very tired. Then I lay beneath a tree and slept through the night. Then I arose with the Sun to walk again. Day and night I searched for the place where I might be fully alone. Yet, in all the forest there was no such place. I have failed you, master.'

'Do you think he failed?' asked Ii-chantu.

'Yes!' was the loud cry that echoed around the Courtyard.

Then a little girl was heard to say, 'But he was not alone!'

Ii-chantu smiled and resumed the story.

'Pass your stick to the others,' said the teacher, 'let it go from hand to hand, and as each holds it, let them understand only you succeeded.'

'Now, little one, tell me why he was not alone,' said Ii-chantu to the young girl who had found the voice to stand apart from the chorus of the others.

'There were trees, and birds, and little crawling things everywhere,' answered the little one. 'How could he be alone?'

'You speak truly,' said Ii-chantu with a chuckle. 'Your words are of the old ways. Let us now go to the end of the story.' Thus did they come to the words of the teacher again.

> *'You are but a student, yet you teach us much. You discovered you could never be alone, that the trees were all around you, the birds ever singing, the nearby stream speaking of its journey, the Sun warming you by day and the Moon lighting your path by night. All spoke of the presence of the Creator and the Web of Life that embraces all of us. We are but strands bound into the whole, part of everything that has ever been, and all that is yet to come.*
>
> *'Carry the unbroken stick always. Let it remind you of the beauty of this day, and hold the thanks of all of us for what you have given to each and every one.'*

When Ii-chantu finished the story, the children left. They were there one moment, then gone the next, as if made invisible by magic.

'At least I know I am really not alone,' said the old one to himself with a laugh. Then he thought of all that moved within the greater realms and whispered, 'This evening all is decided. By early spring we will be gone.'

Darkness settled over the land. Torches, flaming brands attached to high standards, lit the Inner Courtyard for this occasion. The flags of the Noble Houses fluttered in the breeze, and arrayed around them were the leaders of the Middle Kingdom. They came with some excitement, for the city had been overflowing with rumours of long journeys on the land and sea. All would be revealed this night.

The Khan sat with Llana on a raised platform, and the leaders of the many nations who brought the Stone to this very place, sat close by. This was indeed an august occasion. When silence settled over all, the Khan stood to greet those assembled.

'Nobles of the Realm, my people, friends from across the ocean, we greet you. This night we commit the Middle Kingdom to ventures never attempted in my lifetime or the days of our ancestors. Dark and terrible forces move in other lands to destroy the balance that is the essence of life within our land. The Stones raised from the sea must be taken far to the west, to lands recorded in ancient memory and charts that join to the stars, but never seen by the living of today.'

He paused to allow people to consider his words. There was danger in what he proposed. Danger for himself, for those he committed to the journey, and for the nation. But the greater danger lay in doing nothing. To stand aside when evil walks is to condone its actions. That he could not do. The cost was too high.

'I am ordering Commander Mokoio to ready twelve vessels of the Imperial Fleet to prepare for sea. They will escort the Stones, and their guardians, to Su-meria, and the land beyond that is named Egypt. I invite nobles skilled in the ways of the ocean, and their sons, to join him on this expedition into waters unknown. It will be a brave voyage sailed with the guidance of ancient charts. Only fine leaders will see it through.

'My journey is a different one. I travel the Silk Road with those who go to place a sacred marker in the mountains to secure the Web of Life. After that we move on to Su-meria, where we join with the fleet for the voyage to Egypt.

'All these matters are to be pursued with courage. The struggle we engage in is more significant than any war ever waged by our ancestors. The survival of the planet is at stake, not just the land within our borders. The freedom of our minds and hearts, and the future of our children, all hang in the balance. We journey to hold Chaos in check. May we succeed, for to fail is too sad to even contemplate.'

A huge cheer resounded from the walls of stone. Flags were taken up and waved to honour the moment. The Middle Kingdom was to look outward again, and was committed to the stone and all who walked with it. Eroa and Kaho, and those who sat close by, were astounded. To sail with such power was beyond their wildest dreams. They had much to think on now. Ii-chantu knew that too, but held his silence. He wondered if they had lost their way.

Dawn found the Khan sitting with those chosen to travel the Silk Road. 'Everything is arranged,' he said with an air of excitement. 'We will be taken up the River Road of the Yangtze to the beginning of the land trail to the high pass. Pack horses and mounts await us there. Beyond the mountains, in the harsh lands of the Long Desert of the Dragon, a caravan of camels has been engaged to carry us into the hills that open the way to the Roof of the World. There they encamp while we move over the mountains with a yak train to place the sacred marker, the one you call the Tu Ahu. Then we return to the caravan and travel to Tashkent, and on through the highlands and deserts that lead to Su-meria. All this will take the spring months and the early days of Summer.'

He sat back with a happy smile lighting up his youthful face. The influence of the Khan reached far beyond his borders. These arrangements sent Eroa's thoughts back to how the peoples of the frozen north staged their long journey across the winter Tundra to the Inuit Nation.

'We step out in trust, and the help we need is forthcoming,' said Eroa. 'The Wheel that is the Sun turns, and we move with it. May the good go with us. Khan, all you offer is magnificent. Welcome to the trail.'

Meanwhile those gathered to another meeting pored over ancient charts with the help of the Keeper of the Star Maps. The wide ocean called to them, and they needed to walk the trails of the stars to respond. Kaho was overjoyed to have such knowledge for the journey, and a little overwhelmed by the idea of sailing with a fleet of twelve imperial vessels. Yet he knew *Siigaay Kaa* would be ready to match the others before the wind, if not with the paddles. Their long sweeping blades outreached his vessel. The Menehune craft had already proved that on the tides.

'We gain in strength,' he thought, as Mokoio and the Keeper studied another chart covered in symbols new to him. 'But is this kind of strength the answer? I begin to question the wisdom of this way, and need to share my concerns with Utini, Hera, Eroa and Aria.' Thus it was that later in the day Kaho placed his growing unease before his friends.

'In the past, we never moved with an open display of power. Our presence and our purpose has always been hidden behind a veil of innocence. We have always been far more than we seemed, and those who have carried the power have always seemed ordinary in every way.

'Look at Ra, when he toddled up to open the Seventh Gate within the Halls of Stone, and how he moved in later years on the long trail of the whale. A lad of eleven or twelve linking with whale song to guide us through the Octopus. That child completely outmanoeuvred the Commander of the Black Robe forces and the diabolical cunning of the Red Conclave.

'Think of the joining of Pana and Hltanuu across great distance, and the magic wielded by Ii-chantu with such simple grace, and of how he saved us from Kadaraka's Black Robe battle fleet. I could go on and on, and each instance would reveal power shielded within gentleness. That has always been the mark of our journeys and the secret of our achievements.'

'It is true, but tell me more. What is your concern about the Imperial Fleet?' asked Aria.

'It is very large, and by its very presence in foreign waters, will provoke others to aggression. We invite anger by openly moving with a display of force. That is not our way.'

'Are there other matters beyond the first?' she asked, for she sensed a need to probe even deeper. What surfaced here was of huge significance. The journey's end was never more important than the journey itself. How they moved, their deepest intent, was of greater account than anything else. A seemingly good end attained by questionable means was never one that sat well within the dream. When expediency overshadowed truth, when the need of the moment trampled on the needs of tomorrow, pain was gifted to the next generation, to the children.

'The military way, sailing in numbers within a chain of command, brings rigidity to the venture,' said Kaho. 'All advances in the belief authority, and unquestioning response to authority, achieves success in the most efficient and ordered way. It is achievement by control. That is their way but not our way. If we had adhered to such a system, Ra's voice would have been of no account on the sea trails. The commander of the waka would have found no place for the talents of a mere boy.

'We have made room for everyone. Honoured the place of each on the journey, placed none higher than another, and been open to all the tides that flowed. We have honoured the river within each of us, the truth and the magic. We have moved in ways that allowed the spirit of all we touch, and know, to be present in the moment. We have tried to be open to all life, not closed to its presence. We danced the trails.'

'You bring everything into place with simple wisdom,' said Utini. 'Thank you for going back to the roots that feed the wonder of who we are. It is good to see the commander of our waka cloak himself once more in the garb of the forester. You bring us to back to the soils and the waters of the valleys, the sunlight and the gentle rains, the mists, and above all else, the mystery.'

'Kaho has said it all,' added Hera. 'However much of what you say about the fleet also touches into the Silk Road trail. There it is not a matter of numbers provoking anger, but of organisation that may leave no room for the spirit to move. All is tied within a structure that defines and shapes the journey from within this Courtyard. Yet when we leave here, the trail shifts and changes to bring much more into play. The unexpected is ever with us and may present wondrous opportunity. We can not, and should not, plan to eliminate the unexpected. Within that realm dances the magic.'

'Let us discuss this in our wider circle,' suggested Eroa. 'The wisdom of Ii-chantu and Llana is vital for the shaping of these trails. Kaho has voiced concerns that many of us have put aside because they were difficult to face. It is time to bring them into the light of the day.'

The meeting of the circle was a brief one. Kun-Kwii-aan, the Hai-da elder, took the centre to act as Keeper of the Nations. Many spoke, but all with the same voice, one that echoed the concerns Kaho raised earlier in the day. They decided Kun-Kwii-aan, Ii-chantu, Llana, Aria and Kaho would carry their thoughts to the Khan.

Before they could meet with the Khan, Mokoio came to Kaho with exciting news. The Keeper of the Charts had found Hengeland on one of the oldest of their star maps. It lay far to the north-west of Egypt, on the edge of a large landmass that ended beside a huge ocean. It seemed a forbidding place, with ice barriers shown on its northern frontiers, and huge animals with long curved tusks drawn upon its eastern borders. These aspects were of themselves impressive, but it was the drawings of huge shaped stones set atop each other that held the true power. They were the henges of legend, the wonderful structures raised high to honour stone. They were the focus, the essence of the spirit captured on this dry parchment.

'Our scholars have been asked to study the oldest of scrolls and gather more information for us. Now we know Hengeland's location we are able to search with more direction. The Khan is excited by this discovery and talks of sending the Imperial Fleet to explore those waters. The whole world opens to us, and the Great One seems determined to take us to its most distant frontiers. We look outwards again to find inspiration in the challenge of the unknown. Minds moulded within narrowed borders, for too long, stretch to encompass new worlds and new ideas.'

Kaho thought, 'I question the place of a fleet in our work, while the Khan sees it sailing to Hengeland. Something powerful moves here, but still awaits its final shape and form. I must remain open to the widest vision when we sit with the Great One this evening. Ii-chantu and the others need to be told of the Hengeland discovery. It adds new dimensions to the dream.'

Kun-Kwii-aan rose with difficulty to stand before the Khan. Although given leave to sit, he wished to stand to speak of all that weighed him down. Age sat gracefully on his broad shoulders, but his old legs were very unsteady at times. The Hai-da chief put their thoughts before the Khan with gentleness, and was received with quiet concern.

Everyone leaned into the silence that followed, and found it a growing burden until the Khan smiled and said, 'You speak with wisdom. Your words are welcome, and do indeed honour the way you have walked to frustrate the Darkness and hold the balance. You have outmanoeuvred forces capable of crushing you in an instant, have moved with courage and with right spirit to honour the good. Your audacity with the Stone, your simple, direct, uncomplicated demonstration of power, won me over in a moment within this Courtyard. Without words of persuasion, without a single plea or argument, without a single weapon, arrow or spear, you invaded the Middle Kingdom, and changed the course of its history.

'All this I acknowledge. Yet your way is not the only way. Let us use the gift of a powerful fleet to serve the good. Let us go forth with high intent to teach others that the way of peace has greater virtue than the ways of war. Let us honour the journey, let us accept the way we move is more important than the victory. Let us affirm there is no victory unless all sits well with the spirit and is of the wider dream.

'Our way forward is not in the denial of what each has to offer. It is in acceptance of the strengths each brings to the trails. Let the fleet go forward to honour the words placed here with such care by Kun-Kwii-aan of the Hai-da. Let us learn to move as you have moved, to gift power to good purpose, to enter foreign waters to learn, and to foster friendships, for the benefit of all.

'You have opened wondrous worlds for me with your words. The sacred winds of change bring their songs to our people once again, and herald a new dawn. May we have the honesty to look at all we attempt with clear eyes and an open mind. Thank you, my friends of the many nations. Your gentleness and wisdom touches far more than you will ever know, and changes more than you can ever imagine.'

Everyone knew wairua of wondrous power had moved here, a spirit that wove a new vision for all of them. One that brought together wisdom, love and power with good purpose. Some might see it as a cleansing fire, and others as renewal on the waters, but whatever the image, the result was the same. The Middle Kingdom, home of ancient knowledge, was about to reach out to the rest of the world to share, to learn.

All this because an old man, and his family, walked out of the mountains at the Roof of the World, and launched a small craft on the widest of oceans in the belief they would meet five waka that sailed the long tides.

No wonder Mata-u-enga, and the Red Conclave, found this battle for the balance so difficult to win. Trust, intuition, love and respect for life had no place in their world of pain. Anger was a two-edged sword, and envy a spear sharpened at both ends.

Time weighed heavily upon them now. They had tried to distort it to serve base ends, and found only the emptiness of those caught between time.

'Find another way,' said Mata-u-enga. 'Enter other realms to bring these people down and do it soon.'

In that moment he felt utterly alone, and reaching out for the wooden ruler on his table, snapped it in two. Another stick was broken. Another admitted he knew only separation. Another mind adrift within the shadowlands where truth is paradox, and the way ahead is often the way behind, the return to the spirit lost on the journey.

***

'Grandfather, why do they place more emphasis on the way things are done than the result?'

'Only when the chosen way is right, is the result right,' said the old one. 'The means and the end are one and indivisible.

Often we see evil triumph by walking the way of pain to achieve its ends. Yet, its victory is for today alone, it has no place in tomorrow. Only good intent is of the wider dream, of the source that is everlasting.'

'How do we cope with the shadow within ourselves and others?' asked another. 'And what of anger, grandfather, what is its place?'

'It is good to be angry when you see injustice and the misuse of power. That anger cries for change and opens the way to healing.'

'But what of anger that sees a man violate the body of his partner? And beat her and injure her in terrible ways?'

'That anger is born of fear, and has many children of its own. It seeks to rule through violence and the way of pain. It is the child of separation from the self and the world. It is hate turned inwards. It is of the shadows that shun the light. It chains the spirit and destroys joy. It is a very sad anger.'

'How do we heal it, grandfather?'

'Some find within themselves the courage to call up the fears that gave it birth. And to face them squarely and embrace them with love. To still the hand of violence, they must first offer it forgiveness. To be at peace with others, we must first be at peace with ourselves.'

The Challenge of the Way

Journey as the waters go. Learn to flow smoothly through the land. Accept the joy of the rapids, relax in the sparkling pools, languish in the lakes, laugh in the tumbling waterfalls and bathe in their rainbows. Honour the river that flows within each of us.

Never in living memory had so many crowded the harbour and the headlands to farewell the Imperial Fleet. The twelve powerful ships, flying the colourful flags of the houses of the nobles who answered the call, were a wonderful sight. And in the vanguard, the place of honour sailed two vessels of very different lines. Kaho's waka sailed in the place of honour beside Tali-a-tali's wonderful Menehune craft. Their speed under sail was greater than the tall ships that followed, for both found favour in these winds.

'This is indeed the parting of the trail,' said Pana with a sigh. 'What a price I pay for the gift of my far-speaking mind. Yet wisdom says while Hltanuu sails the ocean, I must walk the land. Much depends on us being ever aware of the other's need. Yet I already miss Tali, and our son will soon begin to wonder when he will see his father again.'

Aboard the vessels all was astir. Kaho and the crew were excited to be on the ocean once more. Lashed to the joining platform was one of the carved Stones that sent them on this journey. It was secured with both rope and strong supporting timbers. It would not shift, even in the most violent of storms. Its companion was similarly lashed in the centre of the Menehune waka. Nothing was left to chance, for the Stones were the voyage, their reason for the journey, and life itself in the days to come. If the sea claimed them again, all was lost. Tai and Ra were not there to raise them up. They had chosen the long land trail.

Kaho's main concern was not for the waka, but for Hltanuu and their unborn child. It would arrive on the waters, for the moon of its awakening would soon rise in the east. He feared not the birth, for there were women with the hands to bring the little one into the world. His worry was for Hltanuu, who had become quieter day by day as they approached departure.

Hltanuu sat nearby, close to her aging grandfather, and thought of all that lay ahead. Her concern was not for the child whose restlessness spoke of eagerness to complete its journey. No! Her thoughts were for the old one beside her, who was coming all too soon to the end of his life's trail. She knew when he said goodbye to the Rampart of the Eagles, and sang his farewell chant to his people, he would never return. Age took its toll now, crept ever deeper into his bones to call him home to the stars.

Hltanuu knew each laboured breath he drew was for the little one. He came to each day with the fervent hope he would hold on to life until the little one gathered its spirit from the stars. Only then would he be free to return to the brightest of lights in the celestial realm. Only then could he truly honour life and life renewed through birth, and death. He knew there was no lasting moment within death, just a flow without beginning or end. The trail of the deepest of rivers.

Dawn followed dawn until all sign of land was gone. They were deep within the Inner Ocean, also known as the Yatuka Sea, and sailing for the narrow Straits of Malacca that freed them to the wider ocean. Aboard Kaho's waka, a cry of anguish turned heads and sent Aria hurrying to the platform that held the Stone. A child was making its way into the light. Out of the darkness of the womb, life moved with irresistible power.

Hltanuu lay cradled in Kaho's arms, as he tried to ease the cresting pain. Again and again he spoke to her and held her close. The rhythms that opened the way for the child grew stronger and stronger, for the little one was rushing to meet the tides. When the waters broke to release the sacred flow women lifted Hltanuu high. Aria helped her to stand arms outstretched against the Stone, and in that moment, the new-born one was freed to her waiting hands.

'Your son is beautiful and complete in every way,' said Aria with a joyous laugh. 'He has a lusty cry and strong hands. Take him Kaho, hold him to greet the light of his dawning.'

Bathed in the Sun, washed in the salt waters of the ocean, held aloft to greet the power of a Moon that moved through the brightness of this day, he was marked for the journey into life as a child of the universe.

'You are indeed beautiful, and wise and restless to know all of life,' said Kaho to his son. 'Now I would like you to meet your great-grandfather.'

Kun-Kwii-aan gently cradled his grandchild. He crooned simple words of greeting as he stroked his head with a gnarled hand, and smiled. For he knew the stars that stood overhead to guide this little one into the world, and he found wonder in them. Those birthing stars spoke of distant trails and other journeys, and they sang to him to call him home.

Blessed union, one small hand reaching out to touch one large and worn by age. He spoke so softly, only Hltanuu and Kaho heard the depth of the words. More than lives embraced here. Grandfather Kun-Kwii-aan had called on all his learning, and every dimension of his remaining strength, to reach into the little one sent to honour the Stone. With words of power he joined the spirit of one to the other.

Kaho and Hltanuu were elated as they shared this moment of fulfilment with the old one. They were comforted when Aria and Eroa came close to see if they might help Kun-Kwii-aan return to his station in the stern of the waka. But they were not needed for that journey, the Hai-da elder was already embarking on another. He carefully gave the child into the arms of Hltanuu, embraced his granddaughter with gentleness and warmth, then began to sing his last song. As those parting words were carried ahead of them on the wind, he settled down beside Hltanuu and her son to slip into the long sleep from which he would not return. In the darkness of that night the stars shone with a new brightness to mark the arrival of one who had honoured the long trail of life with integrity. His truth led them on.

With simple ceremony and tears of joy, they gifted Kun-Kwii-aan's body to the tides. Twelve vessels gathered to acknowledge the passing of a chief. The one who had opened the way to the long tides again, who had gifted to his people the waka that spanned the oceans, slipped smoothly beneath the waves. Within the circle of that fleet, two waka shared the moment of last farewell to the sound of a solemn drum. Kun-Kwii-aan had gone home.

The last song of the old one had travelled the rim of the earth before reaching out to the stars. In the village that nestled beneath the Rampart, the old ones of the Nation gathered in a circle of remembrance, and sent word for the village to gather. Then the sad news of his passing was shared with fond words.

'Kun-Kwii-aan, chief of the our people and keeper of the charts for the tides, has gone from this realm. His journey is over. May we always remember the magic of his smile and the wisdom he brought to our days.'

Hltanuu sat with her new-born. 'One life given and one taken away. All is of the balance and held within the hand of time. But there is sadness bound within my wonder and my joy,' she confided to Kaho. 'He led me into the mystery of life with simple words and kindness. I will miss his wisdom and his vision, and will endeavour to honour his wonderful dream.'

'We all owe him more than we can ever say,' responded Kaho. Then set his mind to other's needs by inquiring, 'Have you sent word of our son's arrival, and the passing of Kun-Kwii-aan, to Pana?'

'She knows. We shared much of the birthing travail together. Her words of encouragement were ever present, as were yours and Aria's.'

'I still marvel at Ii-chantu's insistence that Aria and Eroa were to travel the sea trail,' said Kaho. 'Their presence with us is a joy, yet everything I know of the placing of the Tu Ahu says they must be there. Eroa is the Keeper of the Stone Bird, the one dedicated by the Ancients and joined to Utini's stars by prophecy. Together they are the power. Something strange moves here.'

'Fret not,' replied Hltanuu. 'Remember Ii-chantu has said many times the last Tu Ahu is different.'

In three days the fleet would enter the narrow straits that opened onto the wide ocean of the east. 'If Mokoio's words run true, that passage is filled with danger,' thought Kaho. 'The needs of the waka and the pull of my son contest within me. Yet, the safety of the vessel overrides all else, for if we founder in these waters I have no son.'

Meanwhile, on the Yangtze River that flowed into the Yatuka Sea, another fleet, one of many small craft, struggled upstream through swirling tides. Here the River Road was bounded by high cliffs that sent the waters churning through the White Serpent's Gorge. Each boat was pulled upstream with the aid of long ropes pulled by hundreds of men and women who plied a trail cut into the soaring walls of stone. They moved to the rhythm of a chant and the dull beat of a drum. Day and night they hauled the vessels until they breached the narrows that brought the fleet of small craft into a huge valley. Hatsui was name of the land that opened to them.

'Hltanuu comes to her time,' cried Pana as the light of dawn touched the waters. 'Aria attends her and all goes well.'

Thus began the longest morning on the river. While Pana spanned the lands and waters between, they gathered to send comfort. Their joy reached out to embrace the waka when the little one uttered his first cry. And was tinged with sadness as Kun-Kwii-aan departed this realm. They were present in spirit when his body was gathered by the tides and his spirit soared to greet the stars. All gathered to remember the magic of his life and to give thanks for his journey.

'The greatest barrier on our path lies behind us now,' exclaimed the Khan with a broad smile. All the carefully arranged pieces were falling faultlessly into place. 'We will be fourteen more nights on the River Road.' He spoke with pride in their progress, for they proceeded with a sureness that was a comfort to all.

However, in the upper reaches of the river, a dark hand reached into the waters to sow seeds of tribulation. It was of the shadowlands and guided by men who hunched over a long table in distant dark caverns. From that dank place, the Red Conclave sent harsh words deep into the mountains that bordered the Broken Horn of the Moon, the upper gorge of the river. They sought the ravaged heart, the faulted places where recent earthquakes had shattered the stone. Their message spoke only of despair and destruction, and pain strong enough to trigger the release of hurt held too deep for too long.

Silence! No bird song, no whispering in the wind, nothing but the gentle music of the waters moving by. Danger!

A harsh crack shattered the silence. Terror crashed through the little fleet. All rushed on deck, but were instantly felled by a shock wave that smote the earth with awesome power. An enormous earthquake had struck the heart of the land a mortal blow. The first shock cracked rock that protected the summits, and the second sent peak after peak crashing into the waters that flowed through the Broken Horn.

Once again silence surrounded all. An eerie silence that acknowledged hurt sustained, and waited expectantly for the next onslaught.

'Watch the river,' commanded the Khan. 'Make for the shore and watch it closely.'

'I do not understand,' said Ra. 'The danger is over now, all is quiet. The land is at rest again.'

'No my friend, the danger is just beginning. This is nothing compared with what is to follow.'

'More earthquakes? You fear more?'

'No! I fear the river. It is the danger now.'

They made the eastern shore quickly, and moored beside a landing where a path wound up into the hills.

'Wait and watch,' said the Khan. Gather all we can carry and move it high up on the shore, and watch the river while I send a runner to bring people from the nearest village. I will send three others downstream to send everyone to higher ground. All may be in danger.'

Everything asked was done without question. Urgency drove them swiftly, despite their lack of understanding. When the Khan spoke thus, they knew he did so with purpose. When all was stowed high above the water, they returned to find him asking the crew how they might get the boats out of the water. His questions addressed the possibilities with thoroughness. If it could be done, it would be done.

'The river begins to fall,' cried the watch set to that task. 'The flow is less, it falls rapidly now to reveal weed and rock covered not long ago.'

The runner who went to the north found a village, and soon returned with hundreds of people carrying ropes and long bamboo poles. With huge energy and understanding, they followed the directions of the Khan's engineer. Skid poles were lashed in place along the bank and anchored into it with posts. Ropes were attached to the first boat and gathered up by a multitude of men, women and children. Laughter filled the air. A village worked as one to save the Khan. Then came the heave, and the cries of joy that followed as the first craft was hauled onto the skids. Controlled heaving now, all on command, and all as one to allow the engineer and his helpers to keep the craft steady and running true. The watercraft climbed higher with each heave, and all the while the river level fell lower and lower.

The Khan watched in silence. He had gathered all possible power to bring the vessels ashore. Time alone was in the balance now. Time, and the release of distant waters. Time enough if these people had their way, for they worked with calm assurance and trust.

'Khan, are you able to explain the danger to me now?' asked Ra. 'Why does the river fall, and why does it force us to haul our craft out of the waters?'

'It is simple Ra. The earthquake dammed the river in the upper gorge. It toppled tall mountain peaks into the waters and dammed the flow. That's why the river falls away. The ever-lowering tide means far above us a massive wall of water is retained, dammed behind debris that must eventually give way. When the river breaks free, it will sweep down the valley with awesome power and reach.

All in its path will be consumed. That's why we struggle to remove our vessels from the river. Everything must be on higher ground before the dam breaks.

'How do you know all this?' asked Ra.

'It has happened before. Our histories describe such disasters. We are an old Nation and we have survived by learning from our past. There is nothing new under the Sun.'

The villagers worked throughout the day, and into the night by the light of tall torches. When six craft were resting on a high terrace, the Khan said the other four should be abandoned, as the people were too tired to continue. They had outstripped his greatest hopes and would be well rewarded.

All went to their rest amidst an atmosphere of expectation. None knew when the dam might break, yet all knew that was inevitable. The power of water could not be denied.

They heard the river unleashed long before it reached them. Some ran to see its arrival and others ran away, for none knew how high the waters might reach. It was not certain any of the craft were safe.

Ra and the Khan stood with Hera, Tai, Pana and Llana on a rocky outcrop far above the River Road. They saw far up the valley.

'We hear the waters,' whispered Ra. 'Something comes toward us, but the river below is still a mere trickle.'

'Watch closely,' said the Khan, 'the dam has burst. There is no other explanation for that sound.'

Before his words were finished, Llana let out a cry of alarm. She was the first to see the distant wall of water that swept the far reaches of the valley. Filling the river bed it overflowed its banks and moved on to capture village after village in its hungry grasp. Nothing stood before its relentless advance. All hoped the villagers had all heard the warning .

'Call the people higher,' shouted the Khan as he ran down the path to see if everyone was well above the river. Others followed, gathered the slower ones to them and returned quickly to the heights. The cry of the wall of water was like rolling thunder now.

Llana was filled with the memory of another such tide. One that swept through the ravine in the red desert to send them scaling its walls in desperation. The loss of her loved one and grandmother in that raging tide filled her mind and threatened to undo her balance.

'Where is the Khan? Where is my beloved?' was her cry.

'He comes now,' shouted Tai above the roar that filled the valley.

The Khan saw her distress, knew its cause and held her close. Arriving as the waters rounded the last bend in the river, he clutched her to him. The yellow tide that ascended was laced with tree trunks and wreckage that had once been homes. It surged higher and higher until it breached the old bed of the river, and climbed the surrounding slopes to claw ever higher in search of life to drag into its depths. Reaching the upper terrace where the boats were staked to the ground, it flowed more slowly, gathered them in, flowed over their decks, then let them go. The cresting wave passed, the river fell once more to flow in its true bed.

Ra was the first to reach their vessels. He feared their efforts had been in vain, but his shouts of triumph reassured those who followed. One vessel was badly holed by a log, but the others had escaped unscathed. They would soon ride the River Road again. Despite the darkest efforts of the shadow people, the way was not closed.

Pana shared their trials with Hltanuu. She reached her sister at sunset, while Kaho sat with her and their son. They were entrapped by the child's presence, captors to his little hands that reached out as if to clasp at the passing clouds, and servants to his every cry. Such joy, so much contentment gifted by the little one, all unbidden and unexpected.

'They survived the challenge,' responded Kaho. 'The Enclave does not sleep. We must be vigilant on the ocean. Tomorrow we approach the narrow strait that sets us free to the vast eastern waters. Mokoio has sent a fast scouting vessel ahead with strong men at the sweeps. He says in times past, those who have chosen to confine the Imperial Fleet have always made their first attempt in the Strait. We are all committed to avoiding violent engagements. The Khan set down the strictest of codes to keep his captains in check. He expects much of them, and us also.'

By the light of the rising Sun they saw land reaching out to embrace them, and within its headlands, many strange sails. Word of the fleet had called the nations forth to hold it in check. Force moving with force attracted a countering force. Action brought reaction. It was just as Kaho had feared, and now of even greater concern, for he had both a son and a companion to protect. It was time to meet with Mokoio. Somehow he had to convince the warrior in the Commander that the peace maker must triumph to bring a lasting victory. He knew with utter certainty that mind and heart would serve them better than the hand raised in anger.

'Who stands to bar the way?' asked Kaho.

'They fly the colours of old enemies. The past nets us on this tide. Three powerful Nations gather their ships to these narrowed waters to deny us passage. How do we get by without recourse to weapons? The Khan cannot imagine the burden he places upon his Commander and his ships.'

'Speak to me of those you call the enemy. Tell me what you would feel if you knew the Imperial Fleet was loosed upon the ocean. Sit within their vessels and see the world through their eyes,' said Kaho.

Mokoio sat in silence. Kaho's request asked him to see the world through other's eyes. That was difficult to do, yet he instinctively knew it was the mark of a wise leader. To defeat the enemy you must sometimes become the enemy, understand their strengths, their weaknesses and their needs.

'If I was in those other ships, I would be suspicious of any movement by the Imperial Fleet. It has long been an instrument of control, by far the greatest force within the Inner Sea. If confined there, it is a known danger within known waters. If allowed free reign on the ocean, it is a threat of unknown proportions. Fear of motive, fear of being put at a disadvantage would force me into an aggressive stance. I would set aside differences with neighbour nations and combine forces to challenge and defeat the foe in the narrows.'

'What would set your fears aside?' asked Kaho.

'The return of the Imperial Fleet to its home ports.'

'Is there anything else that might serve a wider vision?' continued Kaho.

'If the Imperial Fleet turned for home that might be seen as an act of deception. It could return at any time and break through in the darkness. Such a move serves but for the day, it says little of tomorrow.'

'What is needed to satisfy the interests of tomorrow?' pursued Kaho.

'A lasting understanding. An agreement that sets aside fear, something that is of mutual benefit.'

'How do we begin to put that in place?'

'There is a way. Something that cuts across everything we have ever been to these people. With your help we may serve the Khan to lasting effect and the benefit of all. But the course I offer is dangerous. It may cost both of us our lives.'

When Mokoio had explained his plan, Kaho smiled. It was very simple and he quickly agreed. Thus it was that within a short time one waka, one vessel never before seen in these waters, sailed towards the great array of ships placed across the channel. It was the Hai-da vessel, with Mokoio and five nobles of high rank as guests. Harnessing a strong following wind, it made bravely for the centre of the opposing fleet. Even when the vessels before it set sail and encircled the little craft it continued on, making for the largest vessel, the one Mokoio knew was favoured by the Alliance Commander.

Taking no heed of a warning to stand off, they slowed, turned with grace and came alongside. Vessel was quickly joined to vessel by strong ropes, the smaller one captive of the other by its own consent. Warriors lined the side but were ignored. Speed was essential now, action that kept all the usual responses off balance. Speed to provide the room for hand to reach out to hand without recourse to weapons. Without delay Mokoio, the nobles, Eroa, Aria, Kaho and Tali-a-tali boarded the tall ship without invitation.

On the main deck, three commanders and three women sat behind a formally arrayed bench, covered with a beautiful white cloth. All this arranged quickly when the leaders of the Alliance recognised Mokoio, and knew protocol required them to meet him in a gracious way. Power met power here with soft cloth placed to cover its raw edge.

Tension filled the air. The silence was broken by words of greeting delivered with care, words of welcome that went just far enough to temper anger, but not far enough to extinguish it. Then words in response were delivered by Mokoio, generous words that honoured the peoples gathered around the table, and introduced those who boarded with him. Interest now flitted across the faces of their hosts, wonderment, curiosity about the nations from the east, about the Hai-da vessel and these people of different colour and stature.

Then one of the women stood and asked, 'Why do you sail with such power to reach the wider waters? What is your purpose?'

Instead of Mokoio it was Aria who rose to reply. Mokoio had interpreted the words, and gave way when she asked leave to speak. This was not how the Commander had planned the meeting, but he knew all that happened here was different, that it broke new ground, and was filled with opportunity.

'We voyage to Su-meria, and then on to Egypt with the Imperial Fleet as escort,' began Aria. She paused to allow space for Mokoio to translate.

'We sail without weapons, and journey to honour the Ancients by fulfilling prophecies written in the stars long ago. Our commitment is to the Stone lashed to the deck of our vessel. It is carved with power to serve all nations, for those who carry the wisdom of old know the Web is under threat from gathering Darkness.'

Another pause. At the end of Mokoio's words, a murmur of assent ran through those assembled. Heads nodded agreement. Matters thought upon, but rarely spoken, were revealed here.

'Earthquakes, eruptions and tidal waves are evidence of the stresses laid upon the Mother,' continued Aria. 'The sacred Stone we carry is one of several gifted by those who have long gone from us. It is of the most ancient wisdom and designed to hold the balance. Many nations have put aside their fears and disagreements to bring all this to pass.'

Again a murmur of acknowledgment. They understood the power of stone, but still feared the presence of the Imperial Fleet. Deception is so easily practiced and so hard to put aside. Aria spoke again.

'It is time for the warriors to walk in peace, time to listen to the elders who hold the wisdom of the lore and guard the mystery, and time to recreate the dream of the ancestors. Above all else, it is time to sit with the nations and share the knowledge that will ensure a world of light for our children.'

Mokoio's translation was followed by a long silence. Then those across the table spoke quietly with each other. It was another woman who stood to ask, 'May we greet the Stone?'

Mokoio was encouraged by the turn of events. Perhaps the door was opening to agreements and understandings that would find favour with the Khan and the Middle Kingdom.

The leaders of the three nations were invited to board *Siigaay Kaa* to meet the Stone. They were accompanied by esteemed elders, men and women of standing who walked with the lore of old. Each and every one of those elders had insisted on making this voyage to block the strait. Never before had they accompanied a battle fleet. Those of military mind began to realise more moved here than they understood. Other realms entered the circle.

With ritual slowness, Aria escorted them to the platform. The Stone waited, fully revealed. Kaho had gone ahead to have the crew quickly free it from the protective bindings and the timbers that held it secure. Now the symbols carved deep into the hardness caught the shadows of the lowering Sun, to speak strongly to those who approached.

Cries of surprise echoed over the waters, looks of amazement touched many faces, and urgent words sprang from wisdom keeper to wisdom keeper. Aria knew something of moment was taking place, and was relieved when Mokoio appeared to explain the miracle unfolding before them.

'Each nation sees their most sacred symbol carved in this Stone. A sign unique to their world, and one protected from all eyes except those admitted to the inner school of mysteries. Here it is revealed for all to see. They are baffled by that.

'And there is more. They are shaken by coincidence, they wonder how it is that the symbol of each nation of the Alliance appears on the one Stone. Their minds reel. They feel this is a day of wondrous portent.

'They say none of their carvers have ever cut their symbol into stone. That was forbidden within each nation, but the reason for the prohibition is lost in the mists of the past. Instead, it was painted on reed paper or wood. Yet all knew that merely echoed its true power. Stone and stone alone could join the sacred with the outer realms. Stone and stone alone could honour the symbol that joined their nation to the stars. Only the stone maps linked them to the beginning and the end. Now they see their power set within stone.'

A hush fell over all who stood around the Stone of Lore. It was indeed a day of magic and wonder. And that spirit of openness continued until sunset and beyond. It encompassed the telling of the many journeys of those who first walked the circle, then sailed the trail of the whale and honoured the soaring eagles. The placing of the Tu Ahu to restore the Web and the story of the setting of the carved stone within the Inner Courtyard were all shared until dawn arrived to surprise those who gathered through the night.

When the waka departed to return to the Imperial Fleet, Mokoio invited the three Alliance commanders to visit each and every vessel, to see for themselves that they carried no weapons. The offer was refused. Good intent had opened the way for long talks that would bring all the nations bordering the Inner Sea into a sphere of co-operation. The Stone had spoken with a clear voice, and all knew its message was grounded in truth.

Three days later, Mokoio led the fleet through the narrows and on to the vastness of the ocean. It was a glorious climax to a time of exciting progress on the path of the new way. And the number of vessels that voyaged to Su-meria had grown to seventeen. Each Alliance Nation had gifted one of its vessels for the journey. Each sailed to honour a sacred symbol carved within the Stone.

'What if we had decided to use the Menehune vessel to sail into the midst of the Alliance?' thought Aria. 'Then they would have seen a different Stone. One with symbols that were not of deepest mysteries. But that wasn't how it happened. All was as it was meant to be. It always is when we trust the voice within and go with the spirit.'

Few within the deep caverns could keep their anger at bay when they saw the nations gather in friendship to breach the narrow Malacca Strait.

'We failed upon the ocean, but will triumph in the desert,' cried Mata-u-enga. 'It is time to free the Dragon of Fear. Summon the shadows that feed on death and do it swiftly.'

***

*'How can time shift and shape to create such elegant designs?
How can coincidence bring everything together in such a
wondrous way? Are there no mistakes, and no choices? Was
everything simply planned long ago by a puppet master?'
asked the student.*

*'There are mistakes, and many false turnings,' said
grandfather with a smile. 'We shape the world and all in it.
We create the design, are the owners of the dream and much
more besides.'*

He paused to consider how deep to travel.

*'We all make mistakes, and are made to face them again and
again by the lore of the universe. There is only one journey,
and it is marked by learning. The lesson in life is to learn, to
learn to face the patterns that hide the truth of who we are. To
learn to set them aside and move on. To learn to grow. And to
learn to dance the trails of life.'*

Again he took time to consider his words.

*'When we walk in trust, and face our fears, our journey aligns
with the wider dream, the lore that is universal. Then the way
opens to us, and the elegance that is the mark of truth is ever
with us. That is born of our freedom, our choices, not the
hand of a puppet master.'*

The Passage to Mystery

Respect the tall mountains. Honour their long journey through the countless ages. Remember they are the oldest of the ancestors, for they are of the stone.

Pana was bursting with excitement when she relayed the story of the meeting of the fleets. They sat in a circle around a fire. It was good to leave the river in the evening and rest ashore.

The Khan was thrilled to hear of how Mokoio had won friends when the path was set for war. He was already making plans to foster this co-operation on his return. Ra and Tai missed being there, but knew this was their journey. Tai thought often of Hltanuu and her baby, wondered how her own child grew within the womb, and looked across the flames to the hills and the stars beyond. And all the time the river, and the Wheel that was the universe, moved to bring them through the circle. Everything was perfect in every way.

Soon they would leave the river, and ride over the high pass to the fiery realms of the Silk Road that led into the lands of Taklimakan. Thus did the Khan and Ii-chantu discussed their progress late in the day with Ra and Tai, for all wanted news of the way ahead.

Utini and Hera sat nearby, engrossed in their own thoughts. They were still trying to understand how a Tu Ahu could be put in place without Eroa, Aria and the Stone Bird of the Ancients. Their friends seemed so far away, so secure, surrounded by a fleet that gathered in the nations. How different their journeys. One a multitude sailing on the waters, and the other a mere twelve, beset with children, moving slowly through the land. Yet despite the difference in numbers, between them they held the balance.

Dawn brought expectation. Around the next bend in the river should be the landing where pack mules and fine horses waited to carry them further. The Sun climbed above the early morning cloud of the valley, penetrated the mists that drifted on the waters and brought the first warmth of the day. Nights were colder now, for they were far from the sea and reaching ever higher. Snow topped the distant peaks, and the heavy forest began to give way to fewer trees and more terraces of golden grasses. All was change now.

Expectation realised. The Khan's flag flew from a tent of colourful cloth raised on level ground to await their arrival. Order amidst a wilderness that knew its own order and honoured rhythms bound into the seasons and the beat of the universe. The trail was clear now, a gently curving line that ascended the slopes that rose steeply from the river. Thus did the River Road end and the Mountain Trail begin.

Food waited for them, hot food prepared with care. The Khan had sent a runner through the night to announce their arrival. Those who greeted them with open smiling faces and a wild joy, were little people. Sturdily built and strong, burnt brown by the Sun, a laughing people who danced when they did not ride. There was a skip in their step, a jovial mien that brought cheer to everything. They had ridden far to answer the Khan's call, but that was their way. Home was where they pitched their tents for the night, and their excitement the exploration of ever-changing horizons. They were a nomadic people, a nation born to be ever on the move.

Above all else, they were a happy people who were hardened to the trails and the swift changes that are part of life. One moment enjoying the quietness of the land, and in the next swiftly preparing to survive the terrors of a dust storm in the desert. Enduring the fiery heat of the mid-summers day, and shivering within the deep coolness of the same night. Living with only tanned skins and cloth between them and the tempest, the Sun and the winter snows, and revelling in the challenge. A very hardy people who travelled with all they needed on their horses. A people of the desert, the mountains and the plains, the Kirghze Nation of the Inner Realms. The Khan had called only the best to this trail.

By High Sun they were able to look back from the heights and see the river as a ribbon of light wending its way through the valley far below. Their guides were skilled in all they did, and made even the most inexperienced with horses feel at ease. Their mounts seemed as alert and gentle as their masters. With everything done at a slow walk on the mountain trail, there was time to adjust, time to build confidence and find the balance called for by the journey, and time to see the wider world that opened so dramatically to them.

Two days climbing ever higher brought them into a wide alpine basin. A pause now on the trail. A starkly beautiful land of snow surrounded them. Snow lay underfoot, covered the jagged rocks on every side and towered over them to reach for the blue of the sky. Words of warning from their guides now. The instruction to dismount and hold the reins firmly and close.

Danger lay ahead and they prepared to remove it. They were about to give birth to an avalanche, to deliberately release a huge wall of snow on the upper slopes. It threatened to break free of the mountain and plunge into the valley far below. With minds attuned to the stresses that built within the snowfield, the Kirghze moved with inborn understanding to trigger the danger, before it unleashed itself upon them at a time of its own choosing.

All watched with increasing excitement as the five chosen to set the snow free climbed the heights ahead. Before leaving, each had greeted their chief with the words that were translated as... *it is a wonderful day to die.*

This vast alpine basin, this bright white world, was so breath-taking in its beauty, no one chose to break the silence as five small dark figures trudged higher into the snow. All eyes were on the ones who braved that white wall to keep them safe. Courage wears a cloak of many colours.

They eventually reached a long band of exposed rock. It formed a line of darkness across the whiteness of the basin, an anchor for the snowfield massed around it.

When all five were spaced evenly along the rock, they paused to gather themselves for action. Behind, and above them, was snow they did not wish to disturb. If they triggered the whole field they would be swept away. Their intent was to only touch into the snow below, to cut it loose with the power of sound and stone.

All was beyond time now and into timing. No one moved as all fell to silence. Then, across the wide expanse of separation came a low sound, a song that built in strength and pitch to pierce deep into the mind. It grew ever louder, took on the power of rolling thunder, and at the climax of its ever spiralling ascent, was broken by a sharp discordant cry.

In that moment five large rocks were sent soaring into the sky to land as one on the line where the snow was melded to the rock band that was its anchor. A sharp crack sliced the air. Then a cry of triumph as the upper slope cleaved free of the mountain. Tumult now and thunder of another kind, and a wind so fierce it shook them as it passed by in a rush. Clear words within the turmoil, words to soothe the horses, and words of wonder as a vast field of snow tumbled past. An avalanche, sent on a wild ride to the river lands of the valley by five who sang to the mountain. Five who each gave a stone to set the snow free.

The snow-breakers returned amidst laughter, for the spirit of the mountain had been with them. It was a privilege to sing to the mountains to birth the avalanche. Yet, not all survived the song, for the snow sometimes moved to its own tune in its own time. Nothing was beyond the realms of the unexpected. It had been a good day to die, but that was not the price asked of them. The trail was clear.

During the next five days, young men and women climbed the snow slopes three times to create avalanches to make the path safe. They gifted their all to easing the way of the travellers who journeyed for the stone. And every danger was faced with laughter and song. Thus did they dance the mountain trail to emerge to the foothills beyond, and the red sands of memory. Now the Kirghze sent scouts ahead to find the caravan destined to take them through to the wonders of Tashkent. And their efforts came to nought. It was as if the camels and their keepers had disappeared beneath the sands. One hundred camels and fifty travellers, gone without any sign of their passing.

'Khan, our riders have searched far and wide, have worked their horses to the edge of exhaustion, and still they find no trace of the camel caravan,' said Tovitalih, the esteemed leader of the nomads. 'This defies all understanding, for only three weeks ago we passed them on their way to the appointed meeting place. Yet, there is no sign of them, nothing to say they arrived, nothing to mark their leaving, nothing to place them in the land. They have disappeared.'

'Ii-chantu, do you see behind this mystery?' asked the Khan. 'Do you see an explanation? Anything?'

The old one seemed stronger each day, younger even, from the moment they entered the mountains and reached the snowline. He was returning to the lands of his birth song, the home of his most distant ancestors. Ii-chantu sat very still, giving no sign he had heard the plea of the Khan, and focused on opening his inner eye and the inner voice. He looked and he listened and after a long silence, spoke.

'They are gone from us. Lost to the covering sands. There is blood on that trail and anger. Each and every one is gone. Ancient vengeance walks the night to gather in the unwary. We must move on without delay. There is no camel caravan to take us safely through the desert.'

'What is your need, Khan?' asked Tovitalih. 'How can the Kirghze Nation help you carry the dream of the stone forward? We are here to serve.'

'We need guides on the Silk Road. Can you lead us across the desert, take us to Lop Nur, climb to Qing Zang Gaoyuan, then return through Taklimakan Shamo, and ride on to Taskent? And when that city is reached, go beyond it and over mountains to Mashhad, and through the lands that open the way to Su-meria, and the Wide Ocean?'

'It asks much of us, Khan, and takes us far from the lands of our birth, but we are willing. My people have already sat around the fire and decided on this. Other caravans have disappeared. We know the sands, the mountains and plains and the dangers that stalk the unwary. Vigilance is the travellers' friend, and trust in each other the binding that makes all possible. All that is our Nation, and all we wish for our children, commits us to the journey.

'You will camp here for seven days, gaining rest within this oasis, while our people ride to meet their families to seek aid. To cross the desert and make the long journey to Tashkent, we will need more horses and fodder to see them through the barrens. Water will be no problem, as the rains came in the season. It is not always so. When we return, we will ride by night and shelter from the Sun by day. It will be a harsh ride for those not born to these trails.'

The Khan waited, sensing the Kirghze trail leader was not yet finished. Smiling broadly, the hardened nomad said, 'It has always been my dream to see the ocean.' Tovitalih's laughter rang out across the sands. It evoked delight in response. They were becoming one. Everything was possible within the dance of life.

Dawn found the Kirghze gone. Few had heard them leave to ride the passage of the stars. When they chose to move with stealth, they were the phantoms of the night, the silent ones who roamed unseen across the reach of the nation. Mystery moved them, the disappearance of the caravan was ever in their minds. They sought information from the families who grazed their hardy goats in the valleys that fringed the desert. Surely fifty people born of the shifting sands, and one hundred camels could not simply be covered by the desert.

'All goes well, Master,' reported the Leader of the Red Conclave. 'They suspect much, but know nothing. Your plan will bring them down. They cannot escape the net you weave with such a fine silken thread.'

The ancient design the Darkness unravelled was as much part of the desert as the Kirghze, for it was born of their ancestors. As a twisted mind destroyed the source of life within that realm, the sand shifted to hide the pain created by his actions.

For the East Wind gathered strength to cover all that spoke of death. It was the light bringer, the one born of the rising Sun. The Healing One that whispered only of Hope.

***

The Story Teller sat within the world he had created and looked upon the shifting sands, and thought of the desert's conquest of the greener lands. All turned within a circle of an ageing land and its rebirth. As the desert grew, the mountains thrust ever higher.

'Grandfather, do the Kirghze people still ride the old trails?'

'Yes! They hold to the lore of the desert lands despite the pressures of an encroaching world. That is still their way. But it too will pass, for change shifts in the wind.'

The Child of the Stone

Carve deep the symbols of the sacred as you sing them into the stone. Shape them for the journey, and the light that is the child.

The Imperial Fleet hove to within a sheltered bay. They had come swiftly and surely to this place, guided by navigators of the Alliance Nations who knew these waters well. Those who sailed with the two Stones were overjoyed to ride the tides with such protection. This night they sought shelter from fierce winds heralded by the shape of the clouds in the evening sky.

Sometimes Eroa and Aria sailed on the vessels of the three Alliance commanders. Often elders from those nations joined them on the Hai-da and Menehune waka. Thus was knowledge shared and friendship bound ever closer. This night, on a restless tide beneath the light of a new Moon, discussion opened the way to the final leg of the voyage. Although perhaps several seasons hence, the lure of the destination was ever present in the minds of some.

'Egypt,' said Kaho to the chief commander of the Alliance Fleet. 'What do you know of Egypt?'

'The name itself says much,' was Chuen Tong's reply. 'Egypt means *the place beyond which all else is darkness.* It was an island of light in ancient days. There is mystery in that and we seek the answers.'

'Surely that refers to the realm of ideas, to the world of the mind, not the place of the spirit,' responded Aria. 'Or was Egypt the last bastion of the good when Chaos was loosed upon the age of the Ancients. It intrigues me that one of the Stones seems destined for Egypt.'

'Has it been agreed to make landfall in Kochi and Mumbai on the sunset shores that skirt the Western Ghats?' asked Eroa. He was eager to meet with other nations and gather their support for the journey. Aria also favoured contact, as did Mokoio. They wished to remain open to all possibilities. The Stone moved with power, and it was for them to be aware of its call.

'Yes, we plan to meet with the Imar and his nobles in Kachi, and likewise in the Mumbai if the winds hold fair. Both kingdoms are well known to us, partners in trade and friendly to the Alliance. Our arrival will cause huge interest and excitement. I am sure you will agree, Mokoio,' said Chuen Tong with a laugh.

'How fares the party that travels the Silk Road? How goes the Khan?' asked Chuen Tong. He was eager to know of progress, anxious to meet with the Khan in person for the first time, and fascinated that Hltanuu could mind-speak with them.

'Hltanuu says they have crossed the mountains and rest in the foothills that skirt the desert. The camel caravan that was to carry them onward has not been found. By all accounts it has disappeared forever beneath the sands. Yet, all is not lost, for the Kirghze Nation agrees to guide them over the long trail to Su-meria. They have not ventured that far before, but at this very moment prepare for the challenge. The cry of the stone reaches into many lands and calls together many peoples.'

'And how grows the child born on the tides of this voyage? Has the little one received his name, and when is he to be presented to the fleet? He claims a place in many hearts.'

'That one is very strong and as restless as the ocean. We prepare for the day of naming,' responded Aria with a smile. 'As for presenting him to the fleet, that is a custom unknown to us. Will you speak more of it?'

'First I would like to say more about the child. This son of the tides is of the realms of change. His birth heralds rebirth, the joining of the most ancient of lore with today and tomorrow. That is why the elders sailed with us. Signs and portents led them to our vessels, called them aboard and prepared them for the revelations in the Stone, and the arrival of the child. Do not see the Stone and the child as things apart. They are forever joined in ways mysterious and wonderful. And to be honoured with ceremony.

'Kaho, excuse me for speaking thus of your child,' said Chuen Tong with a smile. 'I was led on by the occasion, and now realise it is best the rest remain hidden until Hltanuu is present, and others who hold the sacred close.'

When that gathering came to pass, it took all present into the deeper realms of stone and left the parents of the child with much to consider. As soon as all the elders, commanders, seers and friends had departed, Kaho and Hltanuu found a quiet place to speak of their son.

'Is he truly the guardian of the Stone that is to be gifted to Egypt?' asked Hltanuu. 'I feel as if my child has been wrenched from my breast. How do they know his chosen task? It is too much to understand and almost too much to bear at this moment.'

With uncanny timing Aria arrived to sit beside them. Clearly her mind had been touching into theirs, for she took up the conversation as if she had been present.

'Hltannu, a stone is a stone and a child a child,' said Aria. 'Each makes a journey and knows the power of the spirit. Let the stone be the stone and let the child be the child. If their paths entwine, if they hear the same song and choose to walk as one, each the mentor of the other, that will be of their making, not ours.'

'Aye, we look too far ahead,' responded Kaho. 'Let us put the wider realms aside to ensure our little one has a wonderful childhood. Let him be surrounded by our love and know joy.'

'Meanwhile we have to choose his name, or a thousand others will choose it for us,' added Hltanuu.

They spent the evening with Aria and Eroa beneath the stars. They knew that whatever the future of their babe, he was blessed by many tides and the love of many peoples. They looked ahead with confidence.

Dawn broke to the cry of seabirds from a gathering ashore. The horizon was cut by the rise of the Western Ghats that spoke of land uplifted high to catch the rains. Green and luxuriant was the coast that beckoned, and set within it was Kochi.

'I favour Kun-Kwii-aan-Alintcha,' were the first words Hltanuu shared with Kaho that day. 'For our son, the name for our son.'

'It sounds beautiful, but what does it mean?'

'Light of the Great Whale, or song of the Great Whale,' explained Hltanuu. 'The light and song are of the same family, and often share the same word. The song creates light and the light creates song.'

'Then Kun-Kwii-aan-Alintcha he shall be,' said Kaho. Both knew the boy would be called Kun by his friends and only carry his full name at special times. That sat well with them too. Kun-Kwii-aan, the child's great-grandfather, the old one they missed so much, would be with them always in that name.

Later in the day they rounded a headland to enter the waters of Kochi. Arrayed in battle order was another fleet. It stood off from the city and flew flags of welcome. Chuen Tong, with Mokoio's agreement, had sent a fast vessel ahead to prepare the way. It had given the Imar two days to prepare for their arrival. He wanted no grounds for misunderstandings.

The Imar awaited them on the royal landing. After long consideration, it was decided to send the Hai-da waka with the Stone to represent the fleet and honour the welcome. On board were all the commanders and many of the wisdom keepers. All knew the key to everything was the Stone, and some who looked with an even broader vision placed a child alongside it.

They closed on the landing, where colour, both brilliant and vibrant, joined the drum beat. It was indeed a royal occasion. Protocol embraced the moment. The Imar stood to greet them with words of obvious warmth, Mokoio replied in the name of the Khan, and Chuen Tong followed with a fine speech. Finally Eroa spoke, with Aria standing at his side, while others translated to bring greater understanding to the nations.

Then the Imar, his council, and the keepers of the ancient way were invited aboard the waka. Without explanation they were taken to the Stone laid bare to greet them. Some stood in confusion, failing to understand the occasion, and wondered why a babe in a small basket slept beside it. Others stared in amazement. Those born to the knowledge of the Inner School of Learning saw cut deep within its face the symbol most sacred to them. Revealed to all by the light of the Sun, and bound within carvings of immense power that shone with the colours of renewal.

Few saw that shift in the light, or understood the luminescent magic wrought here was sourced in the sleeping child. He was of the stone and the stone was of him. The Imar caught the eye of his closest adviser in matters of the spirit and saw the joy in his smile. All was confirmed by that glance. The prophecies that brought them to this stone, and this child, were fulfilled in every way. Hope flared, and commitment.

'We thank you for sharing the wonder of the Stone and know there is much to speak of in a quieter place. We understand we gather for a naming, and are honoured to be invited to attend. We see the spirit of this child. It moves to cross the boundaries of nations and the many realms. It walks with healing and in peace.

'May the one who receives his name this day be assured he is acknowledged as a child of this realm, honoured as a son of the family royal, and gifted the freedom of our Inner House of Learning.

'Papers and seals to set this in place will be with him on the morrow. Meanwhile, may he be a happy child, one who sleeps when sleep is needed, and one who plays when the spirit cries out to dance,' finished the Imar with a laugh.

Thus was Kun-Kwii-aan-Alintcha named according to the customs of many peoples, and with the blessings of the many thousands who gathered to honour the moment. And all the while Hltanuu wondered what was to happen to her child. All they said of him was true. He was of the Stone and only content when sleeping near it. Yet he was her little one, someone precious beyond description, a child who had the right to know all the magic of play. She would be strong for him. She would fight to provide him with the balance, with a life. That simply was the mother's way.

In another place, both distant and different, a mother yet to be stirred in her sleep. Pana awoke to the coolness of the desert night. Those who came to the Silk Road were but one day from departure. The Kirghze had returned with fine horses and fodder to see them through the wastelands. Hltanuu was the cause of her awakening. Calling to her from the distant fleet, she broke through Pana's sleep to share her excitement. Good words flowed, words that described astonishing days in the city of Kochi bordered by the Western Ghats.

Pana felt the dryness of the air, looked out on the vastness of the sands, and envisaged the green hills, palms trees and clear blue waters that were all around Hltanuu. Then the words came again. So much shared, the naming, the joining of the little one with the Stone of Lore, the fears of the mother, the sights and sounds of the city. And beyond all else, the love that reached over the mountains to hold them within the dream they walked together.

'Hltanuu shared more of their adventures while you slept. Great navigators bring the fleet to lands both strange and beautiful,' said Pana to those who sat around the dawn fire of the desert to enjoy the first food of the day. 'And all the while, the Stone speaks to each nation encountered. For into its surface is carved their most sacred symbol. This happens with all the nations they meet, and brings gifts, treaties of goodwill, and willing hands to carry the journey forward.

'Hltanuu is both happy and concerned. The elders with the power to see the colours of people, and the spirit that moves to shift and shape the world, tell her the child of her womb is born to be of the Stone. He is its companion and guardian, its friend and its mentor, its interpreter and its confidant. She worries about the future of her little one, and wants to protect him.

'Khan, Mokoio sends his greetings and eagerly awaits your presence in Su-meria. He has much to share, and says the world is changed forever.'

***

'Do I see this clearly, grandfather? Little Kun has been born to answer ancient prophecy, just as were Utini and Hera. His life is dedicated to a special journey. Has he any choice in this?'

'Yes! There is always choice. It can be no other way.'

'But the child seems set upon a course decided years before his birth.'

The old one let them think about that matter, held his words close while their minds flew free. Then he brought his thoughts to the issue.

'That is so, for that is the way of prophecy. Yet, what is foretold is merely opportunity, the chance to move in a certain way because in that moment the doors are open. It does not demand completion.

'The child is born to answer the moment. Yet, in the end it is the child who responds, who takes up the task. That is by choice, not by demand. Some who have walked that road will say there was no other way, that they gladly passed through the door that opened to them. There is truth in that, for the answer in all of this is the call of truth.

'Those chosen to walk to the sacred crossroads find their truth in following the path that opens. They discover themselves on the journey. If they choose another way, that is also of their future, for all is for their learning. Each of us can meet the truth now, or walk away from it and take the longer trail that is the hardest one of all.'

The Silk Road

When all is mystery, open to its source. Turn not aside from the darkness, but embrace its restless shape. Seek answers in the night. Shun it not, heal with love, for there is no other way.

Excited by the progress of the fleet, those who rode the shifting sands went forth at sunset. The next stage on the long trail to meet the ocean had begun.

The Kirghze were in every way at home in the harshness of the desert. Everything they needed for survival was on their horses. The stars guided them through the coolness of the night, and knowledge handed down through countless generations brought them to the water holes that marked the route of the legendary Silk Road. Narrow ribbons of water, welling to the surface from sources deep beneath the desert, were the tenuous threads that wove the trail. Without water there was no trail, only the fiery breath of the Dragon.

The water at the first hole was fresh and cool. It formed a pool at the bottom of a stone-lined shaft, a natural ravine within the rock, honoured and improved by those who first opened the way. The watering place they came to at the end of the third night was fouled. Dead birds, a strange smell, and a nomad symbol of warning carved into a soft stone saved them from sickness or even death. Now they depended on the skin water bags of their guides and the hope the next hole was safe. However, it too was closed to them, and when the horsemen Tovitalih sent ahead returned three days later, they brought news of the poisoning of the next two wells.

'We begin to see how the caravan that came to guide you west disappeared,' said Tovitalih, the Kirghze leader. 'They perished in parched lands made impossible to cross by the hand that cut the brightest threads of life by destroying the water. An evil mind brings the Darkness to the desert. A shadow stretches across the nations to deny your journey. It is all powerful, challenges your right to life, and more.

'It confronts our nation, denies us right of passage, pollutes the springs of life itself, and closes the trails of our ancestors. This act is an abomination, a violation of the lore of the desert, that is unmatched in memory. We relish this challenge. We commit all we are to the overthrow of those who stand to block your way and ours.'

'Do you have a plan? Can we continue on? Like you, I am determined to overcome those who threaten the world we know,' said the Khan in a quiet voice. Strength gathered where the shadow had sought to sow only fear.

'Leaving the first water hole pure was both cunning and cruel. It committed us to the road, led us on to the second hole and water fouled, and forced us to travel in hope to the third. And all the time we used our reserves of water and rode further and further from a pure source. That is what brought the camel riders down. If the truth walks here, the first water hole at the other end was also clear, and all that followed fouled. They were lured too far from water to escape a trap set with diabolical intent. When the end came, the sands moved to cover everything.'

The sturdy Kirghze chief surveyed the wide horizons, and smiled upon the heat and shifting red sands that might soon become their death shroud. The sands covered and the sands revealed. There was indeed another way, an answer bound in lore both ancient and sacred. It was held in songs long thought lost by his people, but kept safe by those asked to ride with the knowledge of the ancestors. It was long and dangerous, and would test them to the limits, but it was there for those with the courage to accept the challenge.

'Gather closer, come into a tighter circle that you might see what I draw in the sand,' he said quietly. 'It is time to share a song that has not been sung for a thousand years or more. Yet it will bring the brave through to Nor. There is another trail, one kept secret from all travellers, and even hidden from our own. Only those chosen to lead are gifted knowledge of this way. They carry it as a shield, the final hope of the nation should we all be driven into the desert by powers too strong to overcome. When death cloaks the sands we hold the wisdom to survive.'

'Tovitalih, you are about to share your inner secrets, to take away the ultimate shield of your people,' said the Khan. 'Consider that, and take heed of my words. Draw nothing on this smoothed sand. Hold the song within yourself, keep it secret and lead us on in trust. You alone need to know the way, we will follow. Reveal nothing by word or hand, deny the Shadow access to our deeper design. Hold hope close and keep it warm.'

The chief stood to acknowledge the words of the Khan. He was clearly moved by the trust set before them and the wisdom of this way. 'Follow in trust, my friends, and know I lead you in truth. We shall overcome. Be brave, and know we shall overcome.'

In the darkest of the night they left the Silk Road to honour another. Silence covered their trail, for Tovitalih had asked his people to cover the hooves of the horses with coarse hessian cloth to hide their footprints. And when the last riders had moved on, a small team walked behind to smooth the sand with small swatches of tied fronds gathered from the last oasis. The first winds of the day would complete this work of concealment. If any followed they would walk into mystery, would conclude another party had disappeared beneath the sands forever.

'The first well is two days hence,' confided Tovitalih to Ra. They often rode together, for they found much of interest in each other. One born of the driest of lands, and the other of the mountains and gifted with the songs of the whales. One a navigator across the trackless sands and the other a trail seeker on the long tides of the ocean. Although of different lands they were both joined to the stars that guided the lost one home. Their worlds were in the end the same, bounded by the light of the universe, by the need to join star to star. And in the end, to reach that wondrous understanding that allowed them to hold a star and a stone in the same hand.

'Why have others not found the well?' asked Ra.

'Wait and see, my friend, wait and see. It is very difficult to penetrate its secret. Only your beloved, the one named Tai, has the magic to hear the song of these waters. The child that moves within her will be very special, for it will drink from springs of the sacred way, the life cord of the Kirghze Nation. When your daughter arrives to sing her first song to these stars, when she suckles at the breast of the mother, let it be understood by all, she first drank of our sacred waters. Thus will we claim that child as our own, as a daughter of our people.'

168

'What makes you certain the unborn is a girl child?' asked Ra.

'It is written so. Was bound in prophecy long ago. This trail that opens is an ancient one, and all who walk it are of the dreamtime we know and honour. It was written and comes to pass. Even the poisoning of the waters was foretold. A disaster that brings all into alignment. That is why I smiled when faced with the prospect of death, the end of the journey for all of us. Until that moment, all was uncertain. Signs sent by the ancestors may be misread by the unwary. Ego intervenes to push all out of shape. Misdirection was my fear. Too much Tovitalih and not enough room for the spirit of the Great One to move. But the closing of the Silk Road set the seal on all that brought us to this moment. Decisions clouded by confusion became clear. There was no other way. We were forced to travel the hidden trail to honour the most ancient of dreams. Your daughter belongs to us, my friend.'

The chief's laughter reached all, for they rode close to give nurture to each other. The unknown beckoned and they gathered courage and endurance to meet it. Tai smiled, thinking Ra and Tovitalih must be having a good time. Tovitalih was, but Ra rode on in thoughtful silence. He wasn't sure what the chief meant, and wondered if they were to lose their daughter to this trail. 'You had better be a boy,' was the thought that came to him. 'Yes, a boy would put all to rights.' But he doubted even that.

When Tovitalih announced they had reached the hidden water hole, dawn was nearly on them. All their water was gone, eked out through the night and shared with care to ensure the weakest were not denied. Utini noticed few of the Kirghze drank of it. The safety of their charges seemed far more important than their own. He vowed to bring all the power at his command to aid these people, and to ensure they were remembered for their journey.

'Where is the water hole?' asked Ra. 'I see only a simple rock amidst an ocean of sand, my friend.'

'Ask Tai, ask her to walk the sands to open the way. She is of the waters,' responded the chief.

Thus it was that Tai dismounted and walked to the rock, and beyond it until she covered twenty paces toward the rising Sun, and pointed to the sands.

'Dig here, water wells up beneath the sands.'

Within moments many hands worked with simple bowls to shift aside the covering that separated them from the stream of life. Deeper and deeper they went, and came at last to a flat rock one stride across, and shifted it aside to reveal a stone-lined well and the coolness that was of water. Joy abounded, as a leather bucket tied to a rope splashed into the dark pool below to be drawn to the bright light of the new day. The oldest of the trails of the ancestors ran true. The Shadow could not deny them passage. The stars had brought them to this place, and the stars would lead them on.

Night after night they rode, and each dawn came to another hidden well. This route was at least twice as long as the Silk Road, but certain in every way, for it was a true trail of the spirit. All knew they rode to the hoof beat of ancestors and drank of waters dedicated to the survival of a way of life, to freedom and the joy of riding to new horizons. It was a sacred journey, one that brought each and every one to acknowledge their uniqueness, their wider role, their dream and their place within the circle.

The days beneath the shade cloth of their tents were filled with rest and sharing. Nation opened to nation, and within them child to child. Hera's young one was a small, but nimble child who danced through life. Four years old now and ever active, Tia-ho was a joy to all who came into her orbit, and they were many. For she sought out people, went to them without restraint, greeting each with a smile and winning friends with few words.

Pana's son, the one the Hai-da named Eagle Child, was as swift as that bird. He was a little younger than Tia-ho, but lacked nothing for that, for his need was to explore the world without restraint. More often than not, he was to be found amidst the hobbled horses, speaking to them in his chatty way of horse things, and boy things, and fearing not their size as he played at their feet.

The children found companionship in each other, and among the Kirghze youngsters who had joined the party with the families for the Silk Road journey. Tia-ho and Eagle Child took to the trail without complaint, saw nothing strange in days filled with nothing but sand, and long nights on horseback. Their world was one of constant adventure amidst wonderful people. They both enjoyed riding the horses and the attention of the Kirghze who were so affectionate with children. And they loved to sit with Ii-chantu.

'Please tell us another story?' was Tia-ho's plea. She came with Eagle Child, and others who gathered into a circle in this shaded place. 'A long one, grandfather.'

The old one did not reply immediately. All watched as he reached over his crossed legs to rummage in his trail bag and carefully remove something held within a colourful silken cloth. Slowly, to build their expectation, he uncovered the treasure held within. A gasp of awe ran through the gathering. A beautiful carving of Buddha was revealed, the one placed with others of power before the Stones of Lore many moons ago.

Those days seemed distant now, another life in another time. Some day he would tell them of the Battle of the Claw.

One small boy was so entranced he moved to sit beside the carving, to look but not to touch. Others in the camp saw the children gathered, and came to join them. Old and young now sat within the circle. When excitement fell to silence the old one spoke.

> *'Long ago, in a land so far away different stars are seen in the sky, a beautiful golden Buddha was made with love and care by the monks of a little monastery high upon a hill. When people heard of the astounding beauty of that treasure, they journeyed over the high passes and through the snows to sit before that wondrous statue.*

> *'The Buddha brought joy and learning to the village and the little monastery that stood above it. The monks had created a place of serenity that gifted peace to all who made the journey*

in the spirit of the seeker of wisdom of the good. For many years the pilgrims came and left with understanding bestowed within the Silence.

'Then word arrived of others who crossed the mountain passes with ill intent. Warriors who sought treasure for their warlord, men who followed a rumour that a Buddha made of gold existed within a simple monastery high upon a hill. The monks knew they could not move the beautiful statue into hiding because it was too heavy to shift. So they sat quietly in contemplation and opened their hearts to the wisdom of the universe.

'Word of the progress of the invaders was passed to them as swiftly as the wind. Fires lit the darkness as the warriors ravaged the land. Terror walked by day and by night. Yet the monks remained within the quietness of their circle, waiting and listening.

'When the army was merely a few days hence, one young monk asked for leave to speak. He explained that those who came to seize the Buddha journeyed with eyes filled with greed. Beauty had no place in their raiding, merely the lure of gold. He suggested they cover the statue with a mixture of mud and mortar to make it appear to be made of simple stone.

'They liked his words and immediately began the work. Bright fires burned within the room to hasten the drying, and dust was carefully sprinkled over the great one's head to age it by the moment. It was completed with but a night to spare.

'When the warrior chief burst into the monastery he was received with calmness and invited to sit before the Buddha. Again and again, as he won his way across the conquered land, he had heard of the golden treasure that awaited him at the end of his journey. When he strode boldly into the sacred room of the great one, his mind reeled in anticipation. He was devastated by the sight of the grey, dusty statue.

'Stone! It's merely a thing of stone! Lies! Lies have drawn me hence. Those who spread them will surely pay.'

Such were his angry words as he left without a single gesture of respect for the Buddha.

When the army departed the monks decided to leave the golden Buddha hidden beneath the covering that looked like stone. In the years that followed, the ravaged countryside, the burned fields, the polluted wells and a long drought brought hardship to the people of the valley. The little monastery suffered so badly it was decided all would leave and only return when the land recovered.

Time moved on, years turned into centuries and still no one came to occupy the little monastery on the hill. Then the day arrived when a wandering group of monks found shelter within its crumbling walls and decided to make it their home. None of them knew of the history of the Buddha and were not enlightened by the villagers, who had decided long ago the secret beneath the stone was best left within the stone. They feared the return of warriors seeking gold.

The monks worked very hard to restore the buildings and bring their love to the people and the land once again. They left the most important task to the very last, for they did not want to rush the cleaning of the Buddha.

A young monk was honoured with the washing, cleaning and scraping of the dust-covered statue. With each sweep of his young arms, the time-weathered surface crumbled away to reveal whiter layers beneath. Excited by the changes wrought by his hands, he worked ever harder. The scraper he wielded cut deeper and deeper into the stone until it was stunning in its whiteness.

Then his face fell. A crack appeared along the line of an arm and ran across the elbow. To his dismay a piece of stone fell away when he touched the break. He was stunned to see the glow of gold beneath the covering that had bound the secret of the monks within. His cry brought all to aid his efforts. Thus was the golden Buddha revealed once more, and peace gifted to the hearts of all who came to know its power.'

Silence followed the story. Most of the younger children moved away, sought another place to play, for they knew of old that Ii-chantu told only one story on any one day.

However, others stayed. Silence grew again. No one spoke to break the spell. They knew more would follow. That was Ii-chantu's way.

'What is the story hidden within the story?'

'Learn to look beneath the surface,' offered one of the girls. 'It is wise to try to see what is hidden.'

'And sometimes it is necessary to hide something precious, to protect it by putting up a barrier to the world. That's why we survive this long ride through the desert,' said another. 'The secret water holes give us life.'

'We learn quite young to hide things within us, too. We do this as children, we make masks to hide behind,' added a mother.

'Sometimes we forget to remove those masks,' responded a youth. 'We keep them on when they are no longer necessary.'

'We can lose ourselves behind masks,' said a grandmother.

The old one let this river flow where it willed. Many found sustenance within its waters. Some saw their own masks for what they were, saw the burden of wearing false faces and began to let them go. Thus did the healing begin and the light pierce the armour of secrets, long worn thin, and doors shut to learning. When the flow began to ebb, the old one carried them to the closing of the circle with words to carry into the night and the new day.

'We all learn to set masks in place. And as you say, sometimes we lose ourselves behind them. But remember beneath the cold covering of stone that shielded the Buddha, was the Beautiful One that had so much joy to offer the world. We are like the statue in the story. As we grow, we need the courage to set aside the masks that served us once, but no longer do. And we need to understand that the Golden One is always within us. It honours the truth of who we really are.'

The Sun moved towards the horizon, the horses stirred and red drifted on the east wind. Memories gathered. It was time to go. Ii-chantu bade all a safe journey into the darkness of the night. The Silk Road opened to them again.

All went forward with purpose. The Khan was pleased, nay he was delighted with their progress. Llana was a strength to him, and they grew closer and closer within this world beneath the stars. Utini and Hera enjoyed the struggle, it was in their natures to respond to challenge, to find the best within themselves and bring out the best in each other. They found time to be with their daughter and share her wonder. Pana was lonely. Again and again her thoughts went out to Tali-a-tali and the Imperial Fleet. Hltanuu often intercepted her searching mind to ask if Pana was all right. This would lead to an exchange of news and the easing of her loneliness. Yet, there was much to do, for her focus was ever on her son, the one who swooped like a young eagle. Ra and Tai found great fascination in the desert and their companions. The child that grew to join them on another tide was ever in their minds. Ii-chantu was quiet, absorbed in all that moved behind the world others saw. His contentment came from their achievements day by day. The finding of the next water hole, moving out with the setting of the Sun, greeting the dawn and honouring the journey.

The nights were long, but filled with satisfaction. Every step brought them closer to the day when they would set the last Tu Ahu in place to complete the Web. So many years had been filled with toil to honour the stone and the balance. Three sacred markers had been placed truly after long and dangerous journeys, and now they came to the last. The prospect of completion, of the end of separation, was almost too much to bear.

'Lop Nur is but one night hence, we have conquered the shadow set across our trail,' explained Tovitalih. 'Tomorrow the red sands will be behind us. It has been hard, this long ride, but harder still for our brave horses. The grain we carried was never enough for this longer journey. For seven days now, they have carried us with too little food to meet the burden. We must rest them, allow them to graze the grasses, while we gather more fodder and news of the mountains, before the climb to Qing Zang Gaoyuan, the Plateau to Tibet.'

Thus did they come triumphantly to the waters of Lop Nur within lands far from the ocean. They stood taller now, were even more committed to the dream, and stronger for the ascent into the legendary heights of Tibet, the land that was the Roof of the World. Ii-chantu and Llana would guide them to the site where the last Tu Ahu was to be created.

That wondrous event sat heavy on the mind of another. Mata-u-enga viewed it with anger that knew few bounds. He could not understand how all the cunning brought against them on the Silk Road had failed. Many black magicians had gathered to the dark halls of the Shadowlands to bring this band of unarmed men, women and children down.

Power seldom seen, and little known, had been harnessed to turn the water of the wells so sour it invited death within the day. Pain of the deepest realms had been melded with envy and anger to shift the balance within the wellsprings. It was the act of a mind so clever it had outgrown and overshadowed all other sense of self. No heartbeat of kindness was present, all vestiges of love had been stripped away, no recognition of the spirit that joined all with the light remained. Only Darkness now, and within that Darkness even greater Darkness.

'Find another way to destroy this ragged band of ill-assorted people who revel in the light. Find their weakness and find it soon,' shouted the commander of the Black Robes.

Ii-chantu heard the words and thought of all that had come to pass in recent days. Little else entered his world now. So much depended on the success of their endeavour. Changing water, the essence of life, into something that became the agent of death, was an act of unbridled evil. A perversion of lore that distorted the lore, to place the universe at risk. Dark minds would spawn even darker deeds, as the sands of time ran out for those who desperately worked to destroy the balance. He must be vigilant. Nay, all must be vigilant.

The mountains beckoned, folded around them, and lifted them ever higher as the horses gathered themselves for the long haul to the pass. They were strong and sure, and lighter without the need to carry water. Not all were called to make this journey. Most of the Kirghze had moved on to make a camp further west, to prepare for the return of the mountain party, and to open the way to Tashkent. Some twenty-four moved toward the plateau beyond the pass. Among them several children, for three generations would be joined at the Tu Ahu to honour the Web. Each strand as important as any other. Little Tia-ho and Eagle Child, and other children who were vital to the vision, and the days to come. Generations joined, nations joined and stones joined to bring all to the stars.

'Ii-chantu says this Tu Ahu is like no other,' said Utini to Hera. 'You and I are called to gather the power and create the joining, without Aria, Eroa, and the Stone Bird of the Ancients, to help us. Do we depart from prophecy so easily and still hope to succeed? Answer me!' was his cry of anguish.

'Dear one, you change not at all,' responded Hera with a wry smile. 'Constancy is the mark of you. Each time we have approached this moment, you have come up with the questions and the expectation I would find the answers. Ii-chantu is the mind behind all that happens now. He announced this journey the very day we joined the two pinnacles in the frozen north to the Pole Star. We all dance to his call, and find no difficulty in that, for we trust his truth.

'Let us ease our minds by asking him for answers,' continued Hera. 'It is time to know more, to prepare for the moment, we are but three days from the location.'

That night they gathered close around a fire of dried yak dung, collected as they moved along the trail. The land was devoid of trees. All around them were rocks, rugged bluffs, little melt-fed streams and flowers that bloomed brightly for but a few days, brilliant splashes of colour amidst the grey. Above them stretched a sky of muted blue with no clouds in view. The air was cool, so all were wrapped warmly to sit in comfort.

'Be vigilant,' said the old one. 'You ask me how the last Tu Ahu will be placed, and all I can say is be very vigilant. Set the normal watch for the night, then double it. Look ahead, scan the horizons and lift your heads to the heights. Be aware of all you do and all that surrounds you.'

Realising words of warning were not enough, Ii-chantu paused. He wanted to give them something to hold on to, something to bond them even closer to the land and its power. Simple acts, that brought new understanding and purpose to each day, were what he searched for. His need was answered and he continued.

'We came safely through the desert because we accepted it, because we travelled its vastness without sending frustration, anger and hurt into the sands. It must be the same in the mountains. In honouring the land, we honour life and give strength to all about us; to the rocks, the flowers, the streams and the creatures that fly, crawl, or swim. And they in turn give healing and strength to us.

'And in recognising the spirit within those things, we are able to send them love. Each rock has a need, a place in the universe where all things are seen as aspects of the Source, the Oneness. It serves and is served. Use your minds and hearts to greet the uniqueness of everything.

'Then we come to ourselves. Let us be grateful for each day, for everything that moves within it. Everything. The events that cause us pain as well as those that give us joy. Remember the poisoned water did not kill us, it merely sent us on a longer trail that made us stronger. Greet everything with gratitude. Join heart and mind with spirit to see the wonders of a world set within the realms of gratitude.'

'Thank you for your kind words, Ii-chantu,' said Utini. 'We will be vigilant, and endeavour to walk with praise, love and gratitude.'

As they left, Hera said to Utini, 'He gifted wisdom, but he didn't answer, did he? We are still no closer to knowing how the Tu Ahu is to be created. Trust is the message he sends us. He doesn't want to show his intent to the Red Conclave. All that really matters, he leaves to the last moment.'

In a deep dank cavern within a distant land, men gathered to probe the secrets of those who travelled the Silk Road. They sat in trepidation before the Master, the all knowing, all powerful Mata-u-enga. Within this day, or the next, the final Tu Ahu would be raised to secure forever the Web of Life. They had searched feverishly for the means to destroy those who rode to frustrate their grand design. Night and day they had given themselves to the appointed task. Yet no one had found the answer.

'We have used the power of the heavens to strike with lightning and it was sent back to us,' said one robed in Darkness. He kept his head down, not wishing to be seen looking at the seared, scarred face of the Master.

'Earthquake and tidal wave did not defeat them either,' said another.

'Nor the battle fleets of Kadaraka and Maldecta,' added one in a whisper.

'Distorting time was ineffective,' contributed someone new to the Red Conclave.

'Sinking the Stones merely added to their power and support,' said the last.

Then the one appointed by the Master to keep the Red Conclave focused to his will, spoke in summary.

'We have attacked in many ways. We have hindered and hurt them, even dealt in death, and still they continue on their path of madness. They appear so weak and ineffectual, are a small band with no weapons, no army, seek no conquest or wealth, are seemingly without ambition, yet they cross oceans, mountains and deserts with disdain for danger and frustrate our plans. Where is their weakness? What will bring them down?'

'Enough! I have heard enough! Your time is all used up,' shouted Mata-u-enga. 'There has to be a weakness. Everyone has a fatal weakness. Find it. Look into each of them and find weakness. Nothing more, just weaknesses. Expose kindness, healing, selflessness, sympathy, nurture and love. Find which of them has those flaws, and discover how to use them to bring this band to ruin. One among them must be vulnerable.'

They met again within that day. The Master waited to hear the name revealed, and was delighted to be told they all carried those weaknesses. They were fatally flawed. They cared for each other.

'Ah! Hurt one and we hurt all,' was his pleased response.

'Tell me how to exploit love, that I might divide and conquer them. Leave me and return the moment you have found the way.'

He waited impatiently and, after a time that seemed all too long, was greeted by words that sent him into an abiding rage. 'You say love cannot be used as a weapon? You say love cannot be used against them? That its power is not set about with rules that allow for exploitation. That it always travels a true line. That it cannot be bent to our purposes. Love cannot be bent! Everything can be bent, twisted and distorted until it takes the shape of its opposite. Go and find a way to bend love.'

Ii-chantu chuckled when he heard these conversations. His every moment was now devoted to listening to the Red Conclave. Although on dangerous ground within the caverns, he had discovered the anger of the Master created so much confusion and fear, he gained entry without alerting them in the usual way.

'Love baffles them,' he said to Hera and Utini. 'They seek our weakness and think their flaw is ours. It is ever so. We think others should see the world as we do, and should be as we are, forgetting we see the world through a tunnel of our own making and call it real.

'Thus do they see love as our flaw. It is what they have rejected, it is to them the ultimate weakness, the supreme loss of power, the turning that leads to defeat and subjugation. Yet in truth love is our greatest strength. Love is the magic that makes us strong. Love given, and love received, sets us free. Love is the greatest creative force in all the universe. Love and life are one.'

'May they continue to run that course,' said Hera with delight.

'How strange are the ways of those who seek to use the Darkness,' said the old one. 'They sit so close within their pain they fail to see all is order, all part of the greater good. We need both the Darkness and the Light. Each in balance, gifting challenge, and in the gifting inviting change that opens all to new realms of creation. Only those who walk with love find joy in that magic. Love transcends all.'

'Are we still in danger?' asked Utini.

'Yes!' replied Ii-chantu. 'Until the circle is joined we are in grave danger. They may still find our flaw.'

'What circle and what flaw?' asked Utini, but before he could turn to address the old one, he was gone. 'I believe he knows my intent to ask an awkward question before I do myself. Hera we are still no further on. Let us sleep, perhaps to dream, and in that realm find answers,' he said with a laugh.

Dawn, and before them a vista of tall mountains that brought meaning to Ii-chantu's words. It was very easy to praise creation, revere all life, and give gratitude for all that came to pass, on such a morning. The day of days had arrived and still they walked in peace, untouched by those who stalked the shadows to bring them down.

Twenty-four rode on to the heights chosen to honour the dream that had sent Ii-chantu and his family on their long walk to the ocean. That had sent them into death and danger, and carried them over the waters to meet the five waka sailing to the Hai-da Nation. And on this day, brought them home again to these lofty mountains. No longer alone in their struggle to uphold the good, they journeyed with true friends who walked in trust.

'Let us pause here,' cried Ii-chantu, who led them forward. 'Let us pause to remember ancestors who gave so much to hold the balance. And let us remember those who walked with us, and gave their lives that we might stand here at this time.'

Only the sound of the wind moving through the rocks and the cry of the crickets broke the silence. Those who stood within the quietness of this wild realm found strength in joining with those who had gone before, felt the continuity of age joined with age, the comfort of the wider view, and the long stretch of life that encompassed the stars.

'Leave the horses,' said Ii-chantu. 'Walk to the flat rock that forms a huge platform. Along the way find one rock. It will call you. Come with that companion to the circle and do this quickly. Remember even the youngest needs to bring a stone. Each is of the dream.'

Far across the mountains, Hltanuu sat with elders who simply knew it was the moment to gather. None were asked to join her. Their arrival, unbidden, was the mark of their understanding and their power. When Aria, Eroa, Kaho and their children entered the circle, none was surprised to see they numbered twenty-four. All sat in silence awaiting Hltanuu's guidance.

In another land, far beyond the waka of the fleet, the Red Conclave met once more. This time it came before the Master with confidence. They believed they had found the flaw that would destroy those who prepared to bring all into balance.

'Master, we have found their weakness. They have erected the other Tu Ahu by using the power of the sacred Stone Bird carved by the Ancients. They do not have it with them this time. We have tracked it across the ocean and find it on the Imperial Fleet that sails for Sumeria. Only that stone can join them to the stars. It is a great distance from those who depend on its power to accomplish union. Separation is the flaw. They have stretched themselves too far.'

'What must we do?' asked Mata-u-enga.

'Stand between them and the stone. Cast a huge shadow over the

Sun and bring night to day. Place the Darkness between the Imperial Fleet and those who gather at the Roof of the World.'

'Let it be done, and quickly.'

Those who came with a stone felt something shift and shape above them. Something ominous and dark began to steal light from the Sun. Within moments, they were plunged into night in the middle of the day. Stars shone forth to bring a chuckle from Ii-chantu.

'This is unexpected, but does not reveal the flaw,' he whispered to Utini. 'Light a fire in the centre of the circle.'

Utini returned and soon brought a bright flame out of a small pile of dried yak dung. He stood waiting for the answers to the many questions that had churned within him over recent days. Hera took his hand. Each held a stone, even the youngest.

'Place the stone before you. Sit with it and wait. When I call you hence, bring your stone to Utini, who will then hand it to Hera. Thus will the colours merge, and prophecy set in the stars be fulfilled. Take no notice of the Darkness. It merely brings the stars to view all that happens here. It wishes to be part of the restoration of the Light, joined once more in the balance.'

Without another word, Ii-chantu signed for Hera to stand beside him in the centre of the circle. Then he called Tia-ho, the child of Hera, and she went to her father with grace and a smile of joy to gift her stone. On receiving it from Utini, Hera placed it in the centre of the circle.

'This child is the seed of tomorrow. This stone is set here in the centre of the circle for all the children of the universe,' intoned Ii-chantu, in a voice that seemed to carry over the mountains and out to the stars. 'It is the most powerful of all stones, the pivot of all that has ever been and will ever be. The past, the present and the future.'

The Darkness closed in upon them, sought to extinguish the small fire that gave them light, and failed. The deeper the Darkness, the greater the lustre of the stars and the brighter the light from the flame. One candle was enough to hold the power of the dream.

Sound. A wave of sound, a pure clear tone, gathered to the little central stone. Its song embraced the earth and the heavens, and reached out to touch the people. It was a seed, a new beginning, a promise of renewal, a thing of unfathomable power and beauty.

It reached across the Darkness to find the ocean where the circle formed around Hltanuu. A cry of joy went around the room, as elder after elder felt the shift in the balance. Each joined now with one who held a stone to form the Wheel of Life. Hltanuu relayed the name, gave it power with a few words, and knew no one now stood alone. Hand reached out to hand across the darkened Sun, family bound to family, and nation supported nation. They healed separation.

The new-born power of the central stone penetrated the square of confrontation formed by the Red Conclave to unleash frustration. They were bewildered and confused by the turn of events. The Darkness was not halting the raising of the Tu Ahu. Twenty-four men, women and children still sat around a faint light to place a stone. It seemed a simple act, something of little consequence, yet it sent a shiver through each member of the Black Robe council. How could these people, who were separated from the stone of the Ancients, continue without concern? Didn't they understand they were powerless? It seemed not.

Consternation ran through the shadow people. More moved here than they understood. The Master would not be pleased. He would have to call terrible and ultimate power into play very soon or he would be too late.

' Eagle Child,' was the next call of the old one. It summoned the little son of Pana into the circle. He followed the lead of Tia-ho, and walked with determination to Utini, carrying in two strong hands a stone so heavy he staggered. Hera stood at the eastern rim of the circle to gift it to the circle.

'With this stone, we mark the sunrise, the rebirth of the land and the people,' chanted Ii-chantu. 'It is of the beginning, the spark that brings flame to the line of life that reaches out to the west. Eagle Child gifts it to the place of the eagles, to the colours that are yellow, and the direction that brings illumination. So be it.'

Hltanuu reeled as the stone that anchored the east sent forth its power. All felt it, absorbed the shock and smiled. This circle was changing the world.

Mata-u-enga almost fell to the floor when the wave that flowed from the stone of the sunrise touched into his chilled chamber. It was like a brilliant fire that sang as it reached out to join with the core of the Central Sun.

'Counter this madness!' he screamed at those who sat in the square. 'They seek light, then let us accelerate the Darkness until it gathers so close it can only explode into an all-consuming blaze. They seek fire, then gift them the fire that fuels the Sun. Align the ultimate power, destroy all that is, consign this planet to oblivion. Let us ride a wave of total destruction to another home, for the universe is limitless.'

Llana's daughter, Lan-tu-chi, who had reached her seed-time years, and taken a new name to honour her journey as a woman, was now called to bring her stone to the circle. It was set in the west as the old one's voice sent words of ancient power to the land once more.

'We place this stone in the west to complete the life line that begins in the east, and moves by the light of the Central Sun to encompass all, and return again. We bring male child and female child to hold the line, and the joining that is of the centre. May they hold the two halves of the whole, and the balance.'

Again Hltanuu felt the thrust of power moving with purpose. It seemed all she described was known to the elders long before they heard her words. Each held a name, and joined with it to support those who sat around the little fire in the mountains. Those who plied the ocean were, in every way, integrated with those who sat at the Roof of the World. There was no separation. The Great Wheel taking shape within the lands uplifted high was destined to encircle the planet and encompass the stars.

Others saw this too, and moved with haste to intervene before it was complete. Within the shadows, Mata-u-enga and his Enclave gathered matter together and drew it into less and less space. By accelerating its song, and exerting immense power by distortion of the Darkness, they reduced it to a form so small and dense, it began to collapse inwards. They were emulating the law that brought death to a star.

'Do we gather enough power to move matter beyond the reach of sound?' cried Mata-u-enga.

'Yes, master! It builds and gathers more and more into its orbit,' was the excited chorus of response.

They knew that if they could bring enough matter into this chain of reduction, it would eventually reach a critical moment. Squeezed close, pressed smaller and smaller, and heavier and heavier as more matter was accelerated into a diminishing space, it would begin to lose its essence, the image of its shape. The law of survival would then come into play, for every thing has the right of survival, even survival itself.

'How elegant,' cried the Master. 'We bring matter to the point where to continue to keep its essence, it must destroy itself and take another form that, in time eternal, will become once more the original shape. Nothing is made of nothing. There is a cycle to all. We intervene to bend that pattern to our purpose. To destroy those who honour the light, with the light.'

He knew the sequence. The rapidly distorting matter would activate the law of reversal of force. Then all that swept inward would come to a point of negation, instantly reverse direction, and expand so quickly it would explode. The death of a star was often marked by light so bright the Ancients named it a Nova. In the blink of an eye, those who manipulated matter within the Darkness could trigger the destruction of the planet, the end of Terra, the death of Gaia.

'Those who walk the realms of pain and cling to the Darkness, begin to unleash the ultimate power,' cried Aria. 'They move to destroy the Mother. If we cannot overcome the forces gathered, there will be no tomorrow for our children. Nothing will remain.'

'Madness born of unbridled anger, moves to deny the circle and obliterate all that exists,' cried one of the elders.

'Join hands!' cried Aria. 'Bring completion to the circle. Send love to block the malformed ones. Summon courage to the struggle. Join and hold.'

Hltanuu felt the circle on the waka redouble its strength, and send it swiftly to the circle in the mountains. They spanned the world now. Struggled with all their power to defeat those who manipulated matter.

'Join and hold!' was the desperate cry that echoed over the waters, through the valleys, over the deserts and into the heights of the mountain.

Ii-chantu was aware of the battle. The War of the Ancients, that tore the continents apart and sank huge areas beneath the tides, paled beside the ultimate act, the possibilities released by those who fought to see the Darkness stand supreme. Chaos beckoned as never before. Star-burst, oblivion, the death of all. He struggled to complete the circle they built on the heights, knowing each stone placed with good intent increased the balance.

'Tovitalih! Gift your stone to Hera to hold the north.'

The Kirghze chief stepped forward. It was done. Then came the words to hold that power in the circle. 'We place this stone to honour wisdom and all who kept the lore of the Ancients pure. White is the colour of its power and purpose. The horse stands strong to guard this realm.'

'Llana! Go to the south.'

'We set this stone in the southern realms to hold innocence safe within the new world. Green is the colour we gift to those who find joy in play, and play in all they do. We ask the mouse to watch over all held within this direction.'

Eight more were needed to reinforce the ring of fire that was the outer rim of the circle. Name after name was called, and each moved with calmness to hold the power that built upon this rock. And those aboard the waka held their circle, and gathered awesome forces within it, to hold the Darkness back.

'Many stand against us, Master. They try to deny us access to matter. They attempt to slow all that happens.'

'Find more power, bring more speed to the thrust of this awesome tide. Find more power. We near the critical moment. Push everything beyond their interference,' cried Mata-u-enga.

Ii-chantu quickly moved stone carriers to stand on the west-east line. Desperate to reinforce the line of life, to proclaim to the universe that hope reigned eternal, he hurried the placement of their stones. Then he gathered the last to the south-north line for the balance.

Courage beneath that cloak of Darkness, the power of each gathered, and that gifted from afar, rapidly brought the Wheel close to completion. Yet nothing was certain, the Darkness was still moving with formidable purpose. Everything now depended on the twenty-four arrayed beneath the mountains. Depended on each binding their love into the land, the waters, and the star-bright sky above. Trust moved now, for the old one depended on each one of the twenty-four to dedicate their stone to the good. There was no time for incantations, only time for intent to meet need.

'How stands the circle of stones?' asked the Master. 'Have they been consumed by fear and fled before the power we bring to bear? Do they acknowledge the end of all, the death we send to complete the destruction of everything?'

'No master, they foolishly hold their ground. They are lost. All passes beyond their understanding. Their minds are captive to their hearts. They believe in each other and join hands to honour love. They dream of a world set free by the power of truth and spirit. All this falseness binds them as slaves to the circle.'

'We have them then,' cried the Master. 'Our speed outstrips their response. Time rushes to its end. We have them on the edge of total destruction.'

Ii-chantu saw the moment through steady eyes. Despair had no place there. The creation of this Tu Ahu was different. It could not be established by the power of the Ancients. The Stone Bird had brought them to this day, but now it gifted the final act back to the earth, to simple time-worn stone scattered over a high plateau. The forces that shaped it were of the mountain, the waters, the skies, the winds, the snow and the Sun.

The hands that brought the stone to the circle were worn and shaped by life to serve. Children's hands grimed by play, weavers' hands stained by dyes, callused horsemen's hands hardened by the reins, sailors' hands strengthened by the thrust and pull of the paddle, old hands wrinkled by passing years, young hands softened with nurture, the hands of chiefs that carried unseen burdens, and mothers' hands both gentle and caring.

All had travelled the rim of a timeless wheel to come once more to this circle set so high in the land. What the Ancients created, then tore down, was being recreated. The magic that brought it into being was of the ordinary, made extraordinary. Stone that had lain in the dust for countless years was lifted up to open the way, and people, who claimed no special rights or virtues, carried it into a space that was like any other, but with good intent, become magical.

It was time to end separation. Time to gift back to the earth all things that were of the earth, to honour the spirit of life within the stone, the waters, the trees, the fish and all creatures of the land, to revere the ordinary and see its sacredness, to acknowledge the oneness of all that is, and will ever be.

Ii-chantu brought those who formed the Wheel to that moment of completion. Only they could accomplish it. Everything was in their hands. Twenty-four were asked to take the responsibility. Each needing to accept the challenge and hold fast. His final words to them were very gentle. No hint of urgency was laced within them. He knew he had to let everything go, that he had to leave space for the spirit to move.

'Remember you are of the dream and the stone. Reach out to the stars, be a child of the universe. Hold to the stone. Hold to a star. Hold to the good. Be at one with all that is. Just be.'

Silence cloaked the rock upon which they stood. Everyone had to find their own way to contribute to the completion of the Wheel of the Universe.

Only those who gathered on the waka to hold the circle really knew what happened in that moment. Hltanuu felt the final joining, but was aware only of her baby son, who shared ancient words of knowing with an unborn child. This was like a waking dream, a vision set within a brilliant blue light that swept around the rim of the circle. She understood that light was a global source of healing.

Aria gave her strength to Ra, and saw him call the power of the whale song into the circle. Wisdom carried on the long tides of the ocean was shared with all, embraced by the circle. And the music of the waves spilled out to greet the stars. Creation born of the waters honoured creation born of the heavens.

Eroa sat with Tai, who was so close to Ra their colours seemed entwined. He felt the purity of the bubbling mountain stream flow into the circle. Its song was for all the streams that flowed to nurture life.

Tali-a-tali stood with his beloved Pana, and looked across to their son. He saw the eagles of the Rampart lift into the skies and bring the magic of flight to place on the rock. Then his vision shifted, and the Stones of Lore were arrayed before them, and Pana brought them into the circle to bind the deepest wisdom of the Ancients into the earth forever. Now the land would speak of the lore, and hold its song safe.

Kaho reached out to Tovitalih. Thus did one born of the forests support one born of the treeless grasslands and the deserts. He saw the chief riding from hidden well to hidden well, to thank the ancestors for the gift of life. They gathered around him, laughed in greeting and led their horses into the circle.

Mokoio stood strongly beside the Khan. He saw the leader of the Middle Kingdom stoop to touch the earth and gather dust into his hand. Trail-hardened and looking robust and alert, his leader let the fine fragments that were once rock, drift across the circle. He acknowledged in that moment that all was change and ever changing. Thus did he bring renewal into the circle. And when he looked at Llana at his side, he gifted to that moment love both deep and abiding. All this happened in an instant that opened to allow the gifting of the spirit of life to the Wheel.

Then Hera looked at Utini. Reached across to take his hand. Within it he held the circle stone of his mother. They touched. Time spun out of time. Prophecy answered to bring completion to the Circle. Joy unbounded filled the land. Darkness gave way to light, night became day. The Sun shone down from a clear sky. The world was in balance.

The last strand of the Web of Life was anchored by the Twelfth Tu Ahu. Sacred threads of many colours vibrated with joy to share once more the Song of the Universe.

> In a distant land the remnant of the Red Conclave hid from the light. They could not stand the brightness of the Sun by day, or even the soft glow of the stars by night.

> The Master had banished them to the wilderness, ordered them to leave their shadowed haven to wander in a world blessed by light. He knew well the terrible punishment he had consigned them to. Healing was abroad, and healing was the last thing they sought.

Death would have been kinder to them, for deep down, that was their chosen journey. Life and death, light and dark, were all awry in those fear-filled minds where the spirit was denied entry, and the heart forbidden a home. Separation was complete in them, it was their fatal flaw. They saw it falsely in others, for they failed to understand the mirror of the soul.

***

Everyone sat in silence. The story touched deep cords that gave birth to new songs. Even the Story Teller was taken aback by the power that had gathered to his words.

'Does the story end here, grandfather?' asked someone in a quiet voice. A note of sadness within it suggested she feared there was no more.

'The balance is saved and the Black Robe danger overcome. That's it then,' concluded another with a sigh.

'No! How easy it would be if it was so,' replied the old one. 'It is true the balance is restored and the Web of Life bound securely to the Tu Ahu once more. But the keys to lock it thus, have still to be placed and activated.'

'What keys, grandfather?'

'The Stones of Lore are the keys. They join all to the Ancients and the wisdom of the ages. Eight strong locks are needed to secure the doors to the eight realms. Only when the last is placed is the Darkness bound within the balance. Mata-u-enga merely retreats from the field, he has not surrendered it to the Light. There are still journeys to be made and stories to be told.'

Their excited voices echoed through the halls as they left to seek their beds that night.

The Gathering of the Nations

Guides help the lost find the trail again. They are many in number but bound by one law. They understand the trail of truth is only revealed on the inner journey.

They lay exhausted beneath a bright blue sky. Exaltation overlaid a deep weariness. Those who had placed the Wheel struggled to find themselves within the momentous events of this wondrous day.

Each had travelled a different trail to arrive in this place. For some it marked the later years of a lifetime of commitment, and for others it was but a beginning.

Mystery brought them here. With a certainty that now seemed both elegant and assured, all knew the trail they followed was set down long ago. And mystery marked the last act of the placing of the Great Wheel. None remembered the power that visited each stone to carve beneath it a recess that accepted its shape perfectly. Now they fitted so well it was impossible to prise them out of the rock that bound all into the Wheel. Time alone might break it loose, or obscure its place, but whatever its fate, story tellers would keep its memory warm.

'Rest,' said Ii-chantu.

'Rest and sleep, and rest again,' said Hera.

'But be ready to move at dawn,' laughed Tovitalih. 'It is a long ride to Tashkent.'

He was right. They did leave at dawn, and it was a long ride, but one that was nothing but joy after the challenge of the desert trail. Nothing hindered them, no threat called for response, no urgency drove them onward. All was quiet, day after day, and night after night.

They found the city beautiful, and a place to rest and think of friends who plied other tides. The news from Hltanuu was that the Imperial Fleet was about to sail from Mumbai to reach the Straits of Oman within one moon. Landfall in Su-meria was but some twenty-five days hence. Pana thrilled to this message. All became caught up in the thought of this rendezvous. Especially the Kirghze who were eager to come at last to the shores of the ocean.

'We leave at dawn,' once again Tovitalih marked their leaving with a laugh. 'I have found a boy to guide us to Mashhad. He is only twelve or thirteen, but says he knows his way home. A lad of mystery this one. Abdullah Abouh is his given name.'

Abdullah was very small indeed. Yet, he arrived with a mule, and as promised, set out for Mashhad with no show of concern. In the beginning his pace was slower then the rest, but when they entered the hills, he gathered speed to roam ahead to find the best path on the twisting trail. He truly knew the way. Although the main caravan route was further south and longer, the one he offered was far shorter, a narrow path to be sifted from many others that criss-crossed the way.

Ra rode up to range alongside Abdullah. He was intrigued by the boy's trail knowledge, and wanted to know more about his life. Tovitalih's information regarding Abdullah was very sparse. It seems the elders in the bazaar had recommended the lad, and that was enough. It was the Kirghze way.

'I am Ra. Greetings to you, Abdullah. May the Sun shine upon your trail and the moon watch over your tent in the night. And may your parents live a long and happy life.' He used the desert language of the Kirghze, a form that was simple and known to many peoples.

'Greetings, Ra. May the cold winds turn aside from you and the rains fall to meet your need. My parents are both dead. It was the will of the Great One.'

Ra was shaken to hear this news. He felt his innocent greeting had hurt the young one. Yet it served both of them well, for during the remainder of the day they shared much. Ra learned of the tragic death of the boy's parents at the hands of thieves, who ambushed them deep within the hills on one of their journeys with their wonderful carpets.

It was a robbery that gained them little, but stole from the young one all that he had and loved. He was an only child, and although there were relatives in another city, he had decided to stay at home. That was two years ago, and since that time Abdullah had made a new life for himself as a guide. The trails came naturally to him, for he understood the alignment of the stars and had a wonderful feel for the shape of the land. It was sometimes dangerous work, but if he chose his parties well, not too risky for one with his skills.

Abdullah learned that Ra was a foundling, a child orphaned by the invasion of the Black Robe forces of the Altec Nation. Although he knew nothing of that war, he felt they walked a similar path, for both had suffered grievous loss. This led the boy to share his dream.

'I really need a good horse to go with my mule. A fine stallion to ride as well as my pack animal. Then I will be able to go further afield, and perhaps one day, become a famous guide, one remembered in stories and known for long journeys into strange lands. I know the Silk Road calls me, also Egypt in the west, the Middle Kingdom in the east, the land of the Kirghze Nation and those beyond. That is what excites me about this party. You come from many places. I hear that in your speech, but know little more.'

'Let us speak of this tonight within the circle of the fire. Perhaps others will share their stories too,' said Ra with a smile.

Thus it was that Abdullah found the courage to speak of his loss, and gain many friends. He was amazed to discover he guided the Khan of the Middle Kingdom. The thought of that disturbed him at the outset, made him question his place, and for a time created doubts about his worthiness. He began to try too hard to please, and for a day or two lost sight of who he was. Then the Khan came and rode beside him, spoke gently, asked for information about the mountains ahead, treated the youngster as an experienced guide, and won a friend.

Now at ease with the Khan, he was knocked off balance once again on learning Tovitalih was the chief of the Kirghze Nation. He felt overwhelmed. All his dreams came together at once. God was with him, and God was Great.

Tai and Hera saw Abdullah both as a guide, and a child who needed nurture. They understood his deeper yearnings, and tried to balance respect for the one who led them through the wilderness, with the warmth and kindness of the mother. Within a few days they had discovered he was actually thirteen. Porea, Aria's daughter, was of a similar age and showed something of the same independent spirit. She soon found in Abdullah a friend.

Thus was the lonely one drawn more and more into a large family. He responded to their caring with an openness that was a joy to see. The Kirghze children and others met along the way, often gathered to his tent to learn string games and watch him make little figures out of twigs bound with bright carpet wools. A trick learned by the child who sat beneath the loom of the mother.

'Tomorrow we see Mashhad in the distance, a mere outline against the sky, and the next day we gain its walls,' explained Abdullah to Tovitalih. 'Do you require shelter for your people and the horses? Should I organise that for you?' asked Abdullah, with a hint of sadness in his voice. He saw the end of twelve wonderful days, and the loss of friends unlike any he had known. He felt at one with them.

'Yes! Do that for us, it would be a kindness,' said the Kirghze chief.

The walled city of Mashhad was all that the boy had told them. And the stables and rooms he found were just right for the party. However the Khan, Llana, Hera, Utini, Ra and Tai accepted Abdullah's invitation to stay in his home. Porea arrived of her own choosing.

'An old retainer of my parents cares for our dwelling in my absence. She expects us, for I sent a message ahead,' were his words of explanation as he led them into a splendid house of impressive size and beauty. This boy was full of surprises. He chose the hard road, the trails through the wilderness when all he needed was here. Shelter, comfort, food, a retainer to care for him, and security.

'He says he needs a stallion,' thought Ra. 'He has the means to buy one, but chooses to wait until he is strong enough to handle such a horse.'

Pana and Hltanuu spoke often at dawn and dusk. As they journeyed ever closer, the excitement of meeting grew stronger. The Imperial Fleet was moving slowly. Not because of contrary winds or difficulties, but because of visits to many nations along the way. As news of the stone was carried ahead by traders, the cry went out from kingdom after kingdom for sight of it. None was denied if a suitable anchorage existed, for no one wanted to set limits on the reach of the song of the stone. Thus was the pace of the journey set, and the magic of it enhanced.

Tovitalih and the Khan sat with Hera, Utini and Llana around the low table in the dining room of Abdullah's home. Ii-chantu rested nearby. They met to plan the last stages of the trail to the sea.

'I have not found a guide yet,' said Tovitalih. 'There are no caravans moving in this season. All travel from the sea, not towards it.'

'But we have a guide,' said Hera. 'We have Abdullah. He knows the way to Teheran. It was one of his father's greatest markets, and he visited it with him several times. They used an old route, but one that is safe and sure. He often accompanied his parents, for travel was the basis of their trade. That is how he learned so much about the different trails. He has the mind for it and the heart.'

'Teheran is more than half way to the ocean,' said Ra, who had joined them. 'Abdullah has a quick mind, and the language to gather information along the route. He could bring us to Qom and Arak and guide us across the mountains to the Tigris River. From there all flows to the sea. I also want him to guide us.'

'But we take him far from his home,' said Llana, who understood the sadness of that separation. 'How will he return, alone?'

'He will not,' said Ii-chantu from the couch where all thought he was asleep. 'He is the one to guide us. It is written. Our young friend has waited many years for our arrival. Let us not disappoint him.'

Thus was Abdullah hired for the last stage of the journey. And in the asking, his dreams unfolded. To remain with them was his greatest wish, to serve them his pleasure, and to bring them to the mouth of the Tigris his biggest challenge. On the morrow they would begin.

Refreshed and provisioned, they left long before the Sun touched the land. Tovitalih saw to that, for he wanted no delay that would add to the burdens of their young guide. The trail opened before them. With unerring instinct bound into knowledge, they were brought to water as needed, and shade, and at the end of the day, a wonderfully sheltered place to make camp. This was the pattern day by day as they crossed this dry and ancient land, and came at last to Teheran.

Abdullah went again and again to the bazaar to learn of the trail to the Tigris. Each day excited him more. There were stories of dangers along the way, water holes to store in memory, marker rocks to remember in sequence, stars to acknowledge and prayers to be said for each day. So much to learn if he was to truly serve those he guided.

'Tovitalih, Chief of the Kirghze, I ask a boon of you,' were Abdullah's opening words. He wasn't always this formal with the one he respected so much. Their relationship had become more like that of father and son. 'Forgive me for this interruption, but God wills it.'

'Does He now,' was the cheerful response. 'Speak more of God's will.'

'I need you to help me choose a stallion. It is time to be mounted on a horse.'

'It is indeed, and I know the very one that will match the spirit you bring to this trail. I have been waiting to hear those words. I saw your need early on, although Ra prompted me from time to time to ensure it was not forgotten. Your stallion already awaits you, my friend. Meet me at sunset. At the stables. Do not be late.'

Thus did Abdullah come, neither too soon, nor too late. He timed his arrival to the moment, for it was a precious one. He had tried to find Ra to go with him, and failing there looked for Hera, Utini, and Llana, and was disappointed over and over again. Even Porea was nowhere to be found. All had disappeared. However, when he entered the courtyard of the stable he knew why. They had quietly gathered ahead of him to be witness to his introduction to the stallion chosen by Tovitalih. No horse was in view. Merely a wonderful circle of friends. All were present, all who came out of the desert, the families of the long trails. Not a single child was missing, no one. It was a moment of honour and honouring.

'Greetings, guide of the blind and lost, greetings, friend of the desert and the mountains, greetings, companion of the trusty mule, greetings from your many friends gathered here at the setting of the Sun,' said Tovitalih with a solemn grace. 'Enough of words. You know we esteem your services highly. Let us now wait upon the horse. Come forth, Shadow Wind, the one named for the softest of breezes to caress the sands.'

A cheer went up when the stable doors opened and attendants led out a beautiful black stallion. It pranced and strained at the halter, but settled quickly on a quiet command. It was a creature of wonder, small for a stallion, but very strong and clear of eye. Abdullah could not believe the magic that danced before his eyes. His horse had come to him. And at the hands of the greatest riders in the world. A gift from friends. The Sun did not set fast enough to hide his tears.

All was not finished. The Khan stepped forward to speak of his joy in the journey and the part played by the boy. Then on the inclination of his head, Ra appeared carrying a saddle crafted with care and love to serve the rider well. More tears, and arms to hold him in his joy. A wondrous trail opened to stretch further than any knew, for although Ii-chantu saw some of its many turnings, he saw not its end.

Qom was reached without difficulty. Their only real concern was for Abdullah, who from time to time raced ahead on his stallion, alone and too much at risk. A quiet word from Tovitalih saw Kirghze youths stationed near the front and poised to ride with the young one when he broke loose. This excessive exuberance lasted for three days, then fell way. The excited boy once again took on the disciplines of the guide. All relaxed once more.

Arak came into view seven days later and was reached at sunset. Set within the heartlands of the Kuhha Ye Zagros Mountains, it opened to the vastness of the Tigris Valley. Several days later, they reined in their horses to look upon a distant ribbon of light that was the river. The waters before them ran to the ocean that brought loved ones closer night by night. Pana was overcome by that thought, and wept openly for reunion with Tali. Others comforted her with tears of yearning. Trails long set apart were soon to be joined once more.

Descending rapidly from the heights on a well-formed trail, they came to Dezful, the gateway to the lowlands, and the green and fertile countryside of Su-meria. They sped across the land now, filled with urgency, and as impatient as Abdullah to embrace each day. Avhaz was reached in two days, and another three brought them to Abadan and the ocean.

No one rested until they rode to the meeting of the waters of the Tigris and the Gulf known as Oman. A fleet was anchored in the shallow waters to greet them. It was arrayed with colourful flags that honoured the journey made and filled them with an overwhelming excitement. Pana and Hltanuu felt it, sent urgent cries for vessels to make for the shore, and waited impatiently for the waka to reach the land.

They came at speed. The waka powered by Menehune hands at the direction of Tali-a-tali, and the waka steered by Kaho. When their proud prows cleaved the wet sands, the Kirghze formed an arc at a distance, to allow kin and friend to meet without interference. Tali was the first ashore, and Pana and her child the first to be gathered in close embrace. Aria somehow leapt onto the land ahead of Eroa, and both were soon joined by Kaho and Hltanuu. The Khan and Llana and the old man were soon overwhelmed by friends eager to greet them. And when the first rush of excitement subsided, came the introduction of new-found friends, the Kirghze and the one named Abdullah.

'God is Great!' was Abdullah's greeting. 'God is indeed Great.'

Many gathered ashore that night to hear the stories told around the fire. It was a time of celebration, a joyous meeting of peoples who had stepped out in trust to bring harmony where discord reigned. They had reached beyond themselves to find courage buried deep, and carry it forward to honour a dream set in the stars long ago.

Dawn found many still asleep upon the shore, and two in earnest conversation. Ra and Abdullah had talked through the night.

'Can you take a horse to sea? Is there a way to transport Shadow Wind?' asked the youngster.

'Not on our waka. We come from lands that know not horses. However, the vessels of the Imperial Fleet are very different. I think some are made to carry the mounted warriors of the Khan. He will have the answer to your question. Do you hope to sail with us to Egypt?'

'Yes! That thought is ever present. I don't know if it's the voyage that calls, or my sadness at the thought of our parting that drives me. Perhaps both. And there is another reason. Tovitalih asks the same question of others. If his people voyage on, I have no one to join for the return to Mashhad. It would be a lonely ride.'

'A meeting is arranged at High Sun,' said Ra. 'You are invited. It may make everything clearer.'

Those who gathered represented many nations. They sat in a wide array of seats and on the deck as best they could. No formality here, no special place for rank, just men and women coming together to chart their way into the future. The centre-piece of all was the Stone and beside it the sleeping babe, Kun, Hltanuu's child.

Everything seen and heard this day by Abdullah and Tovitalih was new and filled with wonder. The motion of the vessel on the waters, the gentle rhythm of the waves, the salt smell of the ocean, its taste upon the tongue, the touch of the sea breeze so different from the desert winds, the cry of seabirds, the Sun shimmering on surging tides, the sound of the waka timbers creaking, the immensity of the space around them and the brightness of the skies. All intriguing and filled with challenge. It had began.

Kaho welcomed them aboard the Hai-da waka and asked the Khan to speak. The Khan welcomed them to the fleet, and then asked Ii-chantu to speak, and others to translate for him. Only the old one held the pieces that created the bigger picture. They were all players in this ancient dance, some as musicians, others as singers or attendants upon the song.

'The last Tu Ahu has been created to tie once more the Strands of the Web. The balance is restored, but there is no lock to hold it secure. We have journeyed far to achieve all this, but are called to go further, to complete the greater design held within the dream. The Stone placed before you is one of the keys that sets the lock in place. There are eight in all. Three are of this voyage, one holds firm on the Island of the Rampart, the others journey to far-off lands, to places of power and mystery known only to the Stone.

'This Stone bears the sacred mark of every nation gathered here, and all who stand between us and Egypt. That is the land that calls to it, and the one that will reveal the secret of its siting. We voyage onward to complete that mission, and gather now to decide how it might best be done.

'This is my message. May you bring wisdom to this Stone and move to the next tide of this trail without delay. Although my bones grow weary, they are still restless for the day the last lock closes to hold all secure.'

The fleet was committed to the next tide, for all the necessary preparation was complete. Yet none knew for certain who voyaged on. It was time for others to speak. Tovitalih rose first.

'We have ridden far to honour this Stone. My people are committed to its journey and wish to go forward with you. At the end of your voyage you come to another desert, the world we know as home, a wild place where we might once again be of service. Are your vessels able to carry our horses?'

Abdullah hung on every word when the Khan stood to reply. It was as if his life was poised on a knife edge.

'Tovitalih, friend of the long trails of the desert, if it is your wish to sail with us, that is possible. On my orders, four vessels have been prepared to receive your people and their horses, and one more. They have fodder for two moons at sea, and carry water. All this was of my dream. Long before we came to the ocean, it was my hope you would sail with us.'

Abdullah could not contain himself. He knew he had to speak, to ask a question in the presence of all the greatness gathered here. 'Khan, you said... *and one more...* Is that place for my horse?'

'Of course. We could not venture onward without him,' replied the Khan with a chuckle. 'There is a place for your horse, and for you, if you wish to make the voyage,' and now he broke into a laugh. 'Horse and guide are one.'

Abdullah was overjoyed. He would have to find Porea to share his news. He was to sail with them. Hera and Utini would be happy, thought the boy, and perhaps even Aria and Eroa would smile upon him. He wanted to know them better, to be at ease with the mother and father of the girl who was now his closest friend. So much adventure to come, thought this boy, who all too soon chose to be a man. So many stars above them this night. Each one bright and beautiful. So many realms opening to him. Shadow Wind, Porea, a sea voyage, friends set upon a quest, life abundant and filled with laughter. God is Greater than Great.

> 'Egypt is a dangerous land,' said Mata-u-enga to the dark cloaked ones gathered to his side. 'Dangerous for them and dangerous for us. The Ancients set savage protection around that land to uphold the Light.
>
> 'All abides in the jaws of the oldest of crocodiles. That is their challenge now, and ours.'

***

'Grandfather, your stories are often of children who are called to carry heavy loads. Ra and Abdullah come to mind. Why is this so? Why should those who are so young be asked to carry so much?'

'It is the way the spirit moves. I believe many children, blessed with huge gifts, have been born to answer the needs of this age. I see them often as I travel the land with my stories. They are the key to all, they are the future. They know how to carry the heavy things lightly. They are born to dance the trails, to come to the challenge with joy and laughter. That is the secret of the peaceful way.'

The Trail of the Crocodile

Test the waters, look deep, probe the inner realms and know all is bounded by the guardians of the spirit.

The beat of the drum brought Abdullah out of a deep sleep. The drum and the movement of the vessel. He slept below deck beside his stallion, where the light would not penetrate until the Sun stood high.

'It is time to greet the new day, Shadow Wind,' he said to the dark one who moved to rise, 'and time to feed you, and clean this holding place. The Khan has gifted all a boy and horse could ask for, and more besides.'

Seven days they had sailed within the confines of the Gulf of Oman. Seven wonderful days that saw him grow more and more at home on the ocean. If the winds held fair they would reach Egypt on the coming Moon.

Porea visited every day. At sunrise, Kaho manoeuvred alongside to deliver her in a tumbling heap on the deck. To the amusement of the crew, she always managed to fall as she boarded. Her arrival had become a major event that called forth many witnesses. Some say the crews wagered on the outcome of her scramble to reach the other vessel. Yet, Porea was not embarrased by their interest, for she always arose with dignity to bow to all assembled.

Perhaps the most amusing part of the charade was Abdullah's repeated attempts to catch her, and his abject failures. He asked Ra how he might make the boarding easier, and was a little surprised by his friends advice.

'Better to let Porea make her own entrance in her own way,' were Ra's words. 'She never hurts herself. My sister has always moved through life from one fall to another, but without concern for such little matters. She is more in balance than anyone I know. Although I suspect you have tilted that a little awry.'

Abdullah knew his horse, Shadow Wind, enjoyed having Porea nearby. Both of them looked forward to her arrival, he was certain of that.

Seven more days at sea, and within them two brief landings to allow other nations to honour the Stone. Each stop gave Abdullah the opportunity to ride along the sands, enjoy the fresh air and the brightness of the Sun. How peaceful was this journey so filled with purpose.

Egypt was still nine days hence, when the skies darkened and a storm struck. Some said it was born of the heat of the desert, for they swore it carried fine sand with it. However, no one spoke of sand when it brought rain so heavy it blocked out all other sound. Shadow Wind was moved to terror by its power. Abdullah and Porea stayed at his side to calm and reassure him through a day and a night. Both were exhausted when the waves fell away and they sailed to the old rhythms again.

'Will your parents be worried?' asked Abdullah, when they went on deck in answer to the drum to meet the sunrise.

'No! They have braved many storms. They know I am in good hands aboard a good ship. They respect you, and in time may come to know you, and like you as I do.'

Silence upon the waters. Then the arrival of Kaho's waka and Aria's cry of good wishes for the day, words sent fondly to both of them. Abdullah began to feel he might never be lonely again.

High Sun, six days short of Egypt. The land edged closer, began to confine the fleet and thus create uncertainty. The Stone called them to Egypt, but as they neared landfall, some felt they needed to know more about its destination. The leaders gathered and discussed the possibilities for a long time.

Eventually Ii-chantu stood and said, 'I see your need and understand it, but the uncertainty is a burden to be borne calmly until the will of the Stone is made clear. This is not the time of the military mind. We cannot sit here and say this or that would be a good plan for the Stone. Only the Stone knows its destination, and only the Stone knows when it is ready to reveal it. Relax, enjoy the journey and trust the Stone. All will be revealed at the right time and in the right way. Anything else is of no account.'

They disbanded to watch the shore-line gather closer still. The Kirghze began to yearn for their horses beneath them and the desert wind flowing through their long hair. Yet they found excitement in the voyage. How their world changed and their horizons widened to meet the challenge of these days.

Ii-chantu sat alone with the Stone. He wanted to know its destination as much as anyone. *What has yet to be is already written...* was the thought that entered his mind, and fast upon it came another... *the Stone has already marked its passage and announced its destination...* That was true, for the carved symbols on the Stone were of each nation encountered on the long sea trail. If the route to this moment was so clearly drawn, so too would be the end. *Look closer...* were the other words that came to him.

The old one asked Tali-a-tali, master carver of the Menehune Nation, to help him examine the Stone. Pana joined them with their little one. They decided to see which carvings remained, when all claimed as sacred by the different nations were put aside. Aria arrived unbidden, carrying a sheet of reed parchment and a stick of charcoal to carefully draw each carving. While this was done, the others went over the Stone, naming each feature claimed by a nation. It was not a long task. In the end, they were surprised to find there was no carving unclaimed. Each matched a stop along the way, leaving nothing over to point to the Stone's resting place. Egypt was not carved into the surface. Ii-chantu was confused, for he trusted the words gifted from higher realms.

'We are missing something. The answer is carved here and we cannot see it,' the old one exclaimed in frustration.

'Perhaps it is hidden in a combination of all that has been carved, something too large to take in when the focus is on one symbol at a time,' suggested Tali.

'There might be one we cannot see,' said Aria quietly. She was looking at the copies of the carvings on the parchment. 'One side is completely hidden from us. We have never seen beneath the Stone. What we regard as the upper side may be the bottom.'

'I think you have the answer to the answer,' cried Pana with a laugh. 'All we have to do is turn it over. Let us ask Hera and Tai to help. With a little magic, it will be easy to do.'

When all were gathered they called Kaho to the platform to explain what they were about to do. He was concerned they might lose control of the Stone and drop it over the side, or through the hull of the waka.

'This is better done on dry land,' was his suggestion. 'When I see a good landing place I'll swing to the shore. Let us be patient and safe. As you told us, Ii-chantu, the Stone will reveal all in its own time.'

Thus was the mystery put aside until late in the day. News of their intention to turn the Stone travelled swiftly through the fleet. When Kaho eventually put into the shore all followed, and by the time the Stone was freed of restraining ropes and supporting timbers, a huge crowd had gathered on the slopes that ran down to the sea. This was not what Ii-chantu wanted. He had envisaged a quiet look into the secrets of the Stone of Lore, not a public occasion.

'The Stone does as the Stone wills,' was his thought, as those around him prepared to move it ashore.

'You do it, Hera,' was Tai's plea. 'I believe my power is best within the water.'

So it was Hera who went into the Silence. With a quiet mind, despite the many hundreds who watched, she moved within the Stone and found its song. Then with care, she realigned that essence to make it lighter. Utini knew when this was done and took command of all that followed. Six men and women stood around the stone, and on his signal, lifted high the companion of the one that had denied the strength of twenty-four of the Khan's guards. They carried it ashore where six others waited to keep the balance when it was turned over. Everything was accomplished with ease. When Hera withdrew from the Stone, those near it gasped, for it suddenly sank deeper into the loose sand as an awesome weight gathered to it again.

'Stand further back,' cried the Khan. 'Let us gather in procession to pass by to greet and honour the sixth side of the Stone. When that is done, let us leave the elders to examine the wondrous carvings now revealed. Much hinges on their study of the pieces of the puzzle that have remained hidden until this day.'

The moving of the Stone, and the silent passing to greet it, left a deep impression on all who were present. They realised the last ones to see those symbols, carved with such power, were the Ancients. Time folded over time to bring everything into the completeness of the universe, and set this Stone, and those gathered around it, within the greatest of circles.

Ii-chantu was grateful to the Khan for seeing the needs of the people, and the elders, and finding the perfect way to meet both. As the last of those who walked quietly by returned to their vessels, he went to the Stone with Hera and Pana. The weight of the moment seemed almost too much to carry. Yet, when he finally found the courage to go close enough to see the carved underside, he could only stand and laugh.

No secret symbol was hidden here, no intricate carving that would test the greatest minds, nothing like that. The challenge had already been met, the test was to have the vision to look beneath the surface, to think of examining the other side, and having the power to do so. Three pyramids were carved into the Stone, and a lion with the head of a man. Beside them stood the figures of a woman and a man. Beautiful, graceful figures of strangely garbed people seen in profile. Yet the most dominant image was that of a crocodile. This fearsome creature encircled everything, protected all within the range of its awesome jaws and long, serrated tail. It was a compelling carving, simple and elegant, and yet laced with power. The place to set the Stone to seal the lock was very clear to the old one. He knew the legend, and thought he held the key to the key.

Everyone wanted to know what the picture carvings meant. Ideas flowed to and fro, but all were well short of the mark. When the Khan turned to ask if Ii-chantu might share his understanding, they were surprised to find him already gone. No one had seen the old one slip away.

The mystery deepened. Before they came to the resting place of the Stone, they would have to pass through the jaws of the Crocodile, a creature as terrible as the Octopus. All this was clear to Ii-chantu, who sought a quiet place to go into the Silence.

Time passed, then in the dark before the dawn, twelve came to the Stone. Four flaming brands had burned at each corner throughout the night, each attended by a sentinel instructed to be alert to danger in the shadows. They thought they were the only ones who witnessed the moving of the Stone, who saw Hera sing it back onto the waka, who observed the binding of the Stone to the timbers to make it secure. But they were wrong. Power calls power to power. Beyond the circle of the flame was the shadow, and beyond the shadow, the Darkness, and within the Darkness, those who moved in their own worlds to satisfy their own needs. The Crocodile stirred.

Kaho cast off the waka on the first beat of the dawn drum, watched with admiration as the crew skilfully set the sail to harness the wind, gave his weight to the steering oar, and smoothly brought them into the protective arc of the fleet. The Khan had ordered this new line of advance. They knew little of what lay ahead, and sailed with charts unused for centuries into waters unseen by any aboard. The unknown beckoned, and within it moved a Crocodile that guarded a world of mystery.

Ii-chantu sat with the Khan, Eroa, Aria and Llana. It was time to probe the mists that shrouded the future.

'Tell us about the Crocodile,' said the Khan. 'It is the power that surrounds the last days of this journey. That is clear to me, but little else.'

'The Jaws hold the power, and the Tail. We have to contend with both to open the way,' replied Ii-chantu.

'Is its power of this world or another?' asked Aria.

'Both. The Jaws are shaped by the land itself. They are of this world and very dangerous. The Tail is of another realm. Its power is always just out of sight, on the edge of day, hidden in the shadowed place just beneath the waters. The Jaws we meet and overcome with courage, and the Tail we counter with wisdom born of the ancestors.'

'Show us the Crocodile on the chart,' said the Khan, as he unrolled the parchment and held it on the Stone.

'We are here,' responded the old man, as he placed his forefinger at the top of a long, narrow stretch of water. 'This is the legendary Red Sea of the old stories. It is the body of the Crocodile, and we have been sailing from the Tail, which is hidden in the southern waters, up to the Head. This dramatic division of the waters that awaits us soon, the two-pronged separation, creates the Jaws. Thus does the land itself form a creature that is of the waters.'

'Have we sailed through unseen danger for days past?' asked Hera. 'The chart shows we have crossed over its tail and voyaged up its body. Was this known to you, Ii-chantu?'

'No! Not in the way I see it now. I knew the sea itself was named for danger, the colour of blood. Only when the Stone was turned did I see its shape and begin to understand all that gathered here. The Tail only strikes when the Jaws have grasped the prey. We ride the back of the creature, are soon to enter its Jaws, and must be ready to deny them power, to protect ourselves from the strike of the Tail.'

'We need to bring all this into a greater circle,' said Eroa. All agreed they should meet in council in the late afternoon. There was much to think upon. Meanwhile the fleet sailed on.

Mokoio was the first to speak after Ii-chantu had shared all he knew of the Crocodile. As Commander of the Imperial Fleet, he wished to do something quickly to overcome the danger that hung over them. Yet, everything he heard made him feel powerless in the face of immense elemental power. So he pleaded for caution.

'I recommend the fleet hove to, that we find a safe anchorage and wait until we have more information. To sail blindly on would be unwise,' said Mokoio grimly.

'It is strange we have not seen another vessel in all our days on these narrow waters,' added Utini. 'This is a fabled trade route, a highway, and it is deserted. If we could intercept a passing boat and speak with its captain, we might find answers to the riddle of the Crocodile.'

So it was decided to hove to and wait. Meanwhile, a party was to probe the shore for information.

'I will go,' said Abdullah. 'The language of Egypt is cousin to my own. Only I can speak with the people. And I have a horse.'

'Go then, but with an escort of twenty Kirghze horsemen,' said the Khan.

'No! I go alone, this is a journey for a boy, not an army. It is better thus. I will be in God's hands.'

Those words had been spoken three days before. Abdullah had been put ashore with Wind Shadow in the dark before the dawn. Two days had been his promise when he departed. Two days away, no more, and now they came to the end of the third.

'He will be all right,' said Aria to Porea. 'Abdullah is a very brave and resourceful boy. I can think of only one other like him at his age, and that's your brother, Ra. As you know, he wants to take a horse to look for Abdullah. We have decided it is still too soon. He may return this very night.'

There was no return that night or the next. It was on the dawning of the day that followed that news of the young one's arrival went through the fleet. He rode in quietly, boarded silently and sat with friends to share the first of his news.

'Forgive me for being away so long. I have travelled far and seen few people, for the lands beyond the coast are very poor. I went inland and was welcomed into the first village, but when I asked of the Crocodile, I was driven away like a thief in the night. The next village was better, but although they fed me, no one would speak of the creature that guards the way to Egypt.

'So I decided to ride back along the coast, and that was when I ran into trouble. In a fishing village on a river I found men who knew the waters. They said word had been sent to them to remain ashore until the passing of this Moon. When I asked why that should be, they said the Crocodile was stirring and would sink all ships upon the ocean. I now knew it was best to keep quiet and wait and listen. One night later, I overheard two elders whispering of the troubles that were about to descend.

'It seems that once in every generation, or thereabouts, an awesome force gathers within the two waterways that are the Jaws. The old ones that spoke so quietly were confused by the appearance of the Crocodile at this time. It came too soon. It broke the age-old pattern. It is always forecast in the stars and the track of the Moon.

'The awakening of the Crocodile begins with the desert winds. When the east wind and the west wind arise as one, and meet within the Jaws to contest the way, the terror of the Awesome One is unleashed. Yet, they are but forerunners of the power that stirs to release the terror. The true danger gathers from the south, in storm-strewn waters that birth a ferocious gale that suddenly strikes north. Within the narrow waters of the Red Sea it is irresistible, a force that sends all ships into the deeps. It is the Doom of this realm.

'Most vessels caught within this storm-tide are wrecked upon jagged rocks that are, in truth, the teeth of the Crocodile. We have only two days to prepare to meet the Ancient One who has claimed so many lives in these waters.'

'Abdullah, we thank you. No one could have done better,' said the Khan. 'Now it is up to us to save the fleet. You have gifted us time and understanding. We must gift in return clear decisions and swift action.'

While Abdullah slept, the commanders and captains of the fleet met ashore. Mokoio held centre place, his was the guiding hand that sought to bring them together to ensure survival. Words were invited and flowed swiftly.

We have no sea room here... the winds will drive us... no sheltered headland... the tempest... we cannot anchor and hold... how can we escape... how... disaster looms...

All this was true. Disaster was set about them on all sides. It was Mokoio who set before them the first words of hope.

'The Hai-da and Menehune vessels are small enough to be hauled ashore if ramps are made to ease the way. The lighter scouting vessels of the Imperial Fleet may also be saved in that way. If all agree, this work should begin immediately and continue throughout the night. This covers seven craft in all. The bigger vessels, and in particular, those loaded with the Kirghze horses, are our greatest challenge. They need a sheltered anchorage and they need it soon.'

'May I suggest something?' said Ra. On Mokoio's nod he continued. 'Send someone to ask the village of the fishing people where a big vessel might find a haven on this coast. Somewhere that could be reached in two days. Their little craft must flee storms from time to time.'

'It may be too late for such a journey,' said the Khan, 'but Abdullah might already have the answer. Wake him and ask.'

When Ra returned, he was excited. Abdullah knew more than they realised. There was no such inlet or headland within their reach, but there was a large island near the entrance to the Jaws. The fishermen had spoken of it as a sheltered place, a storm-haven. With the knowledge they had no other hope, all agreed the remainder of the fleet should sail to the island. However, the first task was to bring the horses ashore.

Few slept that night. Flaming torches lit the shore to reveal long lines of people hauling the smaller vessels higher. All went well, for many willing hands gave their all to move them far above the clutches of a storm ravaged sea. With Hera's help, the Stone was brought to land once more. Rough stockades were constructed for the horses, and people left to tend them. All that could be done was done.

Dawn saw the remainder of the fleet sailing swiftly north in search of the island that was to be their haven. All hoped they would be sheltered and secure before the Crocodile convulsed to loose destruction on the tides. Mokoio led them into the unknown with a quiet determination to save the Imperial Fleet for the Khan. To lose it was to lose more than the vessels. A dream sailed these waters now, one that opened the way to a world the Commander wanted to be part of, and bequeath to his grandchildren.

The island was reached late in the day. As they approached, Mokoio saw it stood athwart the channel, and was high enough to break the south wind. He waited impatiently to round it, to see the hoped-for anchorage, but when they passed the last headland, he was bitterly disappointed. Five pinnacles of rock rose out of the ocean where the vessels might best be held. Vessels anchored there would be driven into them by the surging waves, and wrecked. All seemed lost.

Then he saw their need in another way. The pinnacles might of themselves become their anchors. Fourteen vessels, bound together as one, each giving strength to the other and the whole, might be secured to the five tall rocks. They had a chance. The greatest danger to the craft might become their greatest strength.

Without delay, they worked to weave their survival. Two huge stone anchors were off-loaded on the three pinnacles nearest the island. Heavy ropes bound them securely to the tall rocks that had defied the waves for thousands of years. These were attached to several five-stranded ropes, as thick as an arm, to join the three largest ships to the pinnacles. Now the other vessels crowded in to be tied into one vast raft, a floating platform criss-crossed by lines that wove a strong web.

The first winds that announced the awakening of the Crocodile arrived in the night. Blowing strongly from the west, they carried the hint of sand within their swirling power. Then the east wind gathered itself, as Abdullah said it would, and all was tossed to and fro by the sea in turmoil. The onslaught of the south wind was heralded by a roar unlike anything heard before. It was the wounded cry of a beast, the signal that the Crocodile was loosed to lash all in its path. Unleashed to drive everything into the terror of its Jaws.

'Hold! Bind to the timbers! Secure against these tides! Place the bags!' were the words Mokoio sent to all his captains.

Thus did they meet the Crocodile as one. Instead of fourteen separate vessels at the mercy of the storm, they met it as a raft. Mokoio knew the craft that took the greatest shocks, and absorbed them for the others, were those tied directly to the pinnacles. They had filled huge hessian bags with horse fodder, and bound them with ropes to cushion the impact of hull on hull. Each pounding shock was dulled by those bundles of sodden grass. Yet all knew courage and cloth were not enough. Time and tide held the key. The terrible thrust and pull of the waves would eventually wear all to nothing.

Dawn arrived at the peak of the storm and urged it to heights that made all fear for their lives. Could the fraying ropes hold? Could they stay strong enough to maintain the web they wove? Ropes parted, strained and broke with a whip crack, but not those who tended them. If they died in these waters they would do so bravely, and in the knowledge the Stone was safely ashore. They had brought it over the widest of oceans to the Gates of Egypt. Some felt their task was done. Yet Mokoio, with a greater vision, knew it had just begun. He drove them to the lines again and again, inspired them, kept alive the desire for life, and in the end brought them through.

The east wind was the first to go home, and was soon followed by the west. Then the Crocodile tired, gathered its strength for a last desperate lunge, and fell away. It did not deliver the deadly blow hidden in its Tail. It was over.

Late in the day, when the small waka rounded the island to greet them with joy, they were still untying the weave of ropes that had saved them. That night, the vessels that carried the horses sailed back to the landing. Within another day, all were gathered to sail the length of the Upper Jaw to the land of the Pharaohs, the Great Pyramid and the Lion Man.

Khalij as Suways, the Long Jaw of the Crocodile, opened to them with the new dawn. According to the charts, two days on fair winds would bring landfall within the Egyptian Nation. That was the hope, but the reality was different. As the Sun settled low over the desert lands to the west, a cry went up from the forward lookout.

'Sail Ho! Sail Ho!'

These words echoed over the calm waters to draw all eyes to the north. A strange sail, and an even stranger vessel slowly came into view. Its shape was elegant and its colours splendid, a craft of beauty and speed, a vessel fit for a Pharaoh approached them without fear. One ship sailing into the midst of many.

'This is how our waka must have looked to the Alliance,' said Kaho to Hltanuu, who sat beside him nursing their child. 'This is how we broke through suspicion to find trust and bring us all to this moment. I like what I see. They will make for the Khan's vessel, the biggest in the Imperial Fleet.'

Kaho's last words were soon proved wrong, for although the Khan's vessel was acknowledged by the dipping of the main flag, the new arrival passed on by and came at last to the Hai-da waka. Sailing a perfect curve, it came in close then stopped a mere two long rods away.

'Bring Abdullah to me,' was Kaho's response. He had failed to see the boy was already at his side. 'Greet them, honour them in the customary way, and do it in the name of the Khan, the Alliance and all the nations gathered here.'

Thus did those within the vessel of the Pharaoh stand in ceremony, to be greeted in a formal way by a boy who spoke a tongue that was cousin to their own. Costumes of splendour, adorned with head-dress of exotic style, gave presence to this occasion. All that unfolded here was unusual, intriguing and exciting, an experience to be remembered for all the days to come.

Abdullah's warm words of welcome were answered in kind, and

when all was done, vessel came to vessel to be joined. Kaho waited beside the Stone, to greet those who boarded. The Khan, Mokoio and all the others, who had quietly slipped onto the offside of the waka from small boats, stood arrayed beside him. Once again the Stone was the centre-piece. No speeches now, just an air of wonderment as their guests went with reverence to honour it. Whispered words, amazement and then joy. Those who came to meet them on the tides were now exuberant. The most imposing of all who stood around the Stone, the one dressed in the greatest finery and most beautiful chains of gold, now stepped forward to touch it and speak in a measured way that allowed the boy to translate calmly.

'I am the First Son of the Pharaoh. We have waited a long time for this day. Prophecy is as prophecy decides. The stars speak, and in time we answer. This day, tides released long ago reach these shores to honour the words of our ancestors.

'You came from afar and, without our aid, have conquered the Jaws of the Crocodile. With keen minds and strong hearts you escaped the perils of its awful Tail. You passed the tests set by the old ones to keep the secrets safe. And you arrive with the key to honour the dream.

'We knew of your journey from the earliest of days. We followed those who rode the Silk Road, and knew of the placing of the Wheel to hold the Web and secure the balance. All this came to us from those who travel the old trails secretly in our name. They are the unnoticed ones, traders mostly, but seemingly of little account. Much that is precious can be rolled into a small carpet. And we were always aware that the Imperial Fleet was free on the high seas. News of the voyage passed quickly from harbour to harbour.

'But above all else, we knew of the coming of the Stone. Those who hold its songs awoke with a start, the moment the ones named Tai and Ra called it from the deeps. Their wondrous works released music long put aside, but not forgotten, by those who dedicate their lives to honouring the lore of the Ancients.

'It has carved within it the image of a prophecy set in stone on the wall of the Great Pyramid. All we have waited for is about to come to pass. We greet your courage and the journeys made to bring the Stone of Stones home. Speak of your needs and know they will be answered. Thoth says this in the name of the Pharaoh. So be it, and may it ever be so.'

A crowd gathered on the shore. Word of the fulfilment of the Prophecy reached the villages and the cities and drew men, women and children to witness the wonder of it all. The Pharaoh sent a huge escort of horsemen to bring everyone across the trail to An Nil, the mightiest of rivers, and the city of Al Qahirah. Mounted on fine royal steeds, they rode slowly through a green land on a well-formed road lined with people. And at the head of the long procession was the Stone. Hera rode beside it as if in a trance, while twelve others held it high and walked strongly to bring it to its appointed destination.

Ii-chantu remained hidden in the throng. He wished to be unnoticed at this time, to be free of distraction, to be open to all that was happening and to all that might be. Aria was aware of his withdrawal and kept him constantly in mind. It had been a long, long trail. Better not to stumble at the very end, after so much had been endured to place them in this legendary land. Utini kept close to Hera, as did Tai and Ra, to support her should she tire. Eroa and Kaho rode with Hltanuu, Pana and Tali, who shared the care of their babes. Three generations riding into the future together, all answering the call of the Stone.

The gates of the city opened to them. Huge crowds now, a multitude that reminded Llana of the day they carried the other Stone into the city of her beloved Khan, the one who rode beside her. Songs of greeting, palm fronds gathered and waved to celebrate the closing of an ancient circle, then arrival at the Royal Square and the imposing entrance to the Hall of the Pharaohs. Huge excitement now, and a colourful array of retainers dressed in finery to bid them welcome.

Entrance without delay. Drums beating now, rolling into thunder and opening the way for the pure, soaring song of flutes. Taking up the rhythm of the one who calls the paddles of the waka to rise and fall, and thrust and pull. Then moving on to capture the hoof beat of riders galloping across the grasslands. Changing again to bring in the sound of the rains and the swelling of the rivers in flood. A wonderful majestic world of sound to call the Stone into the presence of the Pharaoh.

Silence. Sudden and complete. The Stone lowered onto the dais raised to honour it. Placed with certainty by twelve who knew they were but caretakers, not carriers. Then the release by Hera. A sound from the Stone as it settled into its weight once more, then silence again.

The Great One stepped down from the High Throne, walked to Hera and stood before her, inclined his head with obvious respect, then stepped closer to embrace her as if a daughter. Tears now. The Pharaoh wept, gave his tears of remembrance to the Stone, gave them for those who kept the prophecy and the lore safe throughout the ages. Then he stood in silence to hold the moment within the sacred.

Stepping back, he smiled to acknowledge the brave ones who met and overcame the Crocodile, and then he spoke. It was a short greeting, but one that took some time to share with everyone, because they had to wait as three scholars translated his words to join all the nations.

'Esteemed friends, who have journeyed far to answer the cry of prophecy, we welcome you to the Halls of the Pharaohs. All around us we see magnificence, the work of craftsmen who knew the spirit of stone and cleaved it to shape power with grace and beauty. Look upon it with wonder, and know the magic that is born of each of us. We are capable of much when we honour the high trail of the spirit.

'And look upon the Stone carried into these Halls. One of the Stones of Lore, brought home to find its place in the universe, to lock the darkness into the balance. Carved with a power that is beyond comprehension. Lost and without purpose until found and transported over the waters by those who sailed in trust. Brought to our land by those who found the courage to listen to the song of the stone and step beyond themselves. Each day facing the unknown and overcoming obstacles that would have defied armies. Moving outside the accepted path, finding strength in the ordinary, and bringing magic to each moment. Changing those met upon the way, by example not by teachings, shifting their view of the world through gentleness, not force, opening the way to another future.

'We honour the Stone and all who gathered to journey with it.'

The Great One waited while these words were shared in three languages, then stepped forward once more.

'We grant the freedom of the Kingdom of Egypt to each of you. We invite you to rest this evening, to prepare for the placing of the Stone at dawn. Then, when all is done as foretold, we ask you to gather here in celebration. We have much to share. May we join as friends to enter the circle and revel in the dance. Peace be with you.'

Despite the length of the day, few slept long that night. There was too much excitement in the air, too much wonderful food to sample, and too much joy echoing through their lives.

Long before dawn, they gathered by torch light. Silent crowds assembled, to create with their flaming brands a sea of light. All were brought into a carefully arranged procession with quiet words. Then, when the Pharaoh arrived, the Stone was lifted high and carried to the waters of An Nil. Here, twelve men and women dressed in long robes of many colours went to the river with ceremonial gourds, and let its waters wash over the Stone with soft words of greeting. A barge pulled into the landing, and the Stone and the Pharaoh's party boarded. Hera sat in the place of honour for the crossing, with Utini at her side.

As those at the sweeps carried them across the current, hundreds of other barges slipped ashore to bring the procession over the waters. They journeyed on, for they planned to greet the dawn light where the Stone was to rest. A winding flow of light that followed those who knew the final destination.

Ii-chantu had felt the presence of something in the dark beyond the flickering light. It had gathered closer as they crossed the river. Now it moved as they moved, and stopped when they stopped. He asked himself, 'Is it another guardian of the sacred, one sent to test them, or of the power of Mata-u-enga, the Dark One?'

'Is there danger?' asked Aria.

'No! I think not. Merely a powerful presence. A shifting shape that accompanies us on the journey. I sense no threat within it, only mystery.'

Now the way ahead was marked by burning brands set on poles in the sand. The end was nigh, and as they came to it, the presence beyond the dancing lights grew ever stronger.

Ii-chantu smiled and said to Aria, 'It is the Crocodile that moves with us, the spirit of that creature hovers in the shadows to protect us from the Darkness beyond. It surrounds all, wraps its tail around the last in the procession, and sets its Jaws high above the Stone. There is no danger in this. At the end of the trail, this creature is all benevolence.'

More light now, not in the sky, but thrown across the sands by many torches placed in a half-moon to illuminate the wondrous carved figure that sat within their glow. A lion crouched in the desert to bid them welcome. It had the face of a man. Ii-chantu smiled. It was as he thought. The legend gifted in the ancient song held true.

> *Lion Heart and Human Kind,*
> *at one with the Stone of Stones,*
> *joined beneath the stars forever.*

The multitude, that was the procession, approached no closer than the arc of flaming torches. They massed behind them, leaving clear the sands before this wondrous work of the Ancients. Across this undisturbed space walked the twelve stone-bearers, with Hera at their side. She was unsure of what was needed now, felt she had but one task to perform, to sing to the Stone that it might move forward. She hoped others knew the journey, for it was not of her mind.

They stood before the clawed feet of the Lion, waiting for completion of the ritual, expecting someone to know the next step. No one came forward. The Sun was now a glow below the horizon. Silence cloaked the approaching dawn.

'Have they lost the song that opens the way?' asked Aria. 'Ii-chantu, why do they wait? The Sun will soon be upon us.'

'The Central Sun is the key, and the sacred winds of the desert, the song, and the touch of a child, the final trigger to all that follows. The Pharaoh knows this. He stands with his people, not as a man apart. He waits for all to move as written. Others, who are still not awake to their role in this, will be called by the Stone to honour the needs of the Stone. Everything is beyond time now. Purpose alone holds sway.'

The silence grew as the Sun brought a bright glow to the east. The first shaft of light struck the Man Head of the Lion, defied the law of passage and curved back to caress the stone. A wind gathered in the east, a gentle breeze that sang of many realms. Then a woman sent up a cry, a wailing sound that was not of this world, one that touched into another. She left the mass of people, walked towards the Stone with a bundle in her arms, and placed her baby upon it in the fullness of new sunlight. The little one uttered a cry of pure delight, and in that instant, the ground shook as something powerful moved within the Lion.

The torches were not strong enough to give witness to all that had happened. Yet one thing was clear. The Stone was hoisted high once more with the child resting upon it, and carried forward until all disappeared into the shadows between the Lion's huge legs. A mother followed, then all were gone. Hera, the twelve carriers, the child and the mother. Those gathered stood within a silence so deep it seemed no one breathed.

A song drifted out of the shadows. It moved over the sands and carried beyond the people to the desert, and beyond the desert to the stars. And when it fell away, a mother walked from the gloom into which she had disappeared. Hltanuu was returning with her laughing child, Kun, and she was followed by Hera and twelve others. It was done. The Stone rested in a secret chamber within the Sphinx.

Mystery was cloaked in mystery upon these sands. A locking stone was placed. A Crocodile of huge presence gathered to watch over it by night, and a giant Eagle by day. And the East Wind visited often to honour the new way.

Ii-chantu smiled. They had achieved so much, and with such gentleness. Two Stones now rested in their pre-ordained homes. One in the Inner Courtyard of the Khan, and the other within the Sphinx. A third lay bound to the waka of the Menehune Nation in the harbour that sheltered the fleet. Hengeland called to it. The dream was incomplete.

The sands of time ran on, as the Moon turned in its circle, and the cosmic winds sang their sacred songs. They were of the Silence.

***

Once again the journey had been made and the stories shared. Once more those who sat to listen had honoured the circle, and the dream of the ancestors.

The old was made new again, and the new founded once more in the old. This was of the returning, the way back that was the way forward, the trail of truth that was eternal.

The Story Teller knew he walked the realms of magic. Every day spoke of its power and its joy. And as they departed he also knew others walked it too. There was a future, there was hope, the gentle way was truly of the power that was tomorrow.

Children of the earth star

seekers of the knowledge of the old ways

bringers of the wisdom of the stars

may the path you follow be guided with love

and magik.

May the trails you seek open to you in

perfect balance with all the laws of creation.

In peace and harmony may your spirit sing

in oneness with all that is,

to the song of the eternal love.

Kerry Grant

OTHER BOOKS BY BARRY BRAILSFORD

All these books honour the theme of journeys into ancient wisdom.
They are available direct from Stoneprint Press

The Tattooed Land shares the secrets carved into the land itself. This
much sought after book is republished as a completely revised edition
that includes the author's latest research. It now spans 2,000 years of
settlement of the South Island of New Zealand, and is based on detailed
archaeological surveys of pa, gardens, villages and trails, the ancient
lore and knowledge of the first peoples, and historical documents.
Hundreds of visuals, consisting of maps, sketches, diagrams and
photographs, take us onto the land to reawaken the past and bequeath
to this generation some of its many gifts.

Greenstone Trails is a fascinating journey along the land trails of the
past. Out of print for some years, it is republished in a completely
revised form to include recent research. We follow in the footsteps of
those who went in search of the precious pounamu. Via Maori
tradition, the narratives of early European explorers, the evidence of
modern archaeology and his own extensive research, the author takes
us along ancient trails across swollen rivers, through sombre forests and
over treacherous snowfields into the heart of the Southern Alps. Along
the way we discover truths about the land, the people and the
greenstone itself. Packed with maps and illustrations, this book will
delight all who love this land and its history.

Song of the Stone is the true story of five remarkable journeys. This
pakeha historian and archaeologist was invited into realms of ancient
and sacred knowledge long thought lost. *Song of the Stone* describes
his fascinating odyssey into the world of the wisdom keepers of
Aotearoa and the North American Indian peoples. It takes us on the
journey to open once again the trail of the stone across the Southern
Alps, for only then could the oldest of the sacred lore be shared in *Song
of Waitaha*.

We travel to the Red Earth of North America and on a great journey to
twelve Indian Nations, to the ancient standing stones of Europe, to
Stonehenge, Mull, Iona, New Grange, Creevykeel and the Roth of Tara,
to those who honoured stone long before the building of the pyramids.
The last journey was the one within himself, the hardest of all.

THE CHRONICLES OF THE STONE

Song of the Circle, the first book of five in the **Chronicles,** takes us back to the great stone builders in the Americas. In the days before the Inca and Aztec Nations was a world that gave birth to children who sailed into the Pacific with a message of hope for the planet. The *Circle* encompasses many realms and opens wonderful gateways to trails of wisdom. It is a quest for truth.

Song of the Whale picks up the quest in Easter Island and carries it forward into the Islands of the Double Sea with the help of the whales. It speaks strongly of the role of the great Whale Nations, the mystery of their long journeys and how they are bound into our own.

Song of the Eagle moves with the ancestors on their long voyages to Kauai & the NW Pacific Nations of the Haida, and the Inuit. Within its pages we soar with the eagles, walk with the totem animals of the First Nation peoples and enter the icy Artic world of the longest night of darkness.

Song of the Silence journeys to China, along the Silk Road to the mysterious land at the Roof of the World, and beyond that realm of power to Egypt. Old trails open to those who walk to restore the balance of wisdom and purpose created by the Ancients. Trails of the spirit that are woven into the wonder of the Silence.

Song of the Sacred Wind, the last book in *The Chronicles,* carries us from the pyramids of Egypt to the Land of the Henges, to Ireland and that wondrous standing stone known as the Roth of Tara. Then it brings all back to Lake Titicaca and the Fields of Cuzco, to the power of *The Circle,* to the magic of the beginning that has no end, the timeless journey born of paradox.